Power Plays

Power Plays

~

Kristin Dodge

Writers Club Press
San Jose New York Lincoln Shanghai

Power Plays

All Rights Reserved © 2001 by Kristin Dodge

No part of this book may be reproduced or transmitted in any form or by any means, graphic, electronic, or mechanical, including photocopying, recording, taping, or by any information storage retrieval system, without the permission in writing from the publisher.

Writers Club Press
an imprint of iUniverse.com, Inc.

For information address:
iUniverse.com, Inc.
5220 S 16th, Ste. 200
Lincoln, NE 68512
www.iuniverse.com

ISBN: 0-595-18115-5

Printed in the United States of America

To my best friend, for always and forever…Andi

Prologue

"Cameltoe! Cameltoe!"

The boys sitting on neon beach towels howled with laughter. A pretty girl flushed as red as her hair as she waded out of the water. Her friend tossed her a towel, which she quickly knotted around her waist.

"Hey, Matt! Are we in the Sahara Desert, 'cause I'm sure I just saw a cameltoe!" The three snickered at the girls' retreating backs.

A.J. nudged Shea. "What does that mean?"

Shea shrugged, rubbing baby oil on her copper arms. "Means the crotch of her swimsuit was riding up. Making it look like a camel's toe." Seeing A.J.'s confused expression, she leaned closer. "You know, like if you pull your panties on too tight and they go up your hoo-hoo?"

"No!" A.J. hugged her knees in delicious shock, thankful she'd left her jean shorts on.

Shea capped the oil bottle and gave A.J. a solemn look. "So be careful when you're coming out of the water. Always check…front and back."

"I will." A.J. peered around Shea, pretending to look for something while watching the now quiet boys through her downcast lashes.

Sun glinted off the lake, making her squint. She was sure this made it harder for anyone to tell what or who she was looking at. Stretching her legs out, she leaned back on her elbows, relishing the first hot day of the Minnesota summer.

Others had the same idea, as Lake Calhoun's beach was blanket to blanket with people. The peals of children's screams blended with the rhythms of a dozen different boomboxes. Half of her classmates were there, she noticed, most pretending not to see each other. Out of the hallowed halls of school, and cresting on puberty's hormonal drive, boys and girls who once co-mingled easily became guarded in the summer heat.

Like Jack. For five years he had lived up the street from A.J., and for three of those years she had nursed a crush of such magnitude it paled even the glossy faces of River Phoenix and Rob Lowe taped to her closet door.

On an icy, windy winter day a few years ago, when the sub-zero temperatures threatened to instantly freeze the skin of anyone who dared venture outdoors, A.J. had sighed at the school closing reports and started to get dressed for her trek downhill to the bus stop. For some reason, the Minneapolis school district hardly ever cancelled school. She was still furious about that fact as the minus-infinity wind-chill blasted her full in the face, knocking her off balance.

She had fallen hard, cracking her tailbone on the ice, then—to her horror—slid the remaining distance to her bus stop. The pain of her fall nearly had her in tears, but the hyena-like laughter of her schoolmates was threatening to break the dam.

"Need some help?" A.J. had looked up into Jack's eyes, such a mystical mixture of blue and gray and green. They were full of kindness, not the false kind like some kids would have when they'd offer a hand and then pull it away with a laugh. Jack looked sincere and worried.

She fell in love immediately.

Though they had been in only a few classes together, he'd always remembered her name and would say hi in passing. Even as his popularity grew, he still remembered her name. She thought he was worth sainthood.

Especially now, when he hung out with Matt Drucker and Bobby Lansky. A.J. knew they'd all been friends since the playpen. What she couldn't figure out was why Jack had grown up so cool surrounded by such immature idiots.

"Could you do my back?" Shea, in the shocker of the year, had sprouted real breasts, which made her available for the "no t-shirt" club. Having already stripped hers off, she swiveled so A.J. could reach her back more easily.

Sighing, A.J. dumped oil into her palm. She was older than Shea by two months, but always seemed to lag behind. Shea was always the trendsetter. Before all the other girls had gone out and permed their hair a la Madonna, Shea's was done, and she was wearing the net crop tops and silver bangles up her wrists. Shea was the one who told A.J. that she was supposed to wear her Forenza v-neck sweater backwards, and that rainbow t-shirts were totally out. She'd also taught A.J. how to pin her jeans at the ankles without the safety pin's head showing.

At this rate, she would probably even get her first period before A.J.

All the girls at school were envious of Shea. How could they not be, with her wavy blonde hair and hazel eyes? The thing they all hated the most was that Shea was actually nice, which was why most of the boys at school were totally in love with her.

After wiping her hands on her "Twins Win" t-shirt, A.J. leaned back on her elbows again. Sweating, she considered taking off her shorts, then quickly dismissed the idea. Instead she reached over Shea, rummaging through the jelly beach bag they had brought.

"What are you doing?" Shea asked, lifting an arm to shade her eyes.

"It's so hot and humid, my hair must look like Michael Jackson's." Fingers touched the plastic arch and she pulled out a yellow banana clip. Combing through her curls with her fingers, she attached the clip, trying to ignore the unbidden wish that she had blonde straight hair instead of an unruly black cloud atop her head. "How's it look?"

Shea surveyed her critically. "A little poofy, but once your hair gets wet it always looks better. Hey, want to go get some ice cream?"

Feelings slightly stung, A.J. shrugged. "Sure, but I didn't bring any money."

"That's OK, I know who's working the stand today. We'll get it for free." With a lightening-quick smile, Shea was standing and starting down the beach, beautiful in her bikini. A.J. felt like the ugly stepsister as she followed behind, jean shorts rolled right above her knee, her t-shirt baggy and draped nearly as far.

Her breath caught in her chest as she noticed that they were walking right toward the boys. Squinting her eyes again, she hoped they wouldn't say anything too terrible as she and Shea passed by.

"Hey, Shea!"

She stopped, smiling easily. "What's up, guys?"

Matt and Bobby were covering their mouths, holding in laughter. Jack elbowed them and said, "Not much. What's going on?"

Feigning indifference, A.J. scanned the rest of the beach. In reality, she wanted to sink into the sand, covering herself over her head. Because that was exactly how she felt around Jack, in over her head.

Jack Wiese. Football player, A-honor roll, good looks. He was just beginning to learn how to use the tools of popularity, and scorned the girls who fell all over him. With cutting humor and a scathing glance, most would retreat in defeat. A.J. truly thought the gossips made more out of what Jack had said or done. The Jack she remembered was kind and generous.

But not so generous as to greet her. Slinking behind Shea, A.J wished they would stop talking. Ice cream had never sounded so desirable in her life.

Without so much as a glance at A.J., Jack talked about what sports camps he was going to that summer and how he saw Kirby Puckett at the Eden Prairie Dairy Queen. She noticed how his eyes kept straying to Shea's bikini top, and wished fervently that she had started her bust-enhancing exercises two months sooner.

"What are you doofus's laughing about?" Startled from her thoughts, A.J. glanced at Shea. She was looking down her nose at Jack's friends, who were still laughing behind cupped hands.

"Ah, it's nothing," Jack said, elbowing the dark-haired boy to his left. A.J. thought Bobby resembled the kid from Stand By Me, the one who always wore thick, black glasses and a sneer.

"Hee-hawww," the kid said, breaking out into new snorts.

"Hee-haw?" Shea raised an eyebrow delicately, something A.J. had been practicing at home in front of her mirror. "Is that the best you can come up with?"

Bobby swiped his mouth with the back of a sandy hand. "We were just talking about who we wouldn't kiss—"

"Shut up!" Jack said, punching him in the arm.

"—and Jack said he'd never in a million years kiss a donkey. And so we asked him who reminds him of a donkey and—"

"I said, shut up!" Flushed red from anger and embarrassment, he leapt on top of his friend, pummeling him with fierce punches.

"—he said she looks like a donkey, with her hair being its tail and her face being its ass!"

"You dumb-ass, I told you to shut up!"

Frozen, A.J. felt the icy hurt of rejection and humiliation sink its glacial teeth into her heart. **They were talking about me**, she thought, blinking back sudden tears. **Jack said that. About me.**

"…we were just joking around," Jack's voice broke through the numbness. His strange eyes held hers directly, for the first time, and she saw an apology written in them.

And then his mouth curled up, the dimple flashing like a mirror in the sun.

"Oh, grow up!" Shea sniffed, turning around so quickly that sand spit off her heels onto the boys' blanket. "Come on, A.J."

As they walked, the smells of coconut oil and lakeweed pierced the fog in which she had shrouded herself. Amid the pulsing beat of a

Eurythmics song and the squeals of the children splashing, she thought she could still hear the boys' laughter. Biting her lip, she fought back tears.

"Don't let them get to you," Shea said, aiming a vicious look at the far blanket. "They're just stupid boys. Anyway, my mom says that when the boys make fun of you, that means they really like you."

A.J. looked at Shea under the canopy of the ice cream stand. She lifted her eyebrow, Shea-style, and they burst out laughing.

"Well, if that's the case, I feel sorry for that redheaded girl," A.J. said, peering into the case to make her selection.

"Why?"

"Because they were calling her 'cameltoe.' They must totally be in love with her!"

The girls laughed together again, but as A.J. choked down her ice cream, she felt its sweet coolness slide past her heart, forever freezing any feelings she held toward stupid Jack Wiese.

Chapter 1

Ornate jewelry sparkled nearly as brightly as the twinkling white lights that glittered throughout the ballroom, creating a façade of cheer and good spirit. The swirl of long evening gowns blended with the black tuxedos like the imagery in a Monet painting. With the distant pop of champagne bottles being opened and the restrained laughter of well-bred party guests, it appeared to be a typical New Year's Eve party.

Unless you eavesdropped on the endless whispers and gossip happening in every corner and every spare table, Jack thought cynically, tossing back a shot of scotch. He motioned to the bartender for another and grimly surveyed the room full of the governor's guests.

The governor herself was standing next to Senator Carver, pausing occasionally to sip from her crystal flute. Though she smiled warmly, Jack recognized the coldness in her eyes. As she leaned in to murmur to the senator, he wished he had learned to lip-read like he had promised himself last year.

"What do you think's goin' on?"

Jack swiveled in his barstool, eyed first his refilled drink, then the long-haired, pierced-earred, tux-wearing man sitting next to him. "Axel, an elephant would look more comfortable in a Mikasa crystal store."

Axel Gallo fidgeted, the cheap fit of the rented suit bunched at his waist. "Don't I know it. Man, I hate these things. Rather be dipped in hot wax."

"And I bet you have," Jack replied, downing his shot with a smirk.

Axel grinned. "Yeah, did I tell you about the time—"

"So what do you think they're talking about?" Jack smoothly interrupted, nonchalantly nodding toward Governor Sheraton and Senator Carver.

Pulling his hair away from his face, Axel became serious. "I think it's obvious. Went upstairs to check the latest reports and polling data." He gulped down some water, wiping his mouth with his tuxedo sleeve. "Not good."

"Not good how? With women? Men?"

"Across the board. Dropped five points. And that's just in a week."

"Damn it." Jack called for another round in a rough voice, then stared at his hands.

"What do ya think's gonna happen, man?"

He shook his head, then straightened up, remembering the endless pairs of speculative eyes that may be on him. "Word has it Senator Carver has already hired a new press secretary. I've given him some recommendations, but you know how he is, especially about who is on his core staff." Standing, he tossed back his third shot, feeling the weight of it and its brothers settling warmly in his belly. "Run upstairs and get out of that monkey suit. Come up with some tracking polls focusing on the midwestern reaction. Then, start the polling data for the general opinions on governmental issues—gun control, education, women's rights, social security—anything that may give us an edge at the debate in two weeks. Also, it doesn't hurt to start preparing for New Hampshire, if we can get that far. Oh, and get in touch with O'Hara. See if he can dig up any dirt."

Relief relaxed Axel's features. "You bet!"

"I'll see if I can do some damage control around here." Jack eyed the room speculatively. "Now, go to work."

"Hey!"

Intent on his new purpose, Jack felt mildly annoyed by the hold-up. "What?"

Axel grinned, showing off the glint of his multiple silver fillings. "Happy New Year."

With a shake of his head, Jack answered, "Not quite yet, my friend. Not quite yet."

*   *   *

"…and so the next time I'm sitting down with our neighborhood farm bureau, just what the hell does Senator Carver expect me to tell them?"

Jack smiled broadly, the alcohol making his mouth as flexible as chewing gum. His thoughts wandered freely without even wrinkling his perfect party face…**I could be toasting the New Year on a beach in the Caribbean, or at the base of the Eiffel Tower, or even—praise God—sleep through it and the next week.** Forcing his gritted teeth to relax, he leaned toward the Democratic senator from Iowa. "Bill, you and I both know it could be a hell of a lot worse."

Senator Spears fumed. "What's worse than your press secretary spouting off about 'hick farmers' on-air? I've got to tell you, I'm thinking of withdrawing my endorsement of Senator Carver. I've got my own constituents to think about."

"Now, let's not overreact," Jack said, seeing the senator approaching. "You have some valid concerns that we are taking care of as we speak. I'll tell you what. Why don't you join the senator tomorrow at the Vikings-Cowboys game at the Metrodome? I'm sure he'd love to take the time to talk over things with you."

Senator Bill Spears puffed a cloud of cigarette smoke at the ceiling. "Well, I was supposed to head back tomorrow…"

"Great, it's settled then. Now, where's that pretty wife of yours?" Gesturing to the bartender, he asked for a bottle of Dom Perignon. "Only thirty more minutes until midnight, and I bet Donna's looking forward to a New Year's kiss. Here, take this and show her how romantic a former Iowa State wrestler can be."

With low chuckles, the appeased senator was ushered aside only moments before Senator Carver approached Jack. "Well done, Jack," he said, raising his glass of mineral water in a mock toast. "One less feather to unruffle tonight."

"I'd rather unruffle feathers than be a stuffed goose," Jack replied, staring directly at the senator. Part of his job as campaign manager was to gauge his boss' moods, read his mind and make decisions based on what he found. Tonight, rather than seeing the faint traces of a worried frown, he saw a victorious glint in the man's dark brown eyes.

"Now, Jack, you worry too much. It's New Year's Eve. Have a drink." Senator Carver waved to the approaching waiter.

"Yes, senator?"

"Scotch, neat. And another Perrier for me, thanks." Turning to Jack, he grinned. "We've got something to drink to."

Jack eyed Steven Carver with suspicion. How many times had he stood to the side of this rugged man, whether ice fishing on Mille Lacs or shaking hands at White House functions. He had watched Steve's dark brown hair frost silver at the temples, and the lines deepen in his face after the death of his wife, Sandra. Through high approval ratings and low morale, Jack had been through enough with Steve to recognize his many public faces.

But he was still sorting out the private faces. Oh, he knew Senator Carver was a caretaker at heart, fussing over his staff like he would his own children, had he been blessed with any. But other than the day of Sandra's funeral, Jack had never glimpsed the grieving, sorrow-filled husband again.

There was no sign of grief on the senator's face now. Accepting his glass of Perrier with a wink and trademark grin, Senator Carver turned to survey the room.

"Great crowd we've got gathered here tonight, Jack."

"Yes, sir." Jack held back from gulping his scotch. Glancing around the room, he felt a smidgen of pride. Even with the current scandal, there had been an enormous turnout for the governor's New Year's Eve party, which was really just a cover for the Democrats' political games. With senators and representatives, judges and diplomats, the room nearly burst with the combined power of its guests.

Governor Sheraton was laughing loudly, head flung back and cropped black hair flying. A woman with dark, curly hair stood in front of her, holding a champagne flute as if it were a Faberge egg. **Who could make the governor laugh like that?** he wondered, staring at the back of the woman. Her hair spiraled past her shoulders, the wild tangle of ringlets a contrast to the simple creamy silk sheath she wore. Her legs were long, her smooth, ivory calves taut in high heels.

"Met her yet?" The senator's low, tires-on-gravel voice interrupted Jack's thoughts.

"Governor Sheraton? Several times, sir."

"Smart-ass. No wonder they call you 'Wiese-Guy'."

Jack thought, **to hell with it**, and drank his shot in one gulp. "At least they are smart enough not to call me that to my face."

"Tough guy, too. Aahhh, looks like an introduction is in order."

She was undoubtedly the most beautiful woman in a room where appearances were more glorified than any religious saint. With a quick wink to the senator, she slowly made her way over to the table, smiling at a state representative, sharing a joke with a reform party lobbyist. It was bewitching to watch as she worked the room with the finesse of a professional.

The scotch has killed more than a few brain cells, you idiot, Jack admonished himself. He silently vowed to stop drinking and arranged his face in pleasant welcome.

"Annika, how wonderful that you could make it, dear." Senator Carver stood gallantly and offered her a chair. She sat gracefully, the front slit of her dress parting just enough to arouse the more primitive section of Jack's brain. "I'd like you to meet Jack Wiese, my campaign manager. Jack, this is Annika Andersen—"

"Our new press secretary," Jack interrupted, holding out his hand in greeting. Something flickered in Annika's light blue eyes, but was quickly repressed. She smiled naturally and shook his hand with a firm grip.

"A pleasure to meet you," she replied, then folded her hands in her lap. He noticed there was no ring on her left hand, then wondered why he was bothering to look. He'd had enough of relationships getting in the way of his real commitment…work. His last romance had lasted two weeks. That was ten months ago.

Senator Carver beamed at Jack. "Can't pull one over on you, can I? I just know that the two of you are going to pull my campaign together and create sparks. Now, Jack," he leaned forward, gesturing with his water glass. "I know you wanted to be in on the hiring process. But when I heard Annika was available I was certain she was the right candidate."

Standing, he motioned to a senator who was trying to get his attention. "I know you two will have a lot to discuss, especially since the Iowa caucus is in two weeks. But for tonight, have fun. It's New Year's Eve! Yes, Senator Hawkins, so glad you could make it!"

They watched the senator walk away, his animated gestures clearing a path. Jack suppressed a chuckle and turned to his new press secretary.

The distance had not done her justice. Up close, she was even more exquisite, like a china doll. Her skin was porcelain smooth, while her hair created the perfect curling frame to her face. Eyes the bluest gift from angels and a mouth that would make the devil weep. Jack imagined tasting her full lips, a rush of lust flooding his blood.

Meeting those icy blue eyes, he again saw the slightest flash. Anger? Wariness? Before his alcohol-clogged mind could begin to sort it out, Annika slid her chair over closer, crossing her legs and revealing enough thigh that he could see the lace trim of the top of her garters. The heat dropped to his groin.

"So, Jack. May I call you Jack?" Annika asked innocently, thick, dark eyelashes falling like feathers against her cheeks. "I am just so impressed with what you've done with the campaign. The senator absolutely gushed over you. 'He is the most innovative, futuristic man I've ever met,' I think his words were." Placing a hand lightly on his arm set off electric shocks, but if she noticed, it didn't show. "With all of your experience and foresight, what advice could you give me?"

What the hell, he thought. **Who wanted to talk about work on their one night off?** Brimming with flattery, he leaned toward her until their bodies touched. "My first advice would be to follow the senator's advice. And, if I remember correctly, he said to have fun tonight."

"He did, didn't he. Well, are you having fun?" She raised one eyebrow, mocking him but at the same time inviting him to share in their private trap. To be politically correct at all times, in all places. It was the unspoken vow of their positions.

He laughed until a wave of dizziness rushed over him. He blamed it on her nearness, the scent of vanilla that he would catch every time someone passed by their table. "I'm not having fun. Yet." He cleared his throat and tipped a hand at the crowd. "So how do you know the senator?"

She licked her lower lip slowly, sensuously. First his gaze dropped, then his jaw. "Hmm. Does it matter?" She smiled. "But back to you. You were saying you weren't having fun." She laughed, a low, husky purr. "We should do something about that, shouldn't we?"

Jack glanced over his shoulder. This had to be a joke. But there was no sign of Axel, just sequins and silks. He looked in her face and saw the undeniable challenge.

Testing the waters, he placed his hand on the bared thigh, stroking the lacy edge with his thumb. "What did you have in mind?"

Annika's eyes met his directly. "I'm the type who prefers more private parties." She placed her hand on top of his.

"Directness. How refreshing," Jack said. "Well, I have a couple bottles of champagne and a beautiful view of the Cities."

"Perfect." Leaning over, she filled his breath with her sweet, vanilla-almond scent. Lips brushed his ear, further igniting his desire. "I'll meet you by the elevators in five minutes."

As nimbly as a fawn, she was out of her chair and crossing the floor, greeting Minnesota's lieutenant governor and his wife. Jack watched her charm them before turning her attention to a print reporter.

"Fifteen minutes, everyone!" Governor Sheraton waved her arms from the corner of the room. "Only fifteen more minutes until the New Year! Please, help yourself to champagne."

Assured that he could now stand up without being accused of smuggling shot glasses in his pants, Jack wound his way through the crowd, ducking around waiters in red vests holding trays of champagne flutes. Nonchalantly watching the crowd, a mixture of high society people absorbed in their own importance, he easily made his escape unnoticed.

She was already there, leaning against the back of the elevator. "Going up?" she asked, voice husky.

As the doors closed behind them, he reached for her. "Do you know I couldn't stop watching you tonight," she murmured in his ear, making the tiny hairs on the back of his neck stand up with pleasure. "Even before we met, I was watching you, wanting to be with you."

She tilted her head back, corkscrew tendrils tickling his hands on her back. Desire gave way to pure lust, and Jack brought his mouth to hers roughly, probing, tasting. She gave back his passion in triplicate, pressing her body close to his, cupping his buttocks in her hands. His fingers tangled in her hair, and he thought he would drown from the scent of her.

A faint *ding* pierced his consciousness, and Annika pulled back slightly. "Your floor?"

Without answering, he bent and lifted her into his arms, her sheath dress slipping up, both garters bared. Devouring her mouth, he stepped out into the hallway, taking long strides to his hotel suite. He was so enveloped in need he couldn't separate from her for a moment, and instead gently set her down by the door and fumbled in his back pocket for the card-key, still nibbling and taking from her lips.

Sweeping her inside, marveling at how light she was, he kicked the door shut behind them. His suite was enormous, kitchenette, fireplace, oak executive table with seating for ten. Down the hallway was a spacious bathroom with a sunken whirlpool tub and a bedroom boasting a king-sized bed draped with silk sheets. Jack couldn't decide which to enjoy first, spreading Annika out on the bed or sinking her into a bubble-filled tub.

She moaned in his ear and all his thoughts took flight. Pressing his hands against her breasts, he rubbed his thumb against her nipple, feeling it rise against the silky fabric. Heart pounding, he knew that soon he would take her right there in the entryway; his need was so powerful.

"So Jack, tell me something," she whispered, caressing the back of his neck with one hand while the other stroked his belly teasingly. "Being a Democrat, are you still afraid to kiss a donkey?"

Her lips engulfed his, drowning out the warning buzzers drilling in his head. Slipping a hand into the lace of her garter, he slowly touched her thigh. "Hmmm?"

"I asked if you were still afraid to kiss a donkey?" Annika pulled away, fingers hooked in his belt loops. "Like when we were twelve?" Her voice still purred seductively, but her stare was cold.

Jack's stomach jolted in alarm, but a moment too late. Bent over, breath expelled in an enormous burst, his testicles beyond pain to the state of fearful numbness. His first coherent thought was whether or not he'd be able to walk with the senator to greet the National Wildlife Federation spokespersons tomorrow.

It hit like the break of the sound barrier. A streak of white-hot pain made him slide down the wall. Nausea invited the four-plus scotches he had drunk to reappear. Blinking back rainbow-hued floaters, Jack squinted at Annika, trying to understand the torrent of words being hurled at him.

"...son-of-a-bitch like you if it weren't for Steve. I knew you'd never recognize me. I've come a long way from being the 'donkey' you and your friends made fun of. How's it feel now, jackass?"

Though slowed by pain and alcohol, his mental gears shifted rustily to work. Trying to breathe was like trying to drink champagne under water. "A.J.?"

Annika stopped pacing and glared at him. "Happy New Year," she spit out from behind clenched teeth. "See you in the morning."

Spinning delicately on her high heels like a fairy, she sailed out the door, slamming it shut behind her. Jack winced, then recoiled as the throbbing ache spread throughout his groin. Breathing a little easier, he tried to sit as still as possible so the nausea would pass.

Faint chimes and shouts of "Happy New Year" flowed over him like the wind. The revelers down the hall sang "Auld Lang Syne" in boozy, off-key voices. Jack thought of the governor's party downstairs and desperately wished he were still there, spinning weaves of golden wishes for politicians just waiting to wrap them up.

Annika Andersen. A.J. Her twelve-year-old face tickled his memory, but never completely surfaced. He'd been a jerk, he remembered, but he had been a jerk to many teenaged girls. Many adult women, too. If each came after him in such an aggressive way, he had better start freezing his sperm if he would ever want to have children.

Listening to the parties, he waited out the pain until he could crawl into the kitchenette. Slipping the fridge open, he pulled out a bottle of champagne, neatly uncorking it without a drop spilled. Jack caught the ridge in his mouth and swallowed deeply, straight from the bottle like a wino.

Coming up for a breath, he toasted the silent, empty room. "Happy New Year," he muttered, then sat back to finish the bottle and coax the memories of A.J. to rise, like champagne bubbles, to the surface.

Chapter 2

It was two hours earlier in California, so she knew Shea would still be awake. Annika just hoped she hadn't drank too much champagne or turned off her cell phone.

Shea picked up on the first ring with a crispness that assured Annika she was sober. "Shea Sheldon, WSFN."

"Happy New Year."

"Not yet, not here," Shea answered with a laugh, talking a little louder than normal. Echoes of excitement rang through the line, making Annika's loneliness feel more tangible. "Hang on, Annika, let me find a quiet spot somewhere." After a few minutes of muffled voices, sudden silence seemed eerie. "Are you still there?"

"Yeah."

"Ya, sure, ya betcha. You're back in Minnesota two minutes and you're talking as if you never left."

Annika laughed, mocking her friend. "Well, now, dontcha know dem Minnesoootens gots strong blood."

"And how is Minne-sooo-ta?"

"Minus five with a minus thirty wind-chill. How's Cali?"

"Seventy-five and gorgeous. The Bay actually was clear today, miracle of miracles." Annika could hear the ice cubes clinking together as Shea took a drink. "How's the senator?"

"Wonderful, as always. I am so happy to be on this campaign. I really think he can make it all the way—"

"And how's Jack?" Shea interrupted so smoothly that Annika almost felt her voice hitch in surprise. **No wonder she's the best television anchor in California,** she thought, **if she can push me off guard.**

"Jack is fine. I just spoke to him, in fact." Her voice didn't waver. It never did when dealing with the press.

"You're lying."

Annika sighed. Reporter or not, her best friend could always see right through her. "I kneed him in the balls."

Sputtering and choking changed to loud laughter. "Annika Julieanne Andersen! You are kidding."

"No, I wish I were." She shut her eyes at the memory, lying back against the starchy hotel pillows. "And don't call me that any more. A.J. is even better than that mouthful." She sighed. "I don't even know if I want to get into it right now."

The smile still curved in Shea's voice. "Come on, you can't leave me hanging."

"Let's just say I paid an old debt."

"Just a few minutes!" Shea called out. "Where were we?"

"Jack Wiese. Where are you?"

"Locked in my producer's bathroom. You should see this place, but that's another story." The rattle of ice cubes shook in Annika's earpiece. "Nik, I told you, Jack changed in high school. A lot happened after you moved to Colorado Springs. Don't hold what some macho Don Johnson-wanna-be twelve-year-old said to you twenty years ago."

Annika fiddled with the phone cord, wrapping it tightly around her finger until the skin purpled.

Shea's sigh whispered over the line. "It really didn't have anything to do with Jack, did it, Nik?"

"Of course it did, Shea. He called me a donkey."

"Twenty years ago!"

"Almost twenty years ago." Unwrapping her finger, Annika sat up straight, pulling her knees to her chest. "But anyway, I'm going to have to work closely with him for the next few months, so I will apologize in the morning."

They sat in comfortable silence, as two old friends do. Shea broke it quietly. "Have you heard anything?"

Hugging her knees more tightly, Annika rubbed her mouth against her nylons. "No."

"Are you still certain of your decision?"

Breathe deeply, she told herself, watching the white of her stockings pinken from her smeared lipstick. "Yes."

"You're going to be a lot more visible now, Nik…"

"I'm fine, really." Annika straightened her legs and swung them over the side of the bed. "I'm going to take a long, hot soak and then tumble into bed for about four hours of sleep before I meet the wolves for breakfast."

Shea didn't laugh. She couldn't blame her. She didn't feel much like laughing anymore either. "Promise to call me?"

"Of course," Annika answered.

"Especially if you've got a juicy scoop?"

She warmed a little to a smile. "No promises there. Happy New Year, Shea."

"Happy New Year, Nik."

She hung up the receiver reluctantly, perched on the side of the bed. Lonely bed, lonely room. Just like hundreds of other hotel rooms.

Get used to it, she chastised herself, and headed for the miniature bathroom, hoping for clean plastic cups and a complimentary shower cap. She had lied to Shea about the hot bath. After her seduction of Jack, she was hoping that the old wives' tale of a cold shower would do her some good.

*   *   *

She decided to arrive in a blaze of red. Not just any red, but fire engine, cherry-shaming, sex-screaming red.

Annika gave herself a final look in the mirror. The black skirt was on the short side, to appeal to the male members of the press, and the blouse was a modest white v-neck by the latest designer, which would probably show up on most of the female television reporters within the next week. But the touchdown was the red blazer. Viewers expected muted grays and blues on the politicians blaring from their televisions.

Senator Carver was no ordinary politician. And this campaign needed a shot in the arm.

Smoothing the black velvet lapels, she smiled at the mirror, judging the effect. **Poi-fect, as Shea would say**, she thought, and grabbed her leather Coach briefcase before leaving the room.

Jack's room was one floor up from her own. As she exited the elevator, a large coal dark man stood in her path, startling her.

"May I help you?" he asked, polite yet assessing her closely with his dark brown eyes.

"I'm Annika Andersen, the senator's press secretary."

The big man smiled. She realized there were two more men in dark suits behind him. Their sidearms bulged under their jackets and they stood with identical caution.

"We haven't met," the front guard replied, engulfing her tiny hand in his great bearpaw. "But ol' Stevie can't talk enough about you. I'm Tony Bailey, head of the senator's secret service."

"Wonderful to meet you," she smiled. "You gentlemen are sure up early."

"No rest for the wicked," Bailey winked. "So no rest for us. Don't worry, we've got plenty of help."

"Help?"

"There are more than fifty agents working for the senator's detail right now. We don't have to guard him all night by ourselves."

Annika felt her old fear lump in her chest. "Is it necessary? I mean, to have so many?"

"Yes, ma'am, but it's no different than any other candidate. In fact, Governor deMarco keeps asking for more protection, but in his case he needs it." The twinkle in Agent Bailey's eye seemed to be in permanent residence. Whether a disarming ploy or genuine trait, nonetheless, it made her feel soothed and safe.

"Well, a pleasure to meet you, Agent Bailey. Have the others arrived?"

"Yes, ma'am, all but the senator. He's on the phone with the governor of Iowa."

"Thanks." Annika walked confidently to Jack's door, the two officers bowing out of her path. Without knocking, she marched inside. The blend of casual chatter immediately stopped.

"Good morning, everyone," she said briskly as she walked to the executive table, found an empty chair and propped up her briefcase. Looking around the table, she met each face with a smile. "Normally I bring bagels, but this morning I thought aspirin might be more needed. Right, Jack?"

With all her bravado, she turned to meet his eyes, courteous smile pasted on her face. He stared back from the head of the table while the others laughed freely. Seconds seemed stretched into minutes as his gaze flickered over her face, her torso. **What does he think he see?** she wondered, holding tightly to her professional attitude. Memories of the previous night tripped across her thoughts, warming her blood and bringing a blush to her cheeks.

Jack broke out in a huge, self-satisfied grin. She flushed a deeper rose. Wonderful. She'd walked right into his game.

"Well, I for one need a gallon of medication," a tiny, Clairol number 39 red-haired woman drawled. "Y'all don't know how I'm feelin' this mornin'. Gem Agliara, darlin', personal assistant to the senator."

Annika murmured her introduction, staring at the petite woman. Sitting in the huge leather executive-style chairs, Gem seemed even more child-like. Except for her attire, a black net top with black bustier underneath. She remembered looking equally ridiculous during her Madonna-wanna-be stage.

She soon found out that Gem hardly ever sat still enough for anyone to notice her lack of taste in clothing. Gem jumped from her seat as if electrocuted and seemed to sprint across the room.

"More coffee, anyone," Gem tossed back over a shoulder, three-inch heels tapping on the marble floor.

"No thanks," the man to Annika's left replied after clearing his throat. "Richard Schwinn, media adviser. Welcome, Annika."

"A pleasure," she answered, shaking his hand. It was as smooth as a worn pebble, matching his sleek pate. Wire-rimmed glasses perched on his nose, gray eyes watery behind thick lenses. Richard Schwinn had led many practicing politicians to success through his innovative advertising techniques. In her quick assessment, she knew he would be an ally, with a little work.

"Axel Gallo," a voice murmured from behind her. She gasped aloud, startled.

"I'm so sorry. Did I scare you?" The wiry man crouched beside her, blonde hair pulled back in a leather thong, gold loop in one ear. His face was gentle, worried. Unlike the others, he was dressed in simple jeans and a sweatshirt. Annika smiled warmly, replacing her mask of professionalism.

"It's all right. I'm Annika Andersen. It's a pleasure to meet you, Axel."

Reassurance spread over his features. Axel stood and found a seat. "I'm the pollster. And boy, do I have news for everybody this morning."

"Wait, shhh," Jack said, reaching for the remote control on the table. He turned up the volume of the television tucked away in the corner.

"...Governor deMarco introduced a health care plan that would ensure low-cost care available for all citizens, regardless of age or economic status." The dark-bobbed hair of the reporter glistened as she waited for the sound bite to begin.

Connecticut Governor Antonio deMarco suddenly filled the screen, his smiling wife holding his hand, their three beautiful, camera-perfect children tucked neatly between the couple. He waved to his supporters, gesturing for quiet while his charming smile urged them on.

"Today, the first day of a new year, could be the first day of a new era for Americans. Imagine a country where every sick child is treated, where our elderly can afford their medications. Instead of hoping and keeping your fingers crossed for a solution..."

"What is that crap?" Jack growled. "He's the one that voted down the health care reform bill."

"...put your trust in me, and I will make it happen!" The crowd erupted in enthusiastic applause and cheers, waving banners and throwing campaign-supplied confetti.

"Back on home turf," the brunette reporter continued, "Senator Steven Carver will be meeting with members of the National Farming Federation in Minnesota today in response to last week's comments by former campaign press secretary Robert Bardikoff."

"Don't show the clip, don't show the clip," Richard chanted.

"Of course they're going to show it." Jack slumped back in his chair and ran a hand through his short, dark hair, making thick locks bristle up like porcupine quills.

"Well, of course he came out ahead in the Iowa straw poll," a slick-haired, weasel-nosed man was saying to an unseen reporter, hands stuffed casually in his pockets. "We've got a vice-president who is Victoria Secret's leading customer, and these hick farmers only vote for the candidates from states they've heard of. Wait, is this mike on?"

"'Wait, is this mike on?'" Gem mimicked, bringing a stack of papers and the coffeepot. "My daddy had a name for folks like him, but it's not somethin' I'd repeat in polite company."

Jack pressed the mute button. The brunette's lips moved, face solemn behind her handheld mike.

"Same old crap," Axel said, mouth full of powdered donut.

"But it's knee-deep around the farmers," Richard Schwinn argued, thumbing his glasses up the bridge of his nose. "We've got the Iowa Caucus in less than two weeks, and a lot of those farmers are going to the voting booths with our crap still sticking to their boots. This situation is calling for major advertising, and I'm talking print, radio, television—across the board. And we're cutting it close on our budget as it is."

Dusting off powdered sugar from his hands, Axel shook his head. "Iowa's not worth the cash. We've got to do some band-aiding and then concentrate on the biggies."

"Good thing the president already ran Martin's crotchless panties up the flagpost or y'all would have more of a mess to clean up," Gem interjected, sliding a bowl of freshly cut fruit between Axel and Jack.

Richard pointed his pencil at Axel. "If we don't take Iowa, we'll lose in New Hampshire. And California."

"Hold on, everyone," Jack said, motioning for everybody to settle down. When all eyes were focused on him, he smiled charmingly. "We're putting the cart before the horse. Axel, what big news do you have for us?"

After wiping his mouth with his sweatshirt sleeve, he passed around pages from the neat stack Gem had delivered earlier. "These are the work-ups for today's polling. I've got people calling across the country to determine the ripple effect of Bardikoff's screw-up. They'll also be checking the response to Governor deMarco's health care plan."

Jack nodded, flipping quickly through the pages. "Axel, add in the question, 'Which candidate will provide funding for safer schools?'. Also, did you get the gun control info. I dropped off?"

"Yep. O'Hara's already checking it out."

"Great. Have him double check on our old pal, Vice President Martin. His silence is making me nervous." Leaning back, Jack's eyes skipped around the faces. He held Annika's stare, then raised his eyebrows lazily. "And what say you, Madame?"

She stood, pulling out her own papers from the leather briefcase, and began to pass them around the table. "Among these pages you'll find the press release announcing my hiring, as well as details on the press conference that will be held at 9 a.m. I've gotten in contact with the Iowa state representative who will be meeting with Senator Carver later and he has assured me the uncompromising support of the farmers."

Jack's widened eyes nearly made her laugh out loud. "Also," she continued, poker-faced, "since the senator has chosen to attend the Vikings game today, I've decided to sit among the press corps, in order to become better acquainted, as well as feed them the latest coup of supportive Iowan farmers. Just in time for the five, six and ten o'clock local news."

She paused dramatically, shuffling papers and replacing a leather binder. "Finally, once I get some hard polling tracks from Axel, I'll invite reporters from C-USN and the *Washington Post* to meet. Any questions?" Surveying the room, she found faces still, eyes respectful.

"Sorry I'm late." Senator Carver walked quickly to the table, hand outstretched for the cup of coffee Gem was already offering. "Miss anything?"

Jack didn't look up, but continued to gaze at Annika. The hot blush of earlier threatened to rebloom, but she forced herself to concentrate. Lifting her chin, she glared back.

After a moment, Jack grinned, a dimple flickering in his left cheek. "I'll fill you in later, Senator. Meeting adjourned."

"Wow," Schwinn whispered. "Think we could talk strategy later?"

"Better do it soon. We have a lot of work to do before the Iowa Caucus." She shoved the extra papers in her briefcase. "How does two sound?"

His eyes blinked fishlike behind his glasses. "I think I'm free."

"Great, I'll meet you back here." She walked swiftly from the room.

Nodding at Agent Bailey with a smile, she pressed the down button, waiting impatiently. Toe tapping, she checked her watch.

"Running late? Or just running away." Jack's voice was like fingertips running along her spine, in turn both sensual and annoying.

"Running late. I have to prepare for that press conference." She pressed the down button again in succession.

"That won't make it come up any faster." The smirk in his voice made her spin on her heels.

"Is there something I can do for you?" she asked, all previous thoughts of apologies dissolving like the Alka-Seltzer tablet she'd taken earlier. Seeing his face again, the sense of vertigo resumed. Each time she blinked, he changed in appearance. Boy. Man. Boy. Man. She blamed it on too much coffee on top of too much aspirin.

The one constant was the color of Jack's eyes, the deep sea-blue-green that flickered nearly gray in the dim light. His constant gaze was unnerving her, but she pulled herself up to her full height and glared back.

"I'm impressed," he said, quietly. "I wouldn't have thought you'd have time to get prepared for today, considering your, uh…**plans** last night."

Swallowing back a smart retort, Annika chose to play it safe. It was, after all, only her first day on the job. "Well, I think you'll find that is one of my many attributes. Always one step ahead."

Challenge sparked in his eyes, and she nearly slapped her forehead in frustration. But it was too late now. **The game, as they say, is afoot**, she mused.

"…going to go?" Jack's sultry smile had her mesmerized, but his tone brought her back to reality.

"Wh—What?" she stammered.

"I said, 'This is your elevator. Aren't you going to go?'" He grinned, the dimple in his left cheek deepening. "Your big press conference and all."

"Yes, of course. Will there be anything else?" Forcing herself to keep her chin up, she stepped into the elevator, pressing the button for the lobby.

"No, but I believe we have some…unfinished business to attend to later," Jack said, his voice purposely low. The elevator doors slid shut silently, hiding the message written all over his face.

It wasn't until she reached the first floor that her heart stopped pounding.

"Excuse me, aren't you the new press secretary?" A man dressed in khakis and a jean shirt fell in step beside her, tape recorder forming a telltale lump in his front pocket.

Taking a moment to breathe deeply and release her thoughts of Jack, she turned slightly.

"I am, and all of your questions will be answered momentarily." She gave the reporter her flashiest smile, disarming him enough that he fell behind. This was what she loved, the false fronts, the fake spin. She excelled at it. Schmoozing with politicians or lobbyists, it didn't matter. Annika's professional mask kept them all at a safe distance, where she told them what to believe and who to believe in.

But for once, she actually believed in the candidate she worked with. It made her act a little more genuine.

A smattering of flashbulbs marked her entrance into the reserved conference room. Smiling serenely, she approached the podium, then slightly turned her head so that the television camera caught her best angle.

"Good morning, everyone. Happy New Year. And, as you can see, I am a new face in this new age. My name is Annika Andersen, and I am the new press secretary for Senator Steven Carver."

*   *   *

The stewardess gave Jack a molasses smile as she placed his glass in the cup holder beside his seat. "Having a pleasant flight?" she asked, the front of her uniform barely brushing his shoulder.

He grinned broadly. **So this is what they mean by flying the friendly skies**, he mused. "Just wonderful, thank you."

"My name's Jennifer, and if there's anything I can do for you…" Her eyes wandered appreciatively over Jack's body.

The intro music to C-USN could bring Jack out of a coma. "Thanks, I'm fine," he replied, snapping into business-mode. Reaching to the instrument panel on the other side of his seat, he increased the volume.

"…promised to meet the demands of increased health care. But where was Governor deMarco when health reform was being argued at the Senate?" Annika's intense features filled the screen, her serious eyes darkened. Gradually, her face relaxed, became sincere. "He was convincing his state senators to vote against the bill, while Senator Carver was a leader in pushing it through. Now thousands of impoverished children are getting immunizations. Now thousands of elderly can afford to live longer, more enriching lives." The camera tightened its view, and as if psychic, Annika stared directly in its lens. "When you give Senator Carver your confidence and your vote, you are assuring your own future."

The screen switched to an obviously miserable, cold reporter standing in front of the Metrodome. "While the Iowa caucus is only two weeks away, Senator Carver took time to meet with representatives of farm bureaus. At one point of the meeting, Senator Carver removed his Vikings jacket to reveal a t-shirt with the slogan, 'MENSA wants you, farmers,' similar in style to the old Uncle Sam posters. The representatives we spoke to tonight are confident the misstatements by former press secretary Robert Bardikoff will be erased from the minds of Iowa voters by the caucus."

Jack laughed aloud, joined by Richard and Axel who were sitting in plush chairs across the row.

"That was a great idea! Which one of you thought of that?" Jack asked.

Richard shrugged his shoulders. Axel chuckled and said, "Probably the big guy himself."

"Actually, I did." The voice, so persuasive and appealing on-air was decidedly cooler in person. Jack released his seat belt and swiveled to stare at her. She had dressed down from the day's press conferences, the long legs now encased in black jogging pants, an oversized Vikings sweatshirt skimming over her bottom, its sleeves rolled up to keep from dragging. Dark spirals of hair were held back loosely in a low ponytail.

Erase the frigid gaze and she would seem almost vulnerable. Like a fallen angel, Jack thought. Or a child lost in a store.

The weight of her gaze, the tip of her head. It seemed all too perfect, too formulated for a cynic like Jack, who had personally witnessed the downfall of several politicians to the everyday sins of greed, sex and idiocy. She had sat in the back of the plane with the travelling press corps, swapping insults with the Redskins fans while oohing over baby pictures of new parents. With her whispered encouragement, Senator Carver had done the same, showing his delightful charm and quick wit to those who had previously only thought of him by poll numbers and campaign promises.

It was brilliant public relations, masterminded by a serious, arrogant, dazzling woman.

"Good work, Annika. I couldn't have done it better myself." Jack lifted his glass in admiration. "Now, if you have a few moments, we could discuss the next week's agenda. I took the liberty of having the flight attendants seat you next to me."

Her smile hitched, then regained its natural appearance. "Of course," she said smoothly, showing only the barest glimpse of white teeth. Nodding to Richard and Axel, she slid into the window seat, carefully avoiding Jack's slightest touch.

Jennifer, the perky flight attendant, appeared at Jack's side. "How are you doing?" she cooed, bending over enough to allow a glimpse of her mountainous cleavage. "Can I get you anything else?"

"No, I'm fine," he replied, turning to Annika. "You?"

She glanced at his glass. "I'll have what he's having. A screwdriver?"

Jack swirled the orange liquid smoothly, the ice cubes tinkling like bells. "Florida orange juice."

"Oh." The surprise in her eyes was quickly quelled. "Orange juice would be fine."

"Compliments of Florida orange growers," Jack said as Jennifer went to fill the order. "They have already thrown their support behind Senator Carver." He swallowed, then replaced his glass slowly. "You seem…surprised."

"Surprised?" Annika almost passed off her innocence with her blue eyes rounded and eyebrows raised. Almost. Jack had excelled at his work by reading faces, even the most skilled ones.

"That's what I said…surprised. As in astonished, bewildered. Shocked."

A telltale twitch at the corner of her mouth gave her away. "I know what surprised means. I just wasn't aware the Florida orange growers had so much political pull."

"You'd be surprised to see how many congressmen will trade favors just to get free o.j." Shifting in his seat, he faced her more directly. "Did you think I drank all the time, at every chance I got?" he said softly, noticing how, just inches apart, her face seemed more beautiful than he remembered from the night before.

Her pupils widened. "Now, why would I think that?" she asked, equally quiet.

"Last night you caught me in a, shall we say, very malleable condition." His raised eyebrow and smirk drew a short laugh from her, which pleased him. "However, since we are going to be working together closely for the next few months, I wanted to make it clear that first, I am not a heavy drinker.

"Second, I am not so easily seduced…

"And third," he said quickly, cutting off Annika's sharp retort, "you owe me something. I don't know if it's an explanation I want, but an apology would be appreciated."

Annika laughed, a short, sarcastic bark. "What should I apologize for? Wounding your incredibly huge ego? Or hurting your manly pride?"

"If last night…" Jack paused, looked around cautiously, then leaned in closer, nearly whispering in her ear. "If last night was all a game based on your anger over something that happened when we were twelve years old, then I'm going to request Senator Carver rechecks the mandatory psych exam."

He watched her eyes, the baby blue deceivingly innocent. Her face didn't twitch as she studied him in return. In their close quarters, he caught her scent, a mixture of sweetness and musk. **If her scent were bottled, Viagra would be out of business,** he thought, arousal spreading through his body with his blood's natural flow.

The switch in his thoughts must have been obvious. Annika dropped into her professional mode as easily as changing her clothes. Damn.

"You're right. What started as a joke turned ugly, and I apologize for any damage…" Her eyes strayed to the front of his khaki pants. "…that I may have caused. Now, about tomorrow's schedule—"

"Why don't you like me, Annika?"

Startled, she stopped rummaging in her briefcase. "What?"

"I mean, everybody likes me. Right, guys?" Axel and Richard glanced up from the day's poll readings.

"Sure, boss."

"I'm sorry, what were you asking?"

"Never mind, Richard. Now, everybody likes me. So why don't you?"

Flopping back into her seat, she hefted her laptop onto the fold-down tray. "Jack, I hardly know you."

"You've known me for twenty years."

"Almost twenty years. And I haven't known you that whole time."

"True." Jack paused, considering. "All right, after you moved—where did you move to again?"

"Colorado."

"Colorado, right. Well, once I was in high school, I became quite popular. President of our class—"

"Homecoming king. I know, Jack." Her voice was bored.

He rubbed his back against the seat, snuggling down for the long flight, and what he hoped would be a long conversation. "How did you know that, Annika?"

She didn't speak for several moments, busy hooking up her modem and power cord before booting up. Finally, she sighed exasperatedly. "If you must know, Shea told me."

"Shea? Shea Sheldon? Boy, did I have a crush on her throughout high school."

"Who didn't," Annika replied, a trace of pride seeping into her tone.

"So, you were asking Shea specifically about me?" This was one long flight that was going to be enjoyable, he thought, settling in for the game.

Annika instantly flushed pink. "Watch out, Wiese, your ego's showing."

"No it's not, I'm just curious." His response was met with a cold stone wall of silence, her fingers busily tapping away on her keyboard. He waited patiently for a break in her rhythm. "You know, I've changed my mind. I think you really do like me."

Waves of pink spread farther up her cheeks until even the tips of her ears were crimson. Still, she typed incessantly. A dark tendril of hair had escaped her ponytail, curling against her flushed cheek. Jack gently wound the curl around his finger, marveling at its soft texture. It took a moment for him to realize she had stopped typing.

Frozen, she stared blankly at her screen. Her jaw was clenched, the muscles flexing spastically. "Jack. Let. Go."

Her face was tight, like a film of plastic wrap had been wrapped around it. Lips once deliciously lush and full were drawn in a flat line.

Reflexively, he dropped the spiral of hair, squeezing into the far edge of his seat.

For a moment, all facades were dropped. He was no longer the cheerful, flirtatious playboy. She was no longer the serene, capable professional. The pain that etched lines along her mouth and made her bite her lip nervously made something in his soul stir.

Just as quickly, the curtain dropped over her features. If he hadn't been reading faces for years, he may have passed off the emotional shift as a figment of his imagination.

As she typed, Jack began pulling his own documents out of his bag, snatching glimpses of her from the corner of his eye. What had hurt her so badly that she needed to hide it so desperately?

"Here's that orange juice," Perky Jennifer announced, leaning over Jack. He coughed from the rose-petunia-pheromone blend of her perfume. Trying to gain his attention, she leaned even lower. Jack waved her off, and she pouted childishly.

"Thanks," Annika said. "Now Jack, back to tomorrow's schedule…"

He followed her lead and buried himself in strategies, deadlines and poll results. All the while, a tickle nudged the back of his thoughts, unanswered questions, unattainable woman. What was he getting himself into?

* * *

He knew they were just pixels. Red, green, blue dots. But kneeling on the floor, nose pressed against the television screen, he swore he could smell her. All honey and vanilla, sunshine and sweetness.

Pulling away as slowly as ice melting, he stared at the screen. Dots merged into solidity, bold colors that made him wince. If it weren't for her voice, her soothing, river babble tone, he would have turned the TV off.

But he knew her words were for him alone.

Sitting on his heels, he stared at her. Suddenly, she stared directly at the camera and smiled. He gasped aloud.

She knew. His heart raced while his hands trembled. Not long, now, darling.

A commercial interrupted his trance, blared disgraceful innuendoes on the heels of such purity. Rage rushed through his body, every vein, every muscle heating in response. Through a haze of sweet vanilla and honey, he kicked the television, over and over, until the blasphemy was silenced and he was wasted with relief.

Chapter 3

Coffee or aspirin. Hell, why not both?

Annika popped a couple tablets in her mouth and chewed furiously, her sour expression reflected in the bathroom mirror. Hastily, she reached for her coffee and swallowed, the heat trailing a path to her belly.

The navy silk blouse she had neatly pressed and hung last night was now crushed in a rumpled ball at the bottom of her suitcase, the victim of underarm deodorant stains. Her favorite lipstick, **Hint of Passion**, fell out of its holder just as she leaned in toward the mirror to apply it. She couldn't decide if she looked more like Ronald McDonald or Charlie Chaplin. After reapplying all of her makeup, finding a suitable outfit and checking the time, she attempted to finish her hair.

When the diffuser broke, Annika decided to surrender to fashion for the day.

Pulling her tightly curled locks back, she twisted and tucked until her long dark hair was coiled into a French twist. She pawed in her makeup bag for some bobby pins, swearing quite unprofessionally.

The sounds of C-USN's intro music wafted through the open door. Grabbing a pen, Annika thrust it into her hair, securing it in a fashion she made famous in college.

She walked into the small bedroom, sitting on the edge of the uncomfortable bed that had kept her awake half the previous night. She surveyed the morning reporter, absentmindedly pressing her tongue into the crevices of her teeth, seeking out the remnants of bitter aspirin.

"...deMarco will be arriving in Des Moines next week, one day before the highly anticipated first debate with Senator Steven Carver of Minnesota. Meanwhile, Senator Carver has been making the rounds with local farming bureaus in an effort to garner further support. C-USN polls show Senator Carver trailing by only two points, but with a two-point margin of error, this could be a very tight race. C-USN Reporter Sandra Carlson, Davenport, Iowa."

Satisfied, Annika switched off the television. No mention of Bardikoff in three updates and the senator's numbers were on the rise. Now, if only Jack would give her some time to work with the senator on his debating skills…

A sharp knock at the door brought her to her feet. Though the entire hotel floor was posted with secret service agents, she still peered through the peephole cautiously.

A blonde woman stood outside, the fishbowl of the lens warping her features. Nervously tapping one foot, she held a pile of papers to her chest like a schoolgirl. She glanced around, as if wondering what to do next.

Annika opened the door. The woman nearly melted with relief, her brown puppy dog eyes blinking quickly.

"Oh, I'm so glad you're here," she said. "Jack said I needed to bring these papers to you before your morning press conference, and since it's already almost 8:30 I thought you might have left. He's already left with the senator for the day, but said if you needed him you could reach him at his cell phone."

Swiftly bypassing Annika, the blonde walked to the small table and dumped the papers with a sigh.

"You've got the press conference at nine o'clock, followed by one-on-one interviews with the local newspapers and television media." She dug in her pocket for a pen and scribbled some notes on one of the pages. "Then, at noon, C-USN's Darren Cross wants to interview you via satellite. It's already been set up through the local affiliate. Larry King is interested in an interview, but I told his people I'd have to check with you first."

Annika shut the hotel door softly, then walked over to the table.

"I'm sorry, but you are…?"

The blonde looked up from her doodling, brown eyes blinking back first confusion, then amusement. "Lauren Larkin. Your assistant?"

"My…assistant?"

"Didn't the senator or Jack tell you? Oh, that's just like them." Lauren straightened up, brushing the wrinkles out of her black skirt. "Let's make this official, then. How do you do, I'm Lauren Larkin, your assistant and princess of spin. It's a pleasure to meet the queen."

Annika laughed, holding out her hand in return. "Whatever it is you've been doing, keep it up!"

Lauren beamed, then gestured to the chairs. "Mind if we sit for a few minutes to discuss the week's schedule? You can also tell me about what ideas you want to feed to the press." She cocked an eyebrow mischievously. "I also run interference and have been known to sway a story or two."

Annika sat down, all traces of her headache dissolving. She chose to believe it was Lauren's doing, rather than the coffee and aspirin. "Lauren, I think you and I are going to go a long way, baby."

"That may be true, but first, you need to take that pen out of your hair and put it to paper. Let's talk debate strategy."

"You read my mind."

*   *   *

His hand hurt. If there was one thing about campaigning that he would abolish, it would be the routine hand-shaking. Needle-like stabs of pain ran through his palm, lighting each nerve ending on fire.

Sitting in the luxurious black Lincoln, Senator Carver flexed his hand, grimacing. It was only one o'clock, and there were several more town hall meetings, school gatherings and media appearances before he could give his hand a rest.

"Here, boss." With a maraca shake, Jack opened the cap of an aspirin bottle. Steven gulped two down without water, then stared out the window, deep in thought. The crop fields were empty, haggard corn stalks crusted over with frost and a slight half-inch of snow. Cows mooed wearily at their passing entourage, steam flaring from their nostrils and mouths in the ten-degree air.

When he had first decided to run for the United States Senate, he had been in the midst of a pain more deep and disfiguring than he had thought possible. Sandra, his beautiful, wonderful wife, had not died peacefully as they do in the movies, but fighting, rejecting pain medications in order to battle each and every malicious cancer cell that invaded her body. Even in death, her face was determined.

After finding out that alternative treatments had been available, just not encouraged by their health management organization, Steven had become irate, calling doctors throughout the country, who in turn blamed greedy insurance companies. When researching an appeal to the Minnesota legislature, he found that women's health issues received one-fourth the finances needed for research that men's health issues received. His focus intensified—if one man is going to be able to have better penile function for one night, by God someone is going to discover a cure for breast and ovarian cancer and save millions of women.

Twin Cities news station KMNN caught wind of his mission and created an award-winning people's interest story. Letters of support came pouring in, and soon Steven Carver found himself easily elected and thereby referred to as Senator Carver.

And now, sitting in the back of a Lincoln towncar, third in a line of five, Steven still felt the power of his mission, though the pain of his personal loss had faded with time to a slow, burning ache in the center of his soul. Through it all, Sandra's death, the whirlwind of publicity and politicians, Jack had been his maypole.

After miles of barren land, with the scattering of farmhouses and decrepit barns, a lone sign was hammered into a farm's border fence…"Carver Can!"

Steven chuckled. "See, we've still got our supporters out there, Jack."

Looking up from his notebook computer, Jack caught a glimpse of the trademark blue and red sign before returning to his typing. "Need all the supporters we can get."

"Isn't there some way we can pass a constitutional law allowing animals the right to vote?"

"Mmmm, I think it's the fourteenth," Jack replied absentmindedly, pulling out the poll data from that morning and comparing it to the figures on his screen.

"Are you sure? I thought the fourteenth allowed public sexual intimacy?"

"Of course, sir." The low battery alarm on his laptop sounded, and Jack swore under his breath. Frowning, he turned to the senator. "What did you just say, Senator?"

Steven laughed outright, the aural equivalent of a full-bodied red wine. "Jack, put that thing away. Forget about whose numbers are bumping whose and whether I need to wear jeans or a suit at the next meeting. I want to know why one of my closest friends is so distracted this morning."

Watching with hawk eyes, Steven allowed Jack the courtesy of gaining his own thoughts while he packed up his laptop and paperwork. Finally, Jack sighed, turning to him.

"It's the debate you have scheduled with Governor deMarco. We are regaining some of our lost points in Iowa, but he's still hammering away at you in New Hampshire." He ran a hand through his close-cropped dark hair, an all-day habit that caused his hair to stand in staggered sticks, making him look more like a freshly awake toddler than a campaign manager.

"We need to increase our advertising in the East, while still keeping an eye out for California's women's issues. Under Richard's advisement, you're scheduled up the ying-yang with small town meetings, leaving us with little time to prepare for the debate.

"The Committee to Legalize Marijuana is holding a rally outside our next hotel. Axel's computer is down. Agent Bailey wants to restrict more of your access to the public.

"And finally," Jack said, covering his eyes with one hand. "I can't get Annika Andersen out of my head."

"Aahhh," Steven began, leaning back in his classic listening pose, hands folded in his lap.

Jack shook his head, waving a hand at Steven. "No, don't start that. It's only that we knew each other way back in middle school."

"I know."

He loved surprising Jack. Like now, when his eyes opened wide and jaw slackened, before he could regain control of his features. It made him laugh out loud.

"You knew? When you hired her? You dirty, rotten..."

"What I knew when I hired her was that she was an impeccable speaker and a master at political strategy." Steven smirked, turning to look out at the endless cornfields. "The fact that she knew you made no difference in my decision."

"Did you know she hates my guts? No, that she hates the swine that feast on my guts?"

"Mmmm, that I didn't." They rode together in silence, each gazing out their own window. Steven could almost hear Jack's thoughts.

He cleared his throat. "So, as your boss, is this prior relationship—"

"Now, it wasn't a relationship..."

"—going to effect the way you handle your job?"

"Of course not. How can you even ask that?"

"All right. Now, as your friend..." Steven crossed his leg, leaning in toward Jack. "Tell me you aren't looking to use her."

"Use her?" Jack exploded. "What the—"

"Oh, come on. She's exotic, she's intelligent, she's beautiful. All the requirements for a one-on-one with Jack Wiese."

"Steven, you insult me. In relationships, I do not 'use'—"

"Allison Hutch. Rebecca Parker. Jennifer Bleichman."

"—the woman." Jack shrugged, then sipped his coffee carefully. "I can't help it that the relationships just sizzle out."

"After you take them to bed."

"That's not true..."

"After you use them." Steven looked out the window, noting the turn exit for Storm City. "After the challenge is gone."

Jack set his coffee cup into the holder. "When you say it like that, it sounds so callous."

"Well, if the shoe fits."

"Hey, watch it! I am not..." He lowered his voice, eyes on the driver's rearview mirror. "I have not or will not ever 'use' a woman. You of all people should know that. Oh, forget it. I don't know why I brought it up with you anyway." He stared out the window, lip nearly in a full pout.

Flexing his hands, Steven felt only mild twinges of pain. "Jack, I've known you for what...ten years? I'm not trying to insult you, buddy." He massaged the fleshy part of his palm. "You've been turning your act around. You and Jennifer broke up, what, a year ago?" He waited while Jack nodded. "I just think that with Annika, you're out of your league. So don't clog your thinking with strategies on getting her into bed, when you need to be concentrating on strategies to get us the Democratic nominee."

Jack turned to him, eyes nearly silver-blue in the morning haze. "Yes, sir. Now, can we tackle some of these complications?"

"Not now, my friend," Steven replied as the car turned toward a small brick building with 'VFW' spelled out on its side in blazing red. A crowd of forty or so people stood outside, waving homemade signs as they saw the car approach. "Right now, we're going to do what I love the most." He waved to his supporters, his smile brightening the dim Iowa morning.

* * *

"Of course he's pro-women, what would make you think otherwise?" Annika asked, swinging her carry-on over her shoulder, glancing at the *NewsSource* reporter that was unsuccessfully trying to manipulate her.

"Well, a few weeks ago he dodged the question on abortion rights."

Annika laughed, her tinkling, merry public laugh. "Barry, he didn't dodge the question. In fact, the question was aimed toward women's health issues in general, which you and I both know the senator is highly committed to." She paused at the hotel's door, placing her hand on his arm. "Senator Carver is dedicated to women's issues. Period."

Barry squirmed under the pressure of her hand, avoiding her eyes and even having the courtesy to blush faintly. "Thank you, Ms. Andersen. I think you've cleared that up for me."

"Good. I'll see you tomorrow, then." Walking briskly, as to avoid further power plays with the press, she headed toward the elevator, itching to get out of her emerald wool suit and enjoy her first night off in a week.

"Hold the elevator, please," she called. Obligingly, the silver doors slid open, revealing the dimpled smile of Jack Wiese. Electricity sparked from his eyes, causing heat to rush to her core. **How could he have this effect on her, in only a moment's glance?** she wondered as she entered the elevator and dropped her carry-on bag to the floor.

As the elevator began its smooth glide upward, she glanced over at Jack. He watched the numbers rise, humming slightly, his hands tucked deep into his pants pockets. Must have been a tough day, she mused, resisting the urge to fingercomb his mussed hair. She recognized the tune as an off-key rendition of "When You Wish Upon a Star," and smothered a smile.

"Saw your broadcast on C-USN," he said suddenly, turning his gray-blue eyes to hers. "Not bad."

The elevator doors slid open on the sixth floor, the top of the small hotel in Sioux City. Agent Bailey was already stationed just outside its doors.

"Evening Mr. Wiese. Ms. Andersen."

Annika smiled at him with genuine pleasure. Such a gentle man, for one so large. He'd talked to her of his kids, now grown with families of their own, and his eyes had glimmered with emotion. "Agent Bailey, how many times do I have to tell you to just call me Annika?"

He grinned, the fleshy jowls trembling in delight. "As many times as it takes. Thanks again for bringing my men coffee last night. It was very thoughtful of you."

"My pleasure." She turned, smile disappearing as quickly as frost in the sun. "My room assignment, please, Jack?"

"Right here." He halted before a non-descript door and opened it with his key, showing an equally non-descript room. Annika held her hand out for the key.

Much to her surprise, Jack just walked into her room and sat down at the small table. Kicking off his shoes, he placed his feet on the bed, flexing his toes.

"What the hell—"

Jack raised a finger to his lips in a silent shush, then pointed at the door.

Seething, Annika shut the door gently, reining in her anger. She spun around, throwing her bag on the bed, narrowly missing Jack's gold-toed socks.

"What the hell do you think you're doing?" she hissed between clenched teeth. She crossed her arms across her chest in her best school-marm imitation, complete with frown and drawn mouth. No one had ever pushed her when she used this attitude as her armor.

Except Jack.

He leaned back in the chair, stretching his arms high above him while an enormous yawn escaped him. He cracked his knuckles, then began to loosen his tie. Annika became transfixed; the tie was designed with red whorls and loops on a black background, with hints of silver threading between. It was an incredibly sensual tie to wear for a long day of campaigning, more appropriate for a drawn-out candlelight dinner before a night of lovemaking.

Shocked by her thoughts, she made sure her features remained composed and fixed Jack with her most furious glare.

He stared back, amusement making his dimple deepen.

"Are you done?" he asked, hands folded in his lap, feet still comfortably raised on her bed.

"Am I done? You are the one who barged into my room, so the question should be, are you done?"

Jack sighed, rolling his neck in lazy circles. "Drop the prison warden bit. It's been a long day, and we have more work to do before it's over."

Business. Of course. She mentally kicked herself as she eased into the chair opposite Jack, promising herself a long soak after this meeting. "What can I do for you?"

"First, pick up the phone and order up some dinner. I prefer steak, medium-rare, but will take any kind of pasta. I heard they make a wonderful clam sauce."

"I'm not hungry," Annika said. Her stomach grumbled. Traitor.

Jack just stared at her, his full lips slightly curved, repressing a smile. Now, his eyes were nearly gray. Odd how the different light changed their hue.

Annika fought the electric sparks lighting between them by burying her face in the room service menu. "As you said, it's been a long day."

"Everyone has to eat."

"True enough." She set down the menu and picked up the phone, placing their order.

"And a bottle of white zinfandel," Jack added. She glared at him over the receiver. He had put his shoes on again and was pulling his laptop out of his bag.

"And a glass of white zinfandel," she told the operator before replacing the phone. She gracefully sat back down, crossing her legs and watching Jack.

He was amazing, she had to admit grudgingly. The campaign had gone extremely smoothly over the past week. Jack's insight seemed to always be two steps ahead of what the voters were thinking. And her fine-tuning the spin fed to the reporters only reinforced Jack's strategy.

They complemented each other in their work. If only the voters knew how much she bristled against him in real life.

"We need to prepare Senator Carver for next week's debate with Governor deMarco." Jack slowly unfolded wire-rimmed reading glasses, settling them over his ears. Rather than change his appearance, the glasses intensified it, making him seem even more distinguished, more handsome, more intelligent.

More pretentious, she mused hotly, shuffling her own notes. "I have some ideas about how to prep the senator."

"I thought you might."

Annika ignored the sarcasm and pulled out a legal notepad filled with her scrawl. "The sooner we can work with him, the better. Have you got the latest poll results from Axel? Nationwide, not just Iowa."

They bent their heads over the papers, ignoring the current that ran between them like the ocean's tide. When the knock at the door startled them, Jack realized he had forgotten about the food. Annika's insightful ideas and breakneck pace kept his mind completely occupied.

"I'll get it," he said, pulling his glasses off and tossing them haphazardly to the table.

He opened the door to Agent Bailey. His frame filled the entire doorway, his smile like pearls against onyx. "Did you two order room service?"

"Yes. Tell them to bring it on in." Jack winked. "Unless you guys need to taste-test it first. Make sure we're not being poisoned."

Bailey shook his head. "Don't care about what happens to you two. It's the senator I've got to worry about." He lumbered off, his bass chuckle rumbling after him.

A teenager in jeans and a t-shirt with the message, "I Got Licked by Nikki Sexx!" trudged in, pulling a cart behind him. "There you go," he mumbled. "Happy eating." Walking like a Neanderthal, he exited the room, slamming the door behind him.

Jack turned to Annika and raised an eyebrow. "What class! And here I thought we were in the middle of nowheresville."

He was rewarded with a laugh, a full, sexy laugh that sounded like the throaty call of an exotic bird. Not the tinkling, angel's bells she fed the press or the public, but a from-the-belly laugh. It stirred the embers of desire he thought he'd banked for the evening.

Turning to the trays, he busied himself with removing the plastic covers. "Let's see, did you order the spaghetti with clam sauce or the spaghetti with clam sauce?"

"I think I ordered the spaghetti with clam sauce," she replied, the echoes of her laughter still husky in her voice.

"Me, too." Jack held up a styrofoam container and removed the lid carefully. "Coffee?"

"Yes, but I did order the wine for you."

"Oh, it's here." Holding up another styrofoam cup, he was surrounded by her laughter again.

"You really know how to treat a lady to a classy dinner, Jack."

The second after she spoke, her face changed. Lips narrowed to a tight line, eyes darted away. The merriment rose like hot air, leaving a chill that was almost tangible.

Jack placed her plate in front of her. "Fresh parmesan, madam? Oh, wait, I forgot my grater at home."

There was not even a hint of a smile as Annika tucked her napkin in her lap. "Thanks anyway."

Sighing inwardly, Jack sat down and began to spiral spaghetti with his fork. "So, I never got the chance to apologize to you."

She swallowed, eyes reserved. "When?"

"The summer we were twelve. I looked and looked for you, but when I biked up to your house, the sold sign was already up."

She chewed slowly, then sipped her coffee. Her ice-blue eyes were frigid. "Oh, really."

"Really." Jack expertly twirled another strand of pasta, inserting it in his mouth without a dab of sauce staining his face. "What happened?"

Annika set down her fork and fiddled with her napkin, tearing off small pieces and placing them on the edge of her plate. "My parents divorced," she said finally. "My mom and I moved to Colorado Springs."

"That had to be hard on you."

She stiffened slightly and picked up her fork. "Not really. I loved Colorado."

"I meant your parents splitting up. Did you get to see your dad much?"

"Not really." The bitterness edged her tone like icicles on a rooftop. "He died a few years ago. I never spoke to him much."

"Did he stay in Minnesota?"

"No. He followed a twenty-something blonde to California, where I heard he got divorced again." She smiled weakly, poking at her salad. "At least he didn't have any more kids. You have a sister, don't you? I think she was two grades behind me. What is her name, again?"

"Jessica."

"Jessica, that's right. Real powerhouse at volleyball and basketball. Shea said she was the only freshman on the varsity team."

Jack wiped his mouth, swallowed against the ache that made it nearly impossible to finish his dinner. "She was, yes. Even got a scholarship to Marquette."

"You always seemed to have such a close family," she murmured, finding another paper napkin and folding it in her lap.

"Just your regular nuclear family," he replied, hoping the sarcasm didn't burn her ears as much as it scorched his own.

They ate for a while without speaking, the faint echoes of the hotel's other inhabitants having the calming effect of Muzak. Jack sipped his wine and grimaced, replacing the cup. Wiping his mouth on a paper napkin, he watched as Annika pushed her plate away, the spaghetti only half eaten. As it was nearly ten o'clock, her makeup had worn off, leaving the translucent ivory skin his fingers itched to touch. Her lips were turned down slightly, a crescent of long-borne hurt.

The strange twist he felt in his heart before deepened, nearly crushing his breath away. He fought it desperately. Damn, put an angry woman in front of him any time, but one who was wounded, in such pain...

Jack reached out, placing his hand on hers, surprising them both. "I'm sorry. About your dad."

She stared at him, luminous eyes bright with unshed tears. With her hair curling darkly to her shoulders, the dark green of her blazer making her eyes seem all the more like the cool blue of the Caribbean sea, she looked like a mermaid. The rush of his restrained desire nearly made him grip her hand like a lifeline. He wanted her, yearned to tangle his fingers in her hair, feel her heartbeat under his fingertips. Let them lose their individual pain in coupled ecstasy.

Annika blinked, and her mood changed. She yanked her hand free as if burned, and scowled darkly.

"I don't need your sympathy. Or your pity." She cleared her plate, then reshuffled her papers. "Or your friendship, for that matter."

Jack's temper rose immediately, and he welcomed the familiar feeling. Much better than lusting for a wildcat and just getting scratched, he thought. "No, what you need is a ride with the senator. Shake the hands of real people, get to know real feelings." He pushed his plate aside, leaning his palms against the table. "Then maybe you could thaw that ice-cold heart of yours."

She gasped audibly, her mouth open in furious horror. A smudge of clam sauce decorated her lower lip. "How dare you! You don't know anything about me. Or my feelings."

"I know you are only sensitive to the press, and it has been medically proven they are born without hearts."

"I am sensitive to the voters' issues, and that's all that matters." Standing abruptly, she stalked over to the door. "If you'll excuse me, I have some things to prepare for the senator's debate."

Jack stood, but only walked to the edge of the bed, leaving a few feet between them. "You'd be better off preparing your television skills. Your appearance on C-USN today was mediocre at best."

"Mediocre? I defused two difficult issues without insulting the host or hurting the political expert."

"But you left too much room for the viewer to create their own opinion of Senator Carver."

"You can't push too hard or it sounds like all the other politicians' hype." Annika rubbed her forehead in frustration then crossed her arms over her chest. "Now, if that's all, good night."

Swift as a cat, he crossed the room, catching her hand on the doorknob. The electricity nearly arced from her hand to his, her deep intake of breath only fueling his want. He pressed his lips to hers roughly, darting his tongue into her hot mouth. For a second she resisted, then opened her mouth and yielded to him, leaning her body into his, the press of her breasts against his shirt an irresistible temptation.

He pulled away suddenly, against his will and with equal roughness. Annika's face was only inches away, her sweet smell beckoning, lips reddened from friction. She searched his face with glazed eyes.

"Sorry," Jack said, desire making his voice hoarse. "You had some sauce...on your lip."

With the flick of his wrist, the door opened. "Goodnight." He was halfway down the hall, nodding to Agent Bailey, before he heard the door slam violently. Its echoes accompanied him to his room.

Chapter 4

"But, Senator, haven't you already vetoed a gun control bill during your campaign? Isn't that a vote in favor of the NRA?"

Senator Carver stared coldly at Annika, his eyes darkening. "No, it's a vote for the safety of all Americans. That bill didn't include assault or automatic weapons. When I am president, the legislation I want pushed through will ban the sale and use of these types of guns, as well as the hollow-tipped bullets known as 'cop killers.' Unlike Governor deMarco, I'm not sticking with the status quo."

Annika smiled, re-crossing her legs. "Excellent job, Senator." She glanced at her legal pad. "Just remember to hammer him on the gun control and healthcare issues. We'll touch on abortion later." A shadow caught her peripheral vision. Turning around, she saw only Richard, who was tapping his watch excitedly.

"We're running over. The kids are going to be here soon."

"Pam, am I almost done?" Senator Carver sat perfectly still in his chair, hair freshly moussed and tousled, the thick matte of stage makeup a stark contrast to his casual khaki pants and button-down jean shirt.

The makeup woman laughed. "Look natural, Senator." When he relaxed his pose, she nodded. "All done."

"Great. Now I'll have a minute to speak to…" His gaze fell on the door, and Annika's heart pounded in her throat again. Turning in her chair, she saw only Lauren, followed by Gem. Damn that man, where is he?

She hadn't been able to fall asleep last night, lips still burning from Jack's impulsive kiss. Touching her mouth, she could have sworn it radiated heat. Her mood had shifted from angry to aroused as often as she had tossed in her bed, until she could finally no longer stand to think about Jack or his kisses and had risen to work on the debate.

Notes, pads of paper and laptop at the ready, Annika waited, wanting to show Jack how little last night had meant to her. Work was what was important, not these power plays between two team members.

Paging through her notes idly, she checked off some of the items on today's to-do list. Gem sidled up smooth as silk and refilled the coffee cup at the table.

"Darlin', if you don't mind me saying so, you look like you took a turn with a tornado."

Annika dropped her notes to her lap and stared into Gem's concerned eyes. "Why do you think that?"

"Honey, you've got circles darker than mud under your eyes and the way you keep tappin' your foot makes me wonder if I should switch you to decaf." Gem put one hand on her hip, the coffeepot dangling dangerously from her hand. "Why don't I call Pam over to touch you up before you go on today?"

Back straight as a pole, Annika nodded, edging her fury even farther behind her thoughts. "Say, Gem," she asked, trying to keep her voice steady. "Where's Jack this morning?"

Gem rubbed her lips together, refreshing their crimson glow, and stared at her, eyes trying to pry the mask off Annika's face. Annika kept her face neutral, fighting the invisible fingers. Finally, Gem just shrugged and scooped up a stack of papers from the table. "I suppose that's Jack's business, darlin'. You take it up with him."

Before Annika could think of a response, the quick woman was across the room, murmuring to Pam. What was it with him that had everyone simpering and protecting him like a pet? They only fed his arrogance, making him think he could have anything he wanted, take anything he wanted.

Like last night.

Gripping to the last strand of her temper, she stuffed notebooks into her briefcase. The shift of her body sent papers skidding to the floor.

"Oh, damn it all to hell!"

"Here, I'll help." Lauren stooped beside her, face flushed bright pink. She hummed softly as she neatly sorted the mess, producing paper clips from her pocket and securing the piles.

Annika eyed her curiously. "You seem awful happy this morning."

"Hmmm? Oh!" Blushing a furious scarlet, Lauren kept her eyes lowered to her work. "Just had a relaxing night off, I guess."

"Really? What did you do?"

"Oh, not much," Lauren said, gently laying the paper into Annika's briefcase. Annika zipped in her laptop, still watching her face. "A nice dinner, um, you know."

"Not really," Annika said, remembering paper plates and styrofoam cups. And a deep, sweet kiss for dessert. No, a forced kiss. As he was being kicked out. She mentally shook herself of the memory. "So, did you go out or stay in?"

"Um, well, stayed in…" Lauren looked up, relief standing out on her face like Braille letters. "Oh, look. Jack's here."

Just the name sent champagne bubbles afloat in her belly. Feeling her own cheeks flush, Annika turned around to meet him squarely.

Heads bent together, Jack and Senator Carver were talking in low voices. Their combined good looks and relaxed attitude made them appear to be modeling for a clothes advertisement. Jack's jeans were well fitted, the hunter green shirt so vibrant a color that Annika wondered if it, like the light, would change the color of his eyes.

He glanced up and held her stare. A confusing mix of heady delight and turbulent anger made her a thunderstorm of emotion. She'd never met a man who could influence her feelings against her will, like the pull of the tides. Her self-possession almost slipped, and she felt herself nearly grin at him.

Then, he winked.

Fury won. Of all the nerve. He was unabashedly the most egotistical, overbearing, assuming man she had ever known. And, as he walked over to where she stood, she vowed to crush his ego like a rose petal under her foot and relish the scent.

"Good morning Lauren," he said, before turning the full strength of his gaze on her. "Annika."

She was right. The hunter shirt did make his eyes appear green, like the deep cut of an emerald. Smoothly, she answered him. "Where have you been?"

"I had a little business to take care of." He carefully selected an apple from the basket on the table and bit into it. A drop of juice clung to his lower lip, drawing her gaze away from his eyes. "Ready to start?"

"Start? I've been prepping Senator Carver for the past hour, no thanks to you."

"Really?" Jack licked his lip and she repressed the heat sparking in her belly. Instead, Annika embraced her anger and let it fly.

"Yes, really. I thought the plan was for you and I both to rehearse with him? Next time, I would like at least the courtesy of a call."

"Lauren, would you see if the senator has any time available now?"

"Yes, Jack."

Annika shook her head furiously. "No, he doesn't have time, and you of all people should know that. You've got him scheduled right down to bathroom breaks."

"If I'm not mistaken, it was you and Richard that scheduled this campaign promo for this morning." He took another bite of apple, cool and calm as if on vacation. "Pam, how are you? Looking lovely, as always."

The makeup woman blushed through her own heavy powder. "Sorry to interrupt, but Gem said Ms. Andersen needs a touch-up?"

Damn Gem! Pam may as well have said that Annika needed a new tampon; the embarrassment was so acute. "I'm fine, Pam. Thanks anyway."

"You know, you actually could use a little..." Jack gestured under his own eyes, which were mischievously twinkling.

"I do not!"

"Late night?" Jack shrugged with mock helplessness at Pam, who turned with a miffed expression. He paused for a moment, watching Annika while chewing thoughtfully. "Thinking about me?"

"Hardly. Prepping for today. Which, as I stated before, you have neglected."

"The senator is ready for a head-to-head with deMarco."

"How can you say that? Don't you realize that this campaign depends on the strength of the senator's stance at that debate?"

"His numbers have gone up two points overnight."

Axel passed by, quickly snagging an orange from the table behind them. "Three points actually."

Jack gestured with his apple. "Thank you, Axel. Three points. That puts us dead-even with the great governor of Connecticut."

"Maybe for Iowa, but what about New Hampshire?" Annika strained to maintain her last bit of control, but her voice was slipping up a notch in volume. "The voters there are a completely different ballgame. Or haven't you looked that far ahead?

"In fact," she said, dropping her voice with deliberate command. "I think you are only looking as far as the next bed you can tumble in along the campaign trail."

Bulls-eye. Jack's eyes slitted, the iris' darkening to a stormy gray. He grabbed Annika's arm roughly, pulling her against him. "You don't know the first thing about me, lady."

Her heart fluttered. The nearness of him was intoxicating, his smell, his strength. The power that he held over her emotions. She wanted him, desperately, while she wanted to shove him away, equally desperately.

Tinkling, merry elfin voices brought her out of her indecision. Young children, wrapped in hefty parkas like Christmas presents, waddled into the room, mothers and fathers lagging behind, unwrapping each child by mitten and hat.

Gem oohed and ahhed over the beautiful cherubs, calling for the photographer of the local newspaper to take multiple photos. Lauren ushered the children like a gaggle of geese to remove the rest of their outerwear, while Gem promised plenty of snacks. As she passed them, she hissed, "Take it to the other room, please," her face losing its Mother Hen appearance for a fraction of a second.

Annika found herself being propelled to the small room adjoining the large auditorium, which housed the televisions they used for gauging public opinion. Jack's hand clamped painfully on her arm. "Let go of me," she said quietly, while smiling generously at the reporters who were trailing in to watch the taping.

"Not on your life," he answered, an equally polished smile set on his face.

He whirled her into the room, shutting the door firmly behind them. She spun around, adrenaline pumping, ready for the fight.

Instantly, his mouth was on hers, insistent, relentless. Her mind fought while her body surrendered, opening her mouth to taste him, explore him. The sweetness of apple slipped against her tongue and only tantalized her more. She clutched him closer.

He knew he would bruise her, knew he should let go. But the ache that had kept him awake half the night had only intensified when he walked in to see her, the burgundy suit she wore reminding him of her full lips. And her transparent attempts to engage him in verbal sparring, well, he just couldn't imagine better foreplay.

She pulled at him hungrily, heat shimmering between them like a desert mirage. Her hair had been twisted up and he yearned to find the pins and release the torrent of black curls, thread his fingers through them endlessly. Instead, he parted the slit of her suit, finding satin soft skin trembling under his touch. With light caresses, he teased the swell of her breasts, drawing a line along the top of her lace bra. Vanilla filled his senses, and he suddenly had a sense of déjà vu.

Pulling away sharply, Jack backed up several feet. He held his hands in front of him, cupping himself protectively. Breathing hard, he just stared at her.

Annika leaned against the door, mouth parted, chest rising and falling as rapidly as his own. Twisted tendrils of hair had escaped their prison, falling against rose-pink cheeks. She raised a hand to her heart, staring at him with those endlessly aquamarine eyes. Eyes that could be as warm as the ocean off the Florida Keys, or as cold as polar ice.

The temperature dropped. A frosty glare met his own.

"I would appreciate it if you could keep both your hormones and your ego in check long enough to get some work accomplished," she said coolly, folding her arms across her chest.

"I'd like to know I can kiss you without feeling like I need protection," Jack retorted. "I left my metal nut cup at home." The public face had already been pasted on, and he wished he could remove it. Running a hand through his hair, he rubbed at the frustration building in his head.

"Maybe I don't want you to kiss me." Her eyes held a direct challenge, but her tone failed to endorse her words.

"You want it as badly as I do," he said hoarsely, the need still tangible. "You just wish you didn't want it. And damned if I know why."

"Don't take it personally, Wiese. I am just not interested in men right now. My career comes first."

Jack snorted. If only she knew how defensive she looked with her arms crossed over her chest, her chin lifted to the sky. "Your career. And what will you have after this campaign is over? Another nice line on your resume?" She visibly stiffened, jaw clenched.

"And you would have another notch on your bedpost."

"Damn you," he said softly, crossing the space between them like a shadow. He gripped her arms, holding back his fury with only a prayer. "I want you. And I'm used to getting what I want." He stared directly at her creamy neck, dropping his gaze to her breasts. Her flush only fueled his desire. "But I don't beg. I have no need to."

Releasing her arms, he stared her down, until she shut her eyes against his intensity. "I won't apologize for kissing you. And I won't apologize for what I feel for you. But if it's strictly business you want, it'll be strictly business you get."

Her lip just barely trembled, like the whisper of wind on a leaf. She opened her eyes, a battle of desire and fear churning until their color turned nearly aqua. What had hurt her so deeply, he wondered, the question that had haunted him throughout the night.

"...held a press conference this morning to address his immediate dismissal as Senator Steven Carver's press secretary."

Jack and Annika both reached for the volume control, he reaching it first. Pressing the button rapidly, they stared at the screen.

It was filled with the ferret-like face of Robert Bardikoff, dressed in a dark suit with a solemn gray tie. Jack swore out loud.

"Shh," Annika said, placing a hand on his arm.

"As a devoted public servant," Bardikoff began, placing his notes on the podium in front of him, "I felt the need to come forth with the true reason behind my dismissal as Senator Steven Carver's press secretary. For the good of the people, and the future of our country, I am humbled to be standing here today.

"The truth is, Senator Carver, while a good and decent man, has battled an addiction to cocaine and alcohol for most of his life." Audible gasps arose from the seldom-impressed media, and the screen erupted with camera flashes.

Annika sagged, her fingers digging into Jack's arm. Quickly, he pulled up a chair and sat her down gently.

"It is with remorse that I announce that the senator is still using drugs while on the campaign trail. Upon my discovery of this fact, I was immediately terminated."

"He has no proof!" Jack swore at the screen. "Why doesn't some reporter ask him for some proof? This isn't the National Tattler!"

Annika leaned forward and turned the television off. She was still quite pale, her ivory skin further accenting the dark shadows under her eyes. But her hands no longer shook, and she seemed buoyed with calm strength.

"Jack. I need you to be completely honest with me. Is any of this true?"

"Of course not!" He hesitated, one loyalty pulling against another, then pulled a chair next to her.

"Jack."

The single word was spoken with humility, sorrow. It disrupted the balance. He folded his hands in his lap and stared at them, wondering where to begin. "After Steven's wife died, he had a very rough time coping for a while. Alcohol helped him get through the lonely nights, while fighting for her causes helped him through the days.

"Finally, it was getting to be a necessity for him to get to sleep. I would go to his house to pick him up in the morning and find him passed out on the couch." Jack shook his head at the memory. "After that, he recognized he needed help. He joined AA, cleaned himself up and saw a therapist to monitor his depression."

Reaching for Annika's hand, he squeezed it gently. "You and I can't imagine the pain of losing a spouse. Can you judge a man by actions he took several years ago? When he wasn't even in public office?"

She raised her head, moisture lining her lashes. "Of course not. The poor man," she sighed, standing up and pushing her chair back. "But people are going to believe this. Why is Bardikoff doing it? What does he have to gain?"

"What does he have to lose? He's been press secretary of three losing campaigns and being fired by the senator just eliminated any of his credibility in the political circle."

"So how do we fight this?" Annika's face was set in determined lines. Jack felt a surge of protective pride.

"You're asking me?" he teased. "Since when have you sought out my opinion?"

Annika shot him a steely glance. "You're right. Now if you'll excuse me."

Without another word, she opened the door, letting in the musical sound of the children. Jack watched her march up to Lauren and whisper in her ear, the posture of a fighter, a winner. **Thank God she's on our side**, he thought, and headed for his room to change clothes.

* * *

"Of all the darn-pickin' things," Gem murmured, scanning through the e-mails headquarters had passed on. The senator had received a number of kooky messages. Like the one from the guy in Oregon who thought God told him to be Carver's vice-president. Or the furious note from the South Carolina leader of the National Rifle Association, threatening to shove each and every bullet in the U. S. of A. where the sun don't shine.

But this one, this one was different. It gave her what her daddy would call the heebie-jeebies. Chills ran slick tentacles up and down her spine.

"Say, Agent Bailey?" Gem called. "You gotta sec?"

The big black man ambled over, eyes winking merrily. "Do you have any more of those delicious donuts? I was hoping you had hidden some away for me."

"No, darlin', but I'll remember next time." She gestured to the page she had put on the desk in front of her. Even the smooth surface of the paper seemed to emit evil vibrations. "I thought you might want to check this one out. Came to headquarters yesterday."

Agent Bailey picked up the single sheet, squinting at the words. "'Wrap yourself in your warm feeling of safety. It makes it so much easier for me. No matter how many people surround you, I'm always there, waiting for you. All it takes is one moment.' This was e-mailed by a 'Changeling'?" He looked at Gem reassuringly. "Should be pretty easy to trace. Don't worry too much about it."

"I know, but it just gives me the creeps. And I've seen some creepy letters."

Agent Bailey laughed heartily, but his eyes became serious. "Thanks, Gem. I'll check into it personally."

As the agent walked away, Gem tried to shake off the crawly sensation, like spiders walking along her skin.

"Hey, Gem!" Axel rushed up, breathless. "We've got ourselves a problem."

"Well, then, here I come, darlin', to save the day." Relieved, she jumped out of her chair.

*   *   *

"In short, Robert Bardikoff's claims are unfounded. He has given no proof, only an earlier statement based on hearsay and groundless accusations." Annika stared directly into the C-USN camera. "Senator Steven Carver does not use cocaine or alcohol. In fact, he is a champion for drug and alcohol rehabilitation services to be available for everyone, no matter what the cost."

Smiling down at her familiar crew of reporters, she raised an eyebrow sarcastically. "I, however, use caffeine and aspirin on a daily basis. Oh, and I also admit an addiction to Ben and Jerry's Chunky Monkey ice cream."

Amid the laughter, Annika waved her arms. "No more questions for today. We'll see you bright and early for tomorrow's briefing on pet shops, pit stops and putting shots. Thank you."

Exiting through the back door, she was met by Agent Bailey. "How'd I do?" she asked, already knowing the answer.

"I'd say that if you take care of the senator's reputation, and I take care of the senator's person, we will both be calling him president soon enough."

Something in Agent Bailey's tone made Annika push aside her self-congratulations and concentrate on his face. As the elevator doors slid shut, she turned to him.

"Is something wrong? Not your family, I hope."

"Oh, no, Ms. Andersen." He hesitated, then met her eyes with a solemn look. "I believe I must speak with you candidly, in the event it becomes leaked to the press."

"Of course. What is it?"

The elevator doors slid open. A secret service agent stood in their path, then nodded at his boss and returned to his seat across from the elevator. Glancing down the hall toward her room, Annika noticed two extra guards posted by the stairway.

Alarmed, she turned to Agent Bailey. "What's going on?"

He motioned her to the doorway of the senator's suite. "Gem got a strange e-mail forwarded from headquarters today. It's not really a threat, but it implies one." He glanced up at the sound of voices coming from behind the door. "We've checked into where the e-mail originated. It was from one of the computers at the Des Moines City Library."

"Can I see the note?"

Unfolding it from his pocket, he handed it to her. She skimmed it quickly, feeling her blood run colder with each sentence. "Changeling," she murmured.

"Ma'am?"

Annika shook her head. Sometimes trying to summon information from years past was like finding a contact lens on the street. "It just sounds familiar."

Passing the note back to the agent, she asked, "Can you trace the e-mail address?"

"We already did, but had no luck there, either. That's the problem with the Internet; you can be as anonymous as you want to be."

"What about anyone at the library? Did they see who sent this?"

Agent Bailey shook his head. "No, but they're going to keep an eye out for us."

"But he'd never go back to the same place," Annika said, rubbing her fingers across her lips.

The door opened, blasting her with a burst of sound. "There's our gal!" Gem yelled. "Where've y'all been? We've been waiting for you!"

The room was filled with strewn papers and scattered laptop computers. Axel and Richard were clapping, while Lauren sat next to the senator on the couch in the informal living room. Gem scooted Annika inside amid a babble of talk.

"Great job!"

"Coffee and aspirin, huh?" Axel held out his own cup of joe. "Cool."

Smiling, blushing, Annika stepped farther into the room. Senator Carver stood up, looking impossibly handsome as he reached out a hand. "Congratulations," he said. "You just saved my campaign. Again."

"Thank you, sir," she answered, feeling her genuine smile leak through.

"Let's celebrate the demise of that damn ol' bastard!" Gem shouted, waving a six-pack of cola. She smiled demurely under the senator's mock glare. "I mean, great work today. Everyone."

"Am I too late for the party?" Jack stood at the door, the shoulders of his long coat dusted with melting snow, his cheeks flushed pink from the cold. Annika's heart somersaulted in her chest.

He walked over to her slowly, a slow grin deepening the dimple in his cheek. "Here. I thought you might need this. Just to get through the night."

Heart pounding, she opened the plain brown paper bag. Then laughed, her full, throaty laugh.

"Anyone for some ice cream?" she asked, waving the container. The others joined her laughter, calling for bowls.

Annika turned to Jack, pressing a finger to his chest. "Just don't forget. Chunky Monkey is mine."

He leaned close to her ear, his cool cheek against her flushed one. "And don't you forget that we have some unfinished business." His voice was low, sending lightening-hot pulses through her body. Then, he had stepped away, to help Gem find spoons, leaving Annika alone to battle the storm that was building inside her.

* * *

He hated himself. Hated what he was doing. But when there were six kids, five needing new clothes, two needing braces, three needing glasses, and a wife needing everything Neiman Marcus had, it was easier to bypass the guilt.

It was 7:06. He'd been standing out in the arctic breezes of Iowa for almost ten minutes. The call was supposed to come in to this anonymous gas station at seven. Did he mean central time or eastern?

Just as he started to worry, the phone rang. He picked it up, hissing as the frozen receiver touched his ear. "Hello?"

"A package of hygiene items will be sent to you in New Hampshire. You'll find what you need in the shaving cream. Just twist off the bottom. Any questions?"

"No…I mean yes. When will the money—"

"Your wife has already received the first installment. She's a good woman, didn't even ask any questions. You've picked a winner."

He bristled at the sarcasm. "Anything else."

"I'll be in touch." The emptiness of the dial tone nagged him to hang up. He carefully wiped the receiver with a handkerchief, then opened the glass door with his gloved hands.

He hated himself. Almost as much as he hated the vice president of the United States.

Chapter 5

The following days blurred into a schizophrenic dream of endless meetings, interviews and guests. Annika loved every minute of it.

Axel's polls showed the senator slipping ahead of Governor deMarco by four points. Even the whispers following Bardikoff's drug accusations were silenced when Senator Carver endorsed a new drug rehabilitation plan developed by the current Democratic Senate members.

As she rode in the back of the black Lincoln, second in a line of five, Annika gazed out the window at the clear sky, looking for Orion's belt. Counting the stars, she slipped into a peaceful daydream. The senator's television ad with the kids was being well received in New Hampshire and the east. Richard's vision for multi-leveled advertising was becoming a reality, a successful one, at that. They were already planning the ads focused on the west, with the assistance of Cleo Speros, a democratic state senator from California.

Dreamily, she fogged the window with her breath. Drawing hearts lazily, she thought about Jack. Over the past few days they had each been so busy they'd hardly spoken. He'd accepted her proposals with the briefest of nods before disappearing on his own.

"What are you thinking about?"

Quickly rubbing her fist against the window, Annika shifted in her seat. "We're going to win Iowa, you know," she said finally, looking at her assistant.

"I know."

"I mean, how can we lose with Senator Carver? He's handsome, he's people-oriented. He's the anti-politician." Casually, she crossed her legs, watching Lauren beneath her lowered lashes. "In fact, the only thing running against him is the fact that he's a single man. There hasn't been a single man in the White House since Buchanan."

"What does that matter?" Annika smiled inwardly at the sharpness of Lauren's tone.

"Oh, I don't know. If you were a mother, would you trust a man to make legislation that would have an effect on your children? Or your health? A man without the support and guidance of a woman by his side?"

Lauren took the bait. "Senator Carver has proven his support of women's issues and rights, as well as the rights of their children," she replied heatedly. "He has surrounded himself with women advisors and respectfully admires them. He knows women better than most of the voters' own husbands. If the voters can't see that, then to hell with them, and they deserve whomever they choose."

She tossed her long ponytail over her shoulder and glared out the window at the passing streetlights. Annika took pity on her, thankful she wasn't so obviously transparent.

"How long have you been in love with him?" she asked, the words as softly spoken as a child's breath.

Lauren sighed, clouding her own window. "For years." She glanced over at Annika with a face lined with regrets. "I met him soon after his wife died. In fact, I helped him start his first campaign. I always knew he would make it farther than he reached.

"And now here we are, several years later. Except now Jack, Gem and I have more work, and even more commitment to Steven."

Annika waited a moment before speaking again. "Does he know?"

She shook her head. "I don't think so. I've faced the fact that I could never compete with his memory of Sandra. And I don't want to." Unbuckling her seat belt, she waited for the secret service agent to come to her door.

Outside the Iowa State University auditorium, several members of the press waited in the bitter cold, along with a crowd of supporters waving signs supporting either deMarco or Carver. Their combined breaths created a cloud of steam that hovered just below the streetlights.

"Nervous?" Lauren asked as the agent opened her door.

"Are you kidding? This is what I live for!" Annika slid out behind her, flashing her trademark smile to the waiting cameras.

*   *   *

"How can y'all tell who's winning?" Gem whispered, shifting her weight from one spiked heel to the other.

"Unless one of them throws a real zinger, you can't tell." Annika smiled, embracing the thrill of the challenge. "Until we get a hold of the reporters in the press room. Then, we tell them Senator Carver won."

Gem chuckled, all whiskey and cigarette smoke. "May as well give my condolences…I mean, my regards to Mrs. deMarco."

Offstage, she had the best seat in the house, in her opinion. After hours of preparation with Senator Carver, she knew what his face would reveal—sincerity, determination and power. He never lost his temper, even when she tried sticking him with hurtful accusations.

"Aren't you just hoping to win sitting on the top of your wife's grave?" she'd asked, purposely hiding the question among others to amplify the shock. Senator Carver had stared at her a long time, until she had almost squirmed under his gaze. Finally, he had replied, voice soft as silk, "I am hoping to win so that other men won't have to put their wives in an early grave, as I did."

After that, Annika had every confidence in his debating ability.

From her vantagepoint, she could see half of the audience, the moderator, and Governor deMarco. Gleefully, she watched as he pulled out a handkerchief and mopped his streaming forehead. The cameras wouldn't catch that, she mused. But the reporters would. It would make for fun spin in the pressroom.

Jack is going to love it. She stopped mid-thought and glanced at her watch. He was incredibly late.

At the hotel he had insisted on taking a separate car, claiming an errand. The senator hadn't even blinked. In fact, no one had seemed surprised.

Now the debate was reaching its peak, and he still hadn't showed up. A pulse began throbbing behind her eyes, her jaw clenched. What would the press say if they knew the campaign manager wasn't even in attendance at the debate?

Deep breaths, she told herself, purposely relaxing her facial muscles. She would deal with Jack later. Right now, she needed all of her concentration to plan her strategy.

The moderator, an esteemed ISU professor and author of several political theory textbooks, appeared nearly intoxicated with personal success. He swaggered to the audience and turned the microphone over to the public, allowing twenty minutes of open questions. A squat, heavy man with a thick beard and unibrow reached up for the mike.

"Yeah, I was wondering, what is your position on the legalization of hemp?"

Annika repressed a giggle. There was always one in every crowd. Unless he stripped naked and started smoking a doobie in the middle of the auditorium, he would be cut from the tape Americans watched while eating their breakfast cereal.

The moderator stepped in, pulling the microphone away from the man, who meekly returned to his seat. A woman stepped up in his place. "Senator Carver, Governor deMarco, good evening. You both claim to have plans for health care reform, but which one of you is going to follow through?" She wiped her eyes quickly with one hand, the only signal of her distress. "My mother died of breast cancer when I was only ten. My older sister couldn't afford to get mammograms, even when the government offered them for just forty dollars. She's dying right now at Our Lady of Peace Hospital."

The audience had become nearly silent, watching and waiting. With a final pull at grace, the woman stood erect, staring at each candidate in turn. "Which one of you is going to make sure that never happens to someone else's family?"

The moderator signaled to Governor deMarco, who leaned forward on his podium, shaking a finger at the woman. "I can make sure that never happens again because health reform is my priority. By deepening Medicare's pockets, men, women and children will be able to receive a higher standard of care."

Senator Carver listened politely, then turned his full attention to the woman, who was now seated in the second row, tears streaming down her face. "I am so very sorry for your pain," he said quietly, his words echoing off the stillness of the auditorium.

"Your mother and sister suffered from one of the main killers of our American women, next to heart disease. My own wife lost her battle with ovarian cancer when she was only 28 years old.

"As your future president, I can't assure you that these deaths will stop. I can't guarantee another family won't feel the same pain as you. Or me." He leaned forward, eyes only on the woman, who now sat still, entranced.

"But I can guarantee this," he said, speaking as if there were only the two of them in the room. "I will fight for a health care system that doesn't neglect the poor or the elderly. I will fight for more dollars being funneled to women's health research." He paused, finally sweeping his eyes over the auditorium, pausing on the individual faces of women scattered throughout the audience. "And I will fight for the protection of all women's health and reproductive rights."

Silence. Then, an explosion of applause. People stood up, wildly cheering. The woman wept more. Senator Carver walked off the stage, ignoring the hands outstretched to him and climbed the steps to the second row. Embracing the sobbing woman, he whispered in her ear.

Annika spun around, searching for Lauren. "Make sure the cameras got that," she ordered, speed walking toward her briefcase. She grabbed her cell phone and pager, stuffing them into her blazer pockets.

"What did I miss?"

She gritted her teeth before turning around. He stood there, undeniably handsome, the glitter of snow melting in his hair. Unlike the rest of the staff, he was dressed casually, his dark jeans and Iowa State University sweatshirt as flattering as a tuxedo on his tightly muscled form.

Annika felt herself relaxing, wanting to lean into him as if magnetized. Instead, she brushed by him. "Catch it on C-USN, Wiese."

He matched her pace with long strides. "Let me guess. Governor deMarco sweated a lot and Senator Carver whipped his butt."

"Lauren," she called over her shoulder. Her assistant dashed to catch up. "I need you to talk to the local reporters. Emphasize the health issues, but downplay any references to abortion. This is the Midwest, after all."

"You betcha," Lauren answered, mockingly.

"I'll talk to the Post, Times and do some TV spots. I know C-USN wants an immediate reaction, plus they are doing their own exit poll."

"Sounds like a plan. I'll see you in the car." Lauren's quick steps echoed in the hallway.

"What can I do?" Jack asked.

Annika turned around, letting her breath out in a huff. "Go crawl back into the hole you dug for yourself." With a slap of her hand, she pushed open the door to the pressroom.

* * *

"We're leaving tonight," she said into the receiver, using her shoulder to hold the phone against her ear. "I'm packing right now."

"Holy confidence, Batman," Shea replied sarcastically. Annika laughed out loud, feeling the weight of pretending roll off her chest like a stone.

"Well, you saw it. What's your professional opinion?"

"Hmm, well, professionally I'd be skeptical. It's almost too LA, having him go comfort that woman. But people eat it up in the movies."

"And your personal opinion?" Annika zipped up her garment bag with a quick snap.

"Personally, I'd vote for him. And hop in bed with him. Say, he is single…"

"He's a widow. Or a widower. Whatever you call it, he's still in mourning." Annika folded each panty, each bra neatly and piled them into her suitcase. "Besides, he's my boss. And I can't even think of him in that way. Anyway…" She paused, biting her lip.

"Anyway…" Shea prompted. "Come on, spill it."

Annika shook her head, nearly losing the phone in the process. "I can't. No offense?"

"I'll trade you?"

"Shea, we promised we'd never let our professional lives interfere with our personal friendship."

"It's really good." The line hummed. "It's about you."

Annika stopped her manic packing and debated. "Off the record?"

"Completely off the record."

"OK, call me back at the hotel. I don't trust these cell phones."

Flipping her phone shut, she tossed it into her briefcase. She scanned the room quickly, then zipped up her suitcase. Propping it and her briefcase against the wall, she waited.

Instantly the phone rang. "Hi."

Heavy breathing filled the receiver. Annika's blood became ice water. She didn't realize she was gasping until the sound of Shea's voice filtered through her fear.

"Nik, it's just me. Oh my God, how could I have been so stupid. I was just trying to make you laugh…God what an idiot I am."

Annika slowed her breathing and tried to still the shaking that palsied her hands. "It's all right, Shea. I, well, just still get easily scared, you know?"

"I know. I am so, so sorry. To show you how sorry I am, I'll let you go first."

She laughed, a weaker version of her earlier merriment. "Oh, you are a peach."

"Don't I know it. By the way, I'm not taping."

"You better not be." Annika sank down on to the edge of the bed, relieving the faintness that still lingered. "OK. Someone on staff is in love with the senator."

"Hmm, Gem? Axel?"

"I'm not telling. You'll have to figure that out for yourself. Your turn."

"You know Jen Mishiko, my assistant? She flew to New York last night with…guess who?"

"I have no idea."

"Robert Bardikoff! She says he got totally smashed and started blaming everyone from Fidel Castro to you for his fall from grace. Isn't that a hoot?"

Annika toyed with the telephone cord, wrapping it around her first finger. "Bardikoff? What else did she say?"

"That's about it. Just ranted a lot before throwing up in an airsick bag." Shea's laughter filled the earpiece. "Jen was sitting across the aisle from him and luckily there were spare seat so she—"

"Wait. Jen was at the meeting we had a yesterday with the Right to Life people."

"Yes, she was doing some research on the senator and governor's stances on women's reproductive rights. Did you know that California and New York lead the nation in abortions?"

"No, I didn't," Annika said absently, pulling her finger free of the cord. "But you say she flew to New York with Bardikoff?"

"Ye-es?" Shea's tone became more serious. "Nik, what's going through that mind of yours?"

A knock at the door made her jump off the bed. Calm down, she told herself. "Just a minute, Shea." She turned to the door and called, "Come in."

Special Agent Marty Garcia poked his head in the door. One of the regulars who tracked the senator, he doubled as the timekeeper. He tapped his watch. "We're running late. You ready?"

"My bags are packed. Let me just finish up this call."

He hefted her bags over his shoulder, signaling with a finger to his lips and walked out, quietly shutting the door behind him. Annika slid her hand off the mouthpiece and asked, "Are you still there?"

"Yes, but I've got to get going. My news editor just paged me. Call me from New Hampshire?"

"Of course."

"And get me an exclusive with Senator Carver?"

Annika smiled. "We'll see, Shea. Love you."

"You, too, Nik. Take care."

As she hung up the phone, she felt her worries nibbling at her brain, like goldfish at breadcrumbs. She walked out of the room, shutting the door gently.

"All ready, Ms. Andersen?"

"Agent Bailey?" She hesitated, almost afraid to hear the answer. "The e-mail you received. From a Des Moines public library?"

"Yes?" His dark forehead wrinkled into carved ledges of ebony. "Is something wrong?"

Annika shook her head, allowing him to hold the elevator door open for her. "I just got a tip that Bardikoff has been in Des Moines. I don't know for how long, but he left last night for New York City. Can you find out what satellite feed he used for his drug accusations on C-USN?"

"Of course. Seems convenient, doesn't it."

The elevator dinged softly, the doors sliding open. Lauren stood in the hallway, suitcases at her side and a smile on her face. Annika smiled back, feeling her professional persona take control.

"And, Agent Bailey? Let's keep this just between the two of us for now, all right?"

"No promises, but I'll notify you first."

"Thanks." Striding over to Lauren, she greeted her warmly. "Have you gotten used to not wearing a purse? No keys, no checkbook to keep track of. I keep wondering what's missing from my shoulder!"

Lauren laughed. "With your huge briefcase, I don't see how you can expect to carry anything else."

While they chatted, Annika's mind wandered elsewhere, wondering what darkness haunted a man to the excess of betrayal.

* * *

"Didn't she get her flu shot?" he asked, drumming his thick fingers on his desk. Piles of papers overflowed like snowdrifts from his in and out boxes, creating a unique filing system that only he could decipher. Which was a good thing, considering the company he kept. Even reporters at the **Washington Post** wouldn't stoop to eagle-eye their neighbors' desks if they could get a tidbit from it.

Checking the crystal clock on his desk, he realized it was 12:30 a.m., way past Miller Time. The clock was inscribed, "Robert Lansky, Pulitzer Prize nominee."

Which meant exactly zilch to his editor, who was arguing in his ear.

"Bob, I know it's beneath you. You've been off the campaign circuit for what, four years now?" The receiver echoed his emphysema-induced coughs, even as Bob heard him inhale deeply from what he knew to be a Camel non-filter. "If Duggins wasn't off on paternity leave, of all things fer Chrissakes, and Mitchell is getting married. With your four-piece article on the infringement of politics on society, I know you've got some free time."

"It's not just that..." A glint of neon orange caught the corner of his eye and he swiveled in his chair. Joe, the night janitor, smiled meekly under his day-glo hat, shrugging his shoulders. Bob waved him in. "Jimmy, you know the history with me and Jack Wiese."

"And I know you to be a fair and impartial man."

"Yeah, but—"

"A Republican, too, fer Chrissakes. No respect for your First Amendment rights—"

"Oh, Jimmy, cut the crap." Bob grunted, flipping through his mess-pile for his calendar. He groaned audibly when he saw the amount of white space filling his next few weeks.

"Jimmy..."

Hack, cough. "Don't make me beg."

"You owe me. Big time."

"Sweet saints, thank you, Bobby. I'll fax over Belinda's information."

"Fine," he grumbled, replacing the receiver. "Just swell."

"Problem, Bob?" Joe dumped the small bucket of trash into his large can. Wadded McDonald's bags, empty Coke cans and a couple of pens tumbled out. **Oh, the life of a reporter just passed before my eyes**, Bob thought.

"Not really. Just going for a little trip." He scooped a stack of papers into his backpack with one sweep. "Won't be much for you to clean up around my desk for a few weeks."

"You really should recycle more," Joe said, pulling the cans from the trash and dropping them into a separate container. "Where are you heading?"

"New Hampshire Primary. Tagging along with the Carver clan. You a Democrat?"

Joe shook his head, the bright hat nearly making Bob's eyes water. "Yes, sir. Gonna vote for that guy, too."

"What is the world coming to?" Swinging his dufflebag over his shoulder, he gave Joe a mock salute. "See you when I get back."

"Have a good one, chief," Joe replied, passing on to the next cubicle.

"I'll try," Bob muttered, secretly wishing Belinda Robertson a speedy recovery.

Chapter 6

Bright sunlight alerted her arcadian rhythms, urging her to rise and shine. Mentally, she stuck out her tongue and gave the thought a juicy razzberry. After a long flight and an even longer night, the morning had melded into day.

So much for a good night's sleep she thought drowsily, fighting the urge to get up by drawing the comforter up closer around her chin. It stank of cheap detergent, with the faint traces of cigarette smoke, while its texture rubbed her throat roughly. Not at all like her mom's, where the down-filled comforter was lined with the softest flannel. Right now she would be snuggled down, letting someone else take care of her for a change, smelling the rich aroma of coffee float up the staircase.

But she was…where, again? Cautiously opening an eye, she looked at the clock. Posted to its digital face was a note declaring, "Manchester, New Hampshire." Groaning, she tore off the note, eyeing the numbers. 10:32. Rubbing her forehead, she remembered the all-nighters she had pulled in college, studying or partying, but still able to function at maximum capacity the day after.

If I could only bottle that feeling, she thought, thinking of the millions that would be piled in her Swiss accounts.

Slumping back into her lumpy pillow, she tried to pry her eyes open. Ahh, Mom's, where she would step out of bed and grab a cup of coffee, taking it and the newspaper back to her warm nest and hibernate. Her fantasy was so vivid; the hardwood floors beneath her feet, the feel of her thick robe around her, that she could almost smell the coffee.

"Good morning, sleepyhead."

Annika bolted upright, heart jackhammering in her chest. Jack sat at the edge of her bed, freshly shaven and wearing casual clothes.

"What gives you the right to sneak in my room like a common thief!" she shouted, pulling the covers up to her chin. "You just about gave me a heart attack!"

"Shh, people are still sleeping. Coffee?" He held out a cup, its contents a beige color. That pushed her even farther off-guard. He had put in cream and sugar, just how she preferred it. Sipping cautiously, she felt the last remnants of dreams slip away, her work mode shifted into gear.

"Seriously, have you ever heard of knocking? Or even of the telephone? It's a very handy gadget—you punch in some numbers and voila, you can talk to someone without barging in on them."

Jack smiled, that damn dimple of his deepening and making her feel hotter under her load of blankets. "I can see the caffeine is mellowing you out." He stood up and walked to a door she hadn't noticed in the early morning's bleary state. "And you left your door unlocked. You see, we have adjoining rooms."

A thrill tickled her tummy, like riding a roller coaster. She quelled it immediately. "So I'll remember to keep it locked next time."

"If you like." Jack's lazy gaze moved over her bare arms, slowly taking in her covered torso. Could he tell she only wore a camisole and panties to bed? Or did he see her, while she slept blissfully unaware? She felt her body tingle under his eyes, her breath catching in her throat.

"You're beautiful when you first wake," he said softly, his words faintly carried over the distance between door and bed. "All wild, tangled hair and sleepy, innocent eyes." Annika felt her breaths coming in quick puffs. He made no move to her, but she knew she would welcome him to her warm bed, wrap her legs around his strong body until they could thrust this relentless throbbing into nothingness.

Because that's all that would be left over after the deed, she thought. Nothing.

And they would get back to work.

Jack seemed to read her thoughts and turned to enter his own room. "Oh, Lauren has your schedule for today all ready. I have a personal errand to run this morning, but will see you around lunchtime."

Welcoming the shift in topics, she swung her legs out of bed, tucking the sheets around her. "What errand? We were supposed to go over our tactics with Richard—"

"We will." Jack stood with his hand on his door, darkly masculine in his rugged navy shirt and jeans. "And, Annika…

"My door will always be unlocked."

He shut the door gently. Annika didn't realize she had spilled her coffee until it seeped through her toes, spreading a thick brown patch in the rust-colored carpet.

* * *

"It's on the corner of Capitol and North State."

"Yes, sir." Agent Marty Garcia turned right slowly. He still hadn't gotten used to driving in the snow and was extremely cautious. A quality Jack wished he could obtain, at least on a trial basis.

But being cautious hadn't gotten him this far in his life. Now, at the height of his career, he had the ears of politicians, the wagging tongues of the media, and the bodies of numerous willing women at his disposal. He was aware of his own good looks purely for the sake of what they could get for him, whether it was air time or a particular female. Steven had taught him about charm, which had also proved to be helpful in both the personal and political lives.

Annika wasn't buying into any of it.

He didn't blame her. His reputation had erupted into mythical proportions. Not that he was an angel, but since the senator had announced his candidacy, Jack had been completely focused on the campaign. Besides, after hearing Steven say that Jack used women then discarded them, he could hardly look at himself in the mirror.

So maybe it was just his ego and not his true feelings. He mentally shook his head.

Was it his ego that kept him awake at night, throbbing with heat? Not unless his ego could spill over into his dreams, hauntingly beautiful memories of Annika, making him wake in the morning to sticky boxers.

She had something that he wanted. Desperately. And her candy was not for sale.

Maybe I'm getting too caught up in keeping my game face, he thought, watching the bare tree branches shake with a gust of wind, jiggling like Jell-O instead of bending and flowing under the current. Jack could sympathize. Annika had frozen him just as easily as a New England winter.

Mulling it over, he realized that Annika's game face might be the real problem. The staff knew the difference between the 'real' Jack and the public persona. Annika hadn't learned when to let her guard down. She wore nearly as many masks as a drag queen during Mardi Gras.

Garcia slowed, the brick buildings looming above their car. Old buildings, old memories, Jack thought. Some things don't ever change.

But he would. As much as he wanted to caress her seashell-tinted skin, breathe in her scent, take her with lips and tongue and hands to places she'd never imagined, he would wait. And torture himself in the process.

"Here you go. What time do you want to be picked up?"

"I'll call. Thank you." As Jack stepped into the chill and turned up his coat's collar, he felt a renewed sense of control.

He would just wait.

* * *

With the move to New Hampshire came the shift in headquarters. The senator's room was a symphony of televisions blaring, people talking and machines humming.

Annika skimmed through the room, aiming for Axel's corner. "How are we doing?" she asked without any preliminary chitchat. She looked for a place to sit, but the only chair next to him was stacked with faxes and polling forms.

"Post-debate exit polls show that the senator nailed 'em. C-USN is sayin' the same thing." He scrubbed at the scruff lining his jaw while staring at his computer screen. His hair hung straight down his back, so greasy it almost created its own dreadlocks. A cup of coffee sat by his left hand, the surface oily with scum.

To her disgust, he reached for the cup and sipped.

"Can I get you more coffee?" she asked, trying to keep a neutral tone.

"What?" Axel glanced at the cup while typing. "Naw, it's just cold. So anyways, nationwide we're holding our own. South…we gotta work on. I'm figuring it out. New Hampshire is pretty psyched about deMarco, but after last night's debate he lost some credibility. I don't have those numbers yet."

The phone to his right rang, and he snatched it like a spider on a fly. "Yeah?" With his other hand, he typed maniacally.

Annika eased away, sneaking the grimy coffee cup with her. She placed it in the sink and rinsed it with water. A sudden burst of water pressure sent a spray across her suit.

"Damn!"

"Hmmm?" Gem was sitting on a high barstool, her leopard-print skirt riding way past her thigh, one shoe dangling from her toe. Her laptop was propped in front of her. It was the only time Annika actually saw her sit still.

"Nothing." She moved closer. "How are you this morning, Gem?"

"Fine, darlin'." But she kept her eyes on the computer screen, her siren red lips a child's crayon stroke across her pale face.

Annika bent over and whispered, "What is it? You can tell me."

Wide eyes turned to her, full of fright. "Y'all can call me crazy, but there's this person who keeps e-mailin' the headquarters."

Annika's skin chilled. "Is it the same address as the first time?"

"You know about that?"

"Agent Bailey thought I should know. Who else knows?"

Gem counted off on her long, red nails. "You, me, Bailey, his men."

"You haven't told the senator yet?"

She shook her head. "Agent Bailey didn't think it was necessary."

Annika tapped her foot, thinking. "What about Jack?"

"I haven't had a chance yet."

"Well, don't. At least, not yet." Annika took a deep breath. "Let me read it."

Turning the laptop slowly, Gem slipped off her stool. "I think Agent Bailey should see this."

As the tapping of her high heels faded, Annika scanned the document. Its message was threatening in its simplicity.

"Can you feel me watch you? I'm close enough now, close enough to touch. Just one moment, one perfect moment."

It was signed, **Changeling**, just as the last one.

Struggling against the panic that was a heartbeat away, she rushed out of the room, lungs burning for air, heart yearning for peace.

Have to go, have to run, have to hide. The mantra kept pace with her footsteps. Voices called behind her, but she ignored them, jiggled the doorknob to her room until its bolt released. She barely made it into the bathroom before she vomited, gagging and retching until she was spent.

Leaning her head against the cold porcelain, she pulled her hair away from her sweaty face then flushed the toilet. Her arms and legs still trembled, but the fear was receding with the nausea.

"Annika, are you O.K.?"

"Yes. No." Slowly, she struggled to her feet, snagging her nylons on the tile floor. She felt the run pull down to her toes and swore under her breath. Leaning against the sink countertop, she turned on the hot tap and filled her mouth with water, swishing out the lingering foul taste.

Spitting, she met Lauren's worried eyes in the mirror. "I'm O.K. I need a new pair of pantyhose."

"Do you need a doctor?"

"No." Annika finger-combed her hair into a loose bunch and secured it with a barrette, staring at her reflection. She appeared calm, capable. Just as she needed to be. "Must have been something I ate. I feel fine now."

"Agent Bailey and Gem are looking for you—"

"Tell them I don't have time this morning," Annika replied sharply, brushing past Lauren. She rummaged through her garment bag, searching for some slacks. "I'm already running late for the morning briefing with the press."

Finding a freshly pressed pair of gray pants, she tossed them on the bed. "Where's Jack?"

"He had a personal—"

"Personal errand to run. What the hell is he doing, anyway." With no modesty, she tugged down her skirt and pantyhose and reached for the pants. "It's not like the rest of us take time off the campaign to attend to our own personal business. I, for one, would like to be able to take a crap without putting it into somebody's schedule."

Standing straight, she blew a wayward curl from her face. Lauren still stood, arms crossed over her notebook, the curve of a smile twitching in her cheek.

"What's so funny?"

"Nothing." Lauren walked to the door, holding it open for Annika. "At least I know you're feeling better."

Her stomach pitched like a tidal wave. Denying it, Annika buttoned her slacks and prepared her game face.

*   *   *

"So there you have it. Pancake breakfasts, ranch tours and school visits." Annika raised her eyebrow and the press corps laughed appreciatively. "Another day in the life of a presidential candidate."

"You mean, Democratic candidate." The voice came from the back of the room, unfamiliar to her now trained ears. She scanned quickly, finding the owner.

"Of course. But I feel it's obvious Senator Carver is ultimately running for president."

"What is your official position on Governor deMarco's allegations that the woman at the debate was planted by your campaign representatives?" The man stood, letting everyone who was twisting and turning in the seats to see him. There were murmurs of recognition by all. Except Annika.

She glanced sideways at Lauren, who was suppressing a smile. Frowning, she addressed the group. "Our official position is that it's completely false."

"How many points did your candidate gain after the debate."

"Nearly ten. This is common knowledge, Mr.—"

"And how many of those points can you attribute to your candidate's posturing for the camera by embracing that woman?"

Annika stared at him, fighting the urge to step down and throttle him. "I don't believe any polls have tracked that specific data."

He stood there, confident, cocky, no notebook or tape recorder. His auburn hair was thinning, his smile was insolent. The class clown picking on the teacher.

She glared back with her best schoolmarm's disapproval. His grin only widened.

"That'll be all for today, everyone. The senator will be available to answer questions later tonight after the Iowa Caucus results come in."

As she stormed out the side door, Lauren at her side, she asked, "Get Agent Bailey to check that guy's press credentials. What a nut."

Lauren laughed. "Don't you know who that is?"

"No. Should I?" She stopped in the hallway, turning to Lauren.

"He's from the **Washington Post**."

"Ms. Andersen, may I have a word with you?" Agent Bailey appeared at her side as if by magic.

"Of course. Lauren, if you'll excuse us." She began walking with Agent Bailey toward the elevator, then called over her shoulder. "Check his credentials, anyway."

"Yes ma'am," Lauren murmured, biting her lip as a smirk threatened to overflow.

Agent Bailey waited until the elevator doors slid shut. "It's about the e-mail."

"I figured as much." Annika dug in her pocket for a mint, hoping it would settle her churning stomach.

"It has been traced to the New Hampshire County Library in Concord. Same password, same log-on name." He wiped his forehead with the back of one beefy hand. No shine in his eyes today, she thought.

"So he's following the campaign."

"It appears so."

The elevator reached their floor and they exited, turning to each other just outside its doors.

"So, what do we do?" Annika asked.

Agent Bailey stood very erect, his bulk radiating capability. "We're increasing security measures. All librarians in the New Hampshire area have been given a bulletin to keep a closer eye on computer users." He shrugged. "Not much else we can do."

Annika sighed. "I suppose not. Are you going to tell the senator?"

"Actually, I thought about it when I drove him to his meeting this morning, since Agent Garcia wasn't available. But, unless we get more information, it's no use."

Agent Bailey shrugged. "He doesn't take threats very seriously." He reached out and clasped her shoulder. "If I were you, I wouldn't, either. Just concentrate on your job. We'll take care of the rest."

Annika smiled at him, stomach calming. "Yes, sir."

As he began to walk away, a flicker passed through Annika's thoughts. "Agent Bailey?"

He turned. "Yes?"

"Why wasn't Agent Garcia available to drive the senator this morning?"

"Mr. Wiese needed him. Some errand, or something."

Annika tucked her triumphant smile away. "Where is Agent Garcia now?"

"On break, I imagine."

"Thanks." Annika pressed the down button several times before the elevator finally arrived.

* * *

"I will not be made a fool. Do you understand me?"

"Yes, sir."

"Good." Vice President Martin inhaled sharply, the stink of cigarette smoke nearly curling out of the phone receiver. "Did you receive the package?"

"Not yet, sir. We've only just arrived and—"

"Goddamn it, pick it up! For Christ's sake, don't you understand? Carver humiliated me, then President Fuller hung me out to dry, letting me just hang here in the breeze until the new president is inaugurated."

You humiliated yourself by hiring a call girl to dress you up in her panties, he thought, checking over his shoulders. The pay phone was discreetly tucked in a tiny corner behind a public bathroom. The only person he saw was an elderly woman hobbling into the ladies', the door catching on her walker. If he were a gentleman, he would go help her. Instead, he turned his back and his attention.

"…or you are up a creek, mister. Are we clear?"

He shut his eyes. "As a window, sir."

Hanging up, he took off his leather gloves and tucked them in his pocket. The woman was still struggling with the door, her leaden legs unwilling to obey her mental commands.

"May I?" he asked and was rewarded with a relieved smile. He pushed open the door just enough for her walker to fit.

"Such a nice young man," she murmured.

He smiled in return and guiltily grasped that thought as he went out in search of his package.

* * *

"What's with the extra security?" Senator Carver waved, a full smile on his face even as he talked through his teeth.

"I was going to ask you that same question," Jack replied. He waited while the senator called out greetings and thanks before folding himself into the car. The senator slid in beside him.

"You mean you didn't order it?"

Jack shook his head. "Agent Barrington?"

The driver glanced in the rearview mirror. "Yes, sir?"

"Has Agent Bailey ordered an increase in security?"

"Yes, sir. Agents Flynn and O'Malley will also accompany you today."

Jack could feel the frustration leaking off the senator like radiator heat. "Why wasn't I notified?" Steven demanded.

"Sir?"

"Never mind, I know you're just following orders." Steven turned to Jack. "Call Agent Bailey after our next meeting. I want to know what the hell is going on." He rubbed his face with both hands. "Where are we going next?"

Jack had memorized the day's schedule. "Edith's Pump and Munch. To show your support of blue collar workers."

Steven rolled his eyes. "I hate that. All that strategy drives me crazy. I just want to meet some people, hear their stories. Maybe try to help them." He sighed. "Well, good thing I'm starving. I hope Edith can cook."

*   *   *

She found him at the doors, zipping up a thick parka. "Agent Garcia!"

He turned, eyes cautious. "Is something wrong?"

"No." Annika paused to catch her breath. Getting out of shape, old girl, she thought. Better take advantage of hotels' free exercise rooms. "I understand you drove Jack to his errand earlier."

"Yes, ma'am."

"Is he still there?" She hoped her eagerness didn't shine through her like a foglight and fiddled with her briefcase.

"No, ma'am. I've already retrieved him."

"Oh." Disappointment swam across her face, loosening her jaw. "Well, where is he, then?"

"Ma'am, I took him to Senator Carver's next engagement, at the food co-op."

"I see." **What now?**, she wondered, watching the short, muscled special agent. Let's see how he takes feminine wiles.

"Agent Garcia?" she asked, rubbing her forehead with her fingers, then peeking out from beneath her hand. "I am so forgetful lately, what with all this going on." She rolled her eyes before winking at him. "What appointment was Jack at this morning?"

Agent Garcia seemed indifferent. His silence weighed on her conscience. **It's none of your business**, she thought, then he spoke.

"I don't think it was an official appointment, but I dropped him off in Concord. Near the library."

"Oh, of course," she mumbled. "Thank you."

Turning around, she walked toward the elevator. The library? Unease rippled at the pit of her stomach.

After she reached her room, she sat down on the bed to think. Jack had run personal errands in Iowa, too. Now today, the day they received the latest threatening e-mail, he was dropped off by the New Hampshire County Library, the same place from which the e-mail had been sent.

Impossible, her mind argued. Jack is working for this campaign. He has known Senator Carver for years.

But do you ever really know a man? A small voice whispered in the back of her mind. **You, of all people, are not a good judge of character.**

Her cell phone rang, making her jump in surprise. "Annika Andersen," she answered automatically, shifting into professional mode with the ease of a racecar driver.

"Is now a good time to meet about tonight's victory party?" Lauren asked.

"The votes aren't in yet, Lauren."

She laughed. "Such a pessimist, Annika. Want to meet in your room and order up a late lunch?"

"I'm already here."

"Great. See you in five."

Annika snapped her phone shut and reached for her briefcase, the nagging doubts and unbridled whispers still echoing in the corners of her mind. Her eyes fell on the door, remembering how easily he had slipped in while she was sleeping.

She snapped the deadbolt in place without any hesitation.

Chapter 7

Among the sparkles of gold stars and drapes of American flags, he thought his tuxedo was a nice touch.

The hundreds that crowded the ballroom were more casual, most wearing jeans, a few in suits and dresses. But not Senator Carver's staff, shining in the spotlight of success. He had insisted they pull out their finest duds and put them on. Even Axel.

Steven waved at the crowd with both hands, as if he was about to take flight. The people roared their approval, and the beginnings of the campaign chant, "Carver Can" contagiously spread through the crowd. He liked to pick out individual faces, mouthing a silent thank you to each. The young girl on her father's shoulders, almond-shaped eyes bright, waving an American flag. He winked at the girl and thanked the father. The elderly woman leaning on her walker, her face the texture of dried apples, a smile beaming through the wrinkles. He blew her a kiss.

His eyes fell on a woman, blonde hair stiff as only wigs can be, the arch of her eyebrows penciled in. Heart aching, he held his hands out to her, silently sending his prayers. She smiled in response before joining the chant.

"Carver can! Carver can!"

Steven looked at his staff who stood next to him like family. Annika and Lauren were standing next to him in an attempt to make voters view him as a family man without the family. Even understanding the strategy, it still sent a pang through his heart.

Axel looked about as comfortable as he'd seen him, clapping and cheering with the others. Richard and Gem stood together, a comedy of opposites. Richard wore his Armani tuxedo, while Gem was wearing her favorite political party dress, a tank-style, thigh-baring, sequined replica of the American flag, complete with star-spangled heels.

God bless America, he thought with a grin. Motioning to the audience, he raised his own hands to applaud his staff.

While the others blushed or preened, Jack stood completely still, eyes glazed. Steven followed his gaze to Annika. A woman of simple taste and elegance, he mused. His eyes flickered over to Lauren and his pulse quickened. And another with style and grace.

Lauren blushed under his stare and motioned to the crowd. He held her stare for a second longer, then turned to the microphone.

"Thank you, thanks. I'm extremely grateful for your support." He laughed. "But it always feels good to support the winning team, right?"

The crowd enthusiastically clapped, cheering him on.

"Well, this is the first step. Iowa voters have set the precedent. They believe that I am the candidate that will keep his promises and meet your needs. What do you think?"

Again, the roar of the crowd was near deafening. Spirals of red, white and blue paper fell from the ceiling, patriotic confetti.

"New Hampshire, you are next!"

* * *

It was already nearly midnight, but Jack felt as alert as if he'd had ten hours of sleep. The adrenaline of the win, the excitement of the crowd. That provided his nourishment.

His eyes drifted over the crowd even as he spoke to a New Hampshire state representative. Guests mingled, the steady chatter a triumphant buzz.

A path broke through the throng. Like the pot of gold at the end of the rainbow, he thought, unable to draw his eyes away.

She was stunning, so much so that he hadn't been able to speak on the ride to the governor's mansion. Fortunately, she and Richard had chatted about the new advertising they had focused on the southern states.

And now, talking easily with the president of a local electronics company, she only mesmerized him more. The gown she wore was navy blue, with long, transparent sleeves that clung from shoulder to wrist. Hugging her body, it covered her from collarbone to shin, but the fit only fired his imagination. He yearned to trace his fingers down the bodice, skimming her hips in search of undergarments. As snugly as the dress grazed her body, he was willing to bet a bottle of Dom that she wore nothing under it.

"Absolutely nothing."

Jack started, then stared at his companion. "I beg your pardon?"

"Governor deMarco did absolutely nothing to improve our state's educational opportunities. In fact, most of our economic progress is due to new business." The state representative swallowed the rest of his champagne, then patted Jack on the shoulder. "That's why Senator Carver has my vote. Keep up the good work."

He meandered off for the bar. Jack sighed with relief. *You're losing your edge*, he mused. *Concentrate*.

But his eyes refused to obey, instead searching her out of the crowd. She was laughing, luscious mouth open, her hair trailing down her back in a cascade of charcoal corkscrews.

Then she glanced at him.

He swore there was a lightening bolt that passed between them. He knew by her eyes, the way the lids half closed, her mouth parting slightly. She could deny it, to him, to herself. But she felt it, too. It was in the slight curve of her neck and the slant of her hip.

She was the first to break eye contact, resuming her conversation with a graceful ease that annoyed him. He could hardly stutter out a response to the bartender, let alone spin and weave and charm.

"Your mineral water, sir."

"Thank you." He sipped slowly, turning back to the crowd. Senator Carver was riding the adrenaline rush, accepting congratulations with Lauren hovering nearby. The creases around his eyes could easily be mistaken for laugh lines, as often as he was grinning tonight. But Jack knew he had gotten little sleep in the past few days.

"He's amazing, you know." Heat rushed to his belly as if he'd just drank a shot of scotch. Annika nodded in the senator's direction. "The final numbers showed him winning by a forty-percent margin. What do you suppose he needs us for?"

"Colorful background," he replied. "Haven't you ever noticed how good looking his core staff is?"

"Speak for yourself."

"I was."

She laughed, her rich, real laugh. "I'd like to think I was hired for my political cunning, my intelligent strategies."

"That, too." He watched her as she surveyed the room. The navy blue of her dress made her eyes even more sharply blue, like the crevices of a glacier. Barely a wrinkle spoiled the line of her dress as it molded over full breasts and flat belly.

"You're killing me," he whispered, the air just brushing her cheek, gently setting a curl in motion. She shivered, her eyes still pasted to the crowd. The twin points pressing against her dress answered one of his questions of the evening. It was like pouring gasoline on an already raging fire. His hand nearly shook from the need for her.

"If that's your idea of a compliment, then I accept." Her eyes flickered. Jack turned to see who she was watching. Agent Bailey was stationed near the doorway, his face neutral, his eyes ever-watching.

Jack felt her tense beside him, humming like a stretched violin string. "Say, do you know anything about the increase in secur—"

She turned to him. "Where did you go to college?"

The question disarmed him, making him immediately defensive. "Harvard."

"Hmm." She sipped from her champagne flute. "I went to Columbia. During freshman orientation, I happened to be paired with Shea. Isn't that a coincidence? After being best friends as children, then separated by time and distance, meeting up again."

"Do you believe in coincidence?"

"As opposed to fate? Or God's will? Or whatever you want to call it? No, I don't think that everything happens for a reason."

Jack studied her, feeling her layers beginning to rebuild. "So it's just a coincidence that you and I are working together, after all these years?"

"Of course." She turned to him, her shoulder brushing his, eyes serious. "But sometimes things aren't coincidence. They are clues pointing out the bigger picture." Her eyes slitted. "For example, if someone overcomes an addiction to alcohol, but he is accused of currently using drugs and alcohol, is it just a coincidence that the question was asked?"

Jack choked on his water. "Wh…what are you saying?"

Her eyes flashed dangerously. She had stepped back, in self-preservation if in fact he were a raving lunatic. The idea stopped his sputtering and made him laugh. "You're serious?"

"Completely."

Jack scanned the faces around them, but everyone was involved in their own company. He leaned close. "Do you really think the senator is using drugs?"

"I didn't say that—"

"Or that it's really straight vodka instead of Perrier in his glass? He won't even have a sip of champagne to celebrate." His protectiveness gripped his throat like a collar. "It's not a coincidence that Bardikoff asked that question when he was at the edge of a cliff, looking down at the wreckage of his career."

"Then why won't you let me tell the press about the senator's past struggle with alcohol?"

They eyed each other warily, gauging the messages that passed between them, unspoken. Like dogs circling, sniffing each other, he thought, trying to suppress a smile.

"How many questions have you had since your memorable press conference."

She squinted at him, then replied cautiously, "Two."

"Any hints? Any allegations?"

Jack could almost see the hairs on her arms bristle. "Look, I know that his medical records are supposed to be kept confidential, but you can't be guaranteed that some day clerk wouldn't sell them to the **National Tattler** for a thousand bucks."

"You're stunning when you're mad."

Annika blinked, once, twice. Then her eyes sparkled like the champagne bubbling in her glass, and she laughed.

"I really dislike you, Jack Wiese."

"No, you don't. You dislike the fact that I know how to play your games."

She stared at him, lifting her eyebrow in a now trademark Annika move. "Games? I'm not playing games. But if I were, you wouldn't even have a chance to ante up."

"Oh, that's right. I forgot about New Year's Eve."

As he had hoped, she laughed again. A few heads turned appreciatively, speculating what the joke was.

"You had that coming, Wiese." Annika drained her glass and placed it on a nearby table. "No, I'm not playing games." Sighing, she crossed her arms in front of her chest. "With you and Steven's relationship, I can understand you wanting to protect him. But do you think this will look any better if it comes out weeks or months from now?"

Jack winked. "Who said I didn't agree with you?"

"But..." Swearing under her breath, she backed up right into a hole she'd dug herself. And damned if Jack wasn't loving the show.

He smirked, drawing out the dimple. "Coincidence? Or could it be I've already thought about this issue."

How could a man be so infuriating, so mysterious, so frustrating? And so obvious, the way he kept skimming his eyes over her figure, like she was the Playmate of the month. It made her feel...so...

Sensual. Sexy. Desirable. She knew what it felt like to be ogled, and also what it felt like to be appreciated. But the way Jack looked at her, she felt worshipped beyond her dress, her hair. He looked into her eyes and something stirred, first in her heart, then in her belly.

Swallowing, she avoided eye contact. But where to look? It didn't help that the man wore a tuxedo like a cowboy wore his hat, a second skin that only amplified his strong sensuality. She remembered the rent-a-tux her prom date had worn, and how there were holes in the pants pockets so he could pull his shirt down. She wondered what she would find if she casually slipped her hand into Jack's pocket, easing into the hole and touching his bare skin.

Flushing at the direction her thoughts were taking her, she held her arms more tightly to her chest. "Where were you today, Jack?" she asked, softly.

Jack smiled at a passing businessperson and murmured, "I've said that it's personal."

"But—"

"Personal. As in private. Confidential. None-a your bidness."

Annika started to protest when she saw who was entering the far side of the ballroom. She swore aloud, quite unladylike, and turned in search of another glass of champagne.

"What is it?" Jack was already searching the room.

"Don't do that!" she hissed. "He is the last person I want to talk to tonight."

"Who?"

"This arrogant reporter from the **Washington Post**." She waved her hand in dismissal. "He shows up out of nowhere, then starts harassing me. In my pressroom! Oh God, he's heading this way."

She ducked her head, smoothing out her dress and hoping the midnight blue would disappear into the background. Jack caught her arm. "Here, just pretend to be talking to me. I'll help you get rid of him."

Grateful, she looked up into his face. He released her arm and slipped his hand behind her back, pulling her close against his body. **So warm**, she thought, before the reporter sidled near.

"Ms. Andersen. Good to see you—"

"Jack Wiese." He held out a hand. "And you are?"

Something flickered across the reporter's face. He had dark blue eyes and what Annika would admit was a ruggedly handsome appearance. He was also a lot taller then he had seemed during the press conference. That and the memory of his impertinence had her pressing even harder against Jack.

The reporter smiled and shook Jack's hand. "I'm from the Post. Belinda's out sick with the flu, and I'm just covering for her."

"I see," Jack said. She felt his hand slipping lower, grazing her hip, sending tingles through her body. "So, what did you think of tonight?"

He shrugged. "It's only one caucus. He's still got New Hampshire, plus all the others. New York and California may hit him hard. California's a completely different climate."

"Yes, I'm sure they're not dressed in parkas and snowboots at this time of year."

"Politically speaking," the reporter replied, smiling at Jack.

"Oh, of course." Jack's hand dropped lower until he was almost cupping her buttock. Desire overwhelmed her senses, increasing her vulnerability. Determined to stay in control, she elbowed him in the ribs, preferring to battle the beast she knew.

"I'm sorry, but I don't believe I caught your name," she said smoothly, stepping away from Jack's warmth.

"It's Robert." He held out his hand. "Robert Lansky." He winked at Jack. "But my friends call me Bobby."

"Bobby Lansky." Annika reached through the cobwebs of thoughts until she grasped the name. Angry, she swiveled to Jack, who was biting his lip to hold in his laughter.

Bobby reached out and pulled Jack into a headlock. "Man, how are you doing? And what are you doing?" They separated, pounding each other's backs. "Can you believe this? It's like a class reunion!"

Annika smiled graciously and held out her hand. "Bobby, do you believe in coincidence?"

"Yes, ma'am," he answered, grinning. She shot Jack a nasty glare, then turned back to Bobby. "Well, coincidentally, my glass of champagne is empty. Will you excuse me?"

Holding her head high, she walked away stiffly, hearing the twelve-year-old boys' laughter mingle with the men's chuckles.

*   *   *

She had a sense of humor after all. It had just been covered by the many layers with which she shrouded herself.

Jack slipped out of his hotel room, eyes gritty, mouth numb. Across the hall the senator's room was already abuzz with activity. He didn't bother to knock.

"Good morning," he croaked, thankfully accepting the cup of hot coffee Gem offered.

"Did you sleep at all, darlin'?"

"Not a wink." Sipping carefully, he squinted at the television screens. "You?"

"Of course! I turn into a fright if I don't get my beauty sleep."

"Me, too," Richard broke in as he passed by.

"Richard! An actual joke! I'm putting this in my dayplanner!" Jack smiled.

"Oh, he's just happy because his ads are polling high next to deMarco's," Axel called from his corner of the room. Richard smiled behind his coffee cup.

"Are you smiling? Actually smiling?" Jack shook his hand vigorously. "What are the numbers?"

"We're leading by five points in the east and south. New Hampshire is holding strong at two." Axel held up a finger when his phone rang. "Gallo. Yeah. OK." He hung up, snatching his coat from his chair's back. "They're waiting for us."

"Now there's a switch. Usually we're waiting for the senator." Jack gulped the rest of his coffee, grimacing against the scalding trail it sent down his esophagus. "Gem? Hold down the fort?"

"Darlin', anything worth havin' in this dump is nailed down anyway, but if you need me you'll know where to find me."

He bent and kissed her cheek. "See you by ten. And, Gem?"

"Hmm?"

"Have some coffee on. Double strength."

*   *   *

Perhaps it was the champagne. Or the excitement of winning. Either way, Annika hadn't been able to take advantage of the two hours she was allotted for sleep.

She stared blankly out the airplane window, her laptop computer cursor blinking expectantly. There were pages to be written today, spin to be fed, interviews to be granted. But finding her concentration this morning was as impossible as seeing a polar bear in a blizzard.

It had to be sleep deprivation. So tired, she couldn't fall asleep. That sort of thing. It wasn't the door next to the dresser, light filtering through the crack at the floor. It wasn't knowing Jack was awake, perhaps working, perhaps thinking of her.

And, damn it, it wasn't the temptation of Jack's open door invitation, or the memory of his slight caresses and closeness at the governor's mansion.

He'd made her laugh. How long had it been since a man had made her truly laugh, letting all fear and self-consciousness slip away? Too long, she mused, watching the members of the press corps stumble up the stairs, most of whom were nursing big hangovers on little sleep.

"Should be as meek and pliant as sheep."

Annika turned, knowing it was Jack even through the huskiness of his voice. His musky, man-scent wafted around him. "What's wrong with you?"

He pointed to his throat. "Too much talking."

Flagging the nearest flight attendant, Annika ordered hot tea with honey and lemon, ignoring Jack's pleas for caffeine. "Tea is caffeinated, too."

"Need more."

"'Need more,'" she mimicked. "You sound like a cave man. 'Go hunt. Want woman.'" She smiled, settling back into her seat. "It'll be a nice, quiet trip to Washington after all."

A grunt was all she received as a reply. It was all she needed to flip her work switch to **on**.

*   *   *

"...what Senator Carver is saying is that education has always been a priority in the eyes of the people. So let's finally do something about it. Pay teachers more and adopt reimbursement plans that reward teachers for their success."

"But, Ms. Andersen, we don't want Uncle Sam sticking his nose in our classrooms." The reverend's nasal twang reminded Annika of the Beverly Hillbillies.

"Our classrooms are full of students with bigger challenges facing them than you or I could have ever imagined as children. Drugs, sex, alcohol, violence. Teachers are getting burnt out, and then they're dropping out. That's why Senator Carver's incentive plans will work by providing teachers with more support. In fact, the National Federation of Teachers has already put their support behind his plan."

The television anchor's voice cut in. "Since you brought up the topic of drugs, what do you make of the former press secretary's accusations that Senator Carver was and is a drug user?"

Annika stared directly into the camera lens. "These accusations are one-hundred percent false. You only have to look at the senator's track record with repeat drug offenders in Minnesota to know where he stands on this issue." Chalky bitterness left its taste in her mouth.

"And that will do it for us. Ms. Andersen, Mr. Polk, thank you for joining us here on Tick Talk. I'm Harvey Tick wishing you a good day."

After the obligatory thank-yous and chitchat, Annika excused herself and raced toward the waiting Lincoln. Lauren was already inside, talking on her cell phone.

"Whew," she said, after hanging up. "I'm glad we're just in Washington for one day. It seems everyone wants a piece of the senator." The bitter edge was not lost on Annika.

"Trouble?"

Lauren sighed. "I'm just being overprotective and silly, I guess. The vice-president wants to meet with Steven...I mean Senator Carver." She blushed crimson, but maintained her momentum. "After the huge scandal, I can't think of any reason why he would want to see the senator."

"Maybe to thank him," Annika said dryly. "Those panties he was wearing were not his color. I see him more as an 'autumn.'"

Lauren chuckled, then gave directions to the driver. As the car began to move in the slow pre-lunch traffic, she shifted in her seat to face Annika. "You know it was Jack's idea."

"To do what?"

"Eliminate the vice-president as competition for the Democratic nominee."

Annika frowned. "So, it was a set-up?"

"Not exactly. Jack knows everything about everyone in this town. It was fairly easy for him to hire a private investigator to shoot the photos. Then, all it took was a whisper before the pictures were splashed all over the papers."

"I wondered." Annika reached for a bottle of water and uncapped it. "It just didn't seem to be Senator Carver's style."

She drank deeply, easing the cracks in her throat that appeared after days of non-stop talk. Rubbing her lips together to refresh her lipstick, she mentally reviewed her next appointments. "Lauren, you said Jack knows everything."

"Yes." She laughed. "That's why you frustrate him so much."

Surprised, Annika blinked. "What are you talking about?"

"You show up, what, twenty years after he last saw you?"

"Almost twenty years," Annika muttered.

"You're beautiful, you're strong, you're successful. I'm not trying to kiss up here." Lauren took a swig from her own water bottle. "It's just, well, you're not his type."

"His type?"

"Disposable. Resistible." She rolled her eyes. "It's completely obvious that Jack is fascinated by you. He's trying to piece you together, kind of like those old Rubik's Cubes. Once he gets all the colors in place, he'll feel more at peace."

"Well, too bad for him," Annika said. "Besides, he doesn't play fair. All this mystery about personal errands and such."

Lauren's mouth puckered, as if she'd just swallowed a lemon whole. Annika pounced.

"You know what it's about. Where is he?"

She just shook her head, speechless.

"Come on, Lauren. It's not a matter of personal interest," she lied, crossing her fingers under the folds of her skirt. "He's been avoiding his duties for days, and I've had to cover for him. I at least have the right to know what he's doing."

Lauren studied her, brown eyes full of indecision. Finally, she sighed. "Agent Garcia, could you take us to 1700 Peachtree Lane? You know, where you dropped Jack off this morning?"

"Yes, ma'am."

"Then you can take me back to the capitol building." She shook her head at Annika. "I don't want to be around to see the fireworks."

Chapter 8

It was a plain brownstone, a single on a street of cookie-cutter homes. As the Lincoln pulled away, Lauren's worried face in the window, Annika hesitated. Looking down the street, she saw a community's effort to keep the neighborhood clean. The gutters held not even a cigarette butt. Shutters were painted, and some homes had potted plants lining their doorstep.

But the wail of sirens pierced the air, a steady reminder of how close they were to purgatory, where both women and men sold their bodies to get high and drugs were as common as candy.

What was Jack doing at this house? His manicured hands, his wrinkle-free pants. This was a far cry from the television soap opera that Jack seemed to step out of each morning.

Regret made her nerves flare. She could just use her cell phone to call Agent Garcia back, head to the capitol to spend time visiting key senators and begging for their support.

But curiosity won the battle, and she walked up the concrete steps. Knocking gently, she waited as a curtain parted and an invisible someone scrutinized her. A shift of a deadbolt and the door opened just a crack.

"Yes?" A matronly woman, face lined beyond her natural age, peeked through the small slit. Suddenly, her eyes brightened, and the door swung open. "You're the senator's press secretary! Ms. Andersen!"

Annika smiled, relief flooding out the electric nerves. "Yes. I'm looking for Jack Wiese."

"Come in, come in. He's talking to the girls right now." She was ushered into a dark hallway, lined with shoes. Carefully, she stepped out of her heels, placing them in the row beside an enormous pair of black high-tops and a tiny set of cartoon-emblazoned sneakers.

The woman beamed her approval. "I'm Mrs. Jensen, the house mother. Sorry if I appeared rude, but as you can understand, we mustn't be too careful about who comes knocking!"

"Of course," Annika murmured, biting back her questions.

"Would you like a tour?" Mrs. Jensen looked so hopeful, she felt she couldn't refuse.

"Yes, please."

Mrs. Jensen led her down the hall, pausing at a doorway. "Here's the kitchen. The women share jobs in shifts, so that everyone is helping. It really builds a sense of support and community that many haven't felt before."

Annika smiled shyly to the two women who were building sandwiches for lunch. The rising level of small voices had caught her attention, and she turned back to the hall.

"Here is our children's room." It was a large space filled with books and toys that would encourage every kid's playroom fantasy. However, the sober, solemn eyes that stared at her were haunting. **No laughter, no smiles**, she thought with bewilderment.

Mrs. Jensen rattled on. "We also take turns with watching the children." Annika stared at one child, a little girl with mocha skin and a ripped, pink shirt. She clung to a teddy bear, her dark eyes filling half of her face. Pulling her eyes away, Annika glanced at the women supervising.

One smiled at her, cautiously, while the other kept her eyes to the floor, the yellow-brown of a fading bruise staining her cheekbone.

"Upstairs are the rooms. Normally our families stay with us two to four months, until employment is secured and an apartment is found." Mrs. Jensen turned and shrugged. "Of course, some don't stay that long and go back." Opening a hallway door, she steadied herself against the railing. "They are always welcome to come back here, if they change their minds."

Numb, Annika followed down the staircase, the faint sound of voices floating past her. At the bottom, she leaned against the wall next to Mrs. Jensen.

Jack spoke quietly, hands folded on the table. The shoulders of the woman sitting near were shaking, and he slowly pulled a handkerchief from his pocket and slid it across the table. There were other tables, with other women sitting, but Annika could not look away.

He murmured something to the woman at his right, who was slowly and methodically scribbling on a piece of paper. She nodded, then met his eyes and hesitantly smiled. Jack returned the smile, the wink of his dimple a mere flash before it disappeared.

Annika took a deep breath, feeling as if a rock had rolled off her chest, pulling her doubts and fears with it. Shame filled its place. She should never have come. It was his private business.

"Ladies, lunch is almost ready," Mrs. Jensen said. The weight of the women's curious gazes fell on Annika. But it was Jack's look of shock, then anger, that pierced her soul to the core.

*   *   *

She refused to beg for forgiveness. Even though the guilt gnawed at her stomach, making her pop a Tums into her mouth, she wouldn't beg.

"I don't blame you for being angry," she muttered.

"Angry? No, Annika, I'm beyond angry. I'm completely, royally pissed off." Jack stared out the window, the muscles of his jaw flickering. "I repeatedly told you it was personal. Private. Yet you pushed anyway, regardless of anyone's feelings other than your own curiosity."

"I said that I was sorry."

"Sorry isn't going to work for me, sweetheart." His gray-green gaze raked her like nails. "I don't think it'll work for any of those women, either, if their boyfriends or husbands find them because of your carelessness."

A new fear pinched her conscience. "Could that happen?"

Jack shrugged, turning back to the window and shutting her out. "What do you care?"

The first seedlings of anger began to sprout. "Believe me, I care. More than you could ever realize."

"Why, because you're a woman? And I'm a man? You think that gives you an automatic inside view of what these women have been through?"

"Yes!"

Jack spun in his seat, lunging against the restraint of his seat belt. He grabbed her arm in a painful grip. "Do you know their feelings of helplessness? Or what it feels like to be beaten, again and again? How they put up with it to protect their children? Do you know what would happen to them if they were found?"

Annika shuddered. "I can imagine."

"No, you can't." She glared at him furiously, and he released her arm. "So the next time you think about invading someone's privacy, think again."

"Like you and the vice president?" The words were released before she could resist. "Or do you only hold others accountable for their actions, while you remain immune to scrutiny?"

Jack hissed between his teeth, a long, drawn-out breath. "There's a difference between the privacy of a public figure and the people's right to know. Or didn't you learn that at Columbia?"

"I learned plenty, including how to spot a hypocrite from a mile away," she answered, the heat still burning brightly.

She matched his glare. A discreet cough interrupted them.

"Sir, ma'am? We're here." Agent Garcia met Annika's eyes in the rearview mirror.

"Thank you, Agent Garcia," she answered smoothly, sweeping out of the car without a backward glance.

* * *

There were no cameras to record their visit. No sound bites, no photos of them shaking hands. Just a meek, mouselike woman who ushered him through the doorway into the main office.

Which was a good thing, Senator Carver thought, because Vice President Martin looks like a wolf when he removes his political mask.

"Vice President Martin," he said, holding his hand out in greeting. The vice president gripped it a little too strongly.

"Welcome Senator Carver. Although, I wouldn't get to comfortable in the White House, if I were you." He released the senator's hand and motioned to a chair. "Sit."

Steven nodded to Agent Bailey, who sent the vice president a look of distaste before leaving the room. He sat in the offered chair. "You wanted to see me?"

"Yes. Surprised?" Martin leaned toward him, teeth bared in a feral smile.

"Of course. I don't imagine you asked me here to announce your support."

The vice president laughed, a husky growl that ended in a phlegm-filled cough attack. He struggled to regain control and sipped from a glass of water. Senator Carver felt a nick of compassion.

"My support. At least you still have a sense of humor." His eyes glittered. "We'll see if you're still laughing when you leave."

Vice President Martin slid a folder across the floor with his loafered foot. Steven watched him cautiously, then bent down to retrieve it. "What's this?"

Martin snickered. "You tell me."

He knew before opening the folder. Keeping his hands from shaking took a lot of effort, but he paged through the papers with feigned nonchalance. Finally, he met Martin's eyes. "So?"

"So. Do you think now is a good time to let the American people know that their snow-white candidate was in a drunk tank for two months?" He sneered. "Or should I wait until you are at the height of the campaign. Say, maybe before New York or California?"

Steven repressed the urge to stalk out of the room. "What do you want?"

"I want you to burn in hell," Vice President Martin growled, shaking a nicotine-stained finger at him. "You destroyed my marriage. You embarrassed my children. You cost me the presidency." He sat back, smoothing out his pants. "But I'll take a pay-off."

"A what?"

Martin laughed. "Drop the innocent act, Senator. A pay-off. A bribe. Something that will keep me quiet."

Steven raised his chin. "What makes you think this is worth a bribe?"

"Oh, I don't know. A former drunk as president would be acceptable. A former drunk who denied having any drug or alcohol problems could be accused of lying to the public. Americans are fickle. They can forgive almost anything, but being lied to."

Martin leaned closer again. "If you get elected, I want to be put on your Cabinet. I don't care what. I want to stay in the game." His eyes darkened. "If you refuse, I'll leak the contents of that folder."

Furious, Steven stood. "Mr. Vice President, I believe you underestimate the American people." He held the folder in one hand, waving it gently. "And, sir, you have greatly underestimated me."

With the rage of a tornado, he threw the folder at the vice president, papers scattering like snowflakes.

*   *   *

Senator Carver slipped into the seat next to Jack. "Our gal is doing a hell of a job with the press. Right now, they're eating sugar cubes out of her hand."

"Probably tainted with strychnine." Glancing up at the senator's surprised expression, Jack waved a hand. "Excuse me. It's been a long day on no sleep."

"I hear you. Try using that as an excuse when you nod off during the Speaker of the House's long-winded speech after an enormous lunch."

Jack laughed. "You covered yourself beautifully."

"Thank you. What is on the agenda tomorrow?"

"Sleep."

"Besides that."

Jack paged down screen after screen on his laptop. "Slow day tomorrow. You have no official appointments until two o'clock."

"Wonderful," Steven sighed, leaning back in his seat. He accepted a glass of sparkling water from the flight attendant. "Thanks, Jennifer."

Jennifer flashed her starlet smile at Steven, then turned her attention to Jack. "Anything for you?" she asked, suggestively sucking on her lower lip.

At any other time, he would have responded to her flirtation. Maybe even bedded her. At least, laughed at her obvious attempts. But as he looked at her, perky, perfect breasts riding high in her uniform, wide mouth beckoning invitingly, he could only think of Annika.

"No," he replied, his tone a bit harsh. Jennifer looked as if he'd slapped her, and the senator frowned at him. He tried to soothe her with a smile, but she was already stalking off to the small kitchenette. Tapping the keyboard, he found no respite from his thoughts.

When he had seen Annika, standing at the back of the room, he had felt as if a window to his most personal thoughts had been pried open with a crowbar. And his fight with her, rather than purging all his hurt, had only amplified it.

But why was he really fighting? Everyone in the core staff knew about Jack's mission. Why did he want to keep it from Annika?

The plane raced down the runway, the pull of gravity like an anchor around his heart. He watched out the window as the cars became toddlers' toys and the lights swam amid the wisps of clouds. As the plane settled into its flight pattern, Jack realized something.

The anchor still weighed down his heart.

Sighing, he turned to the senator, hoping that work would create a diversion. Steven sat, head tilted, snoring lightly. Jack slumped. **Oh well**, he thought, reaching up to shut off the light.

Drawing his hand back, he glanced across the aisle. Annika was staring at him, the message in her eyes unreadable in the increasing darkness. Yet the pull, the power of her was blinding enough.

She looked away, turning in her seat to speak to Richard. Jack felt as if he had lost his jacket, cold chills making him shiver. He wanted the heat of her gaze, wanted the fire of their arguments.

And she wanted it, too. But on her terms.

He typed on the computer, sending an e-mail/page to Bobby. If ever he had a need for a friend to help him pull his head out of his ass, this was the time.

*   *   *

"Say it."

Bobby rolled his eyes, hands on his hips. Holding up one hand, boyscout style, he said, "I swear that everything I hear in this room is off, off, off the record." He sat down on the bed, scooting back so he could lean against the headboard. "Christ, Jack. We're not kids any more."

"No, some of us are far less innocent, while others have completely joined the forces of evil." He handed Bobby a tiny bottle of Jack Daniels.

"I know. I've been praying for your soul every Sunday."

"Touché." Jack twisted the top off a bottle of mineral water. "So when do you get off this bum assignment?"

Bobby shook his head. "Damned if I know. Bored to tears. Can't you tell your candidate to cough up something good, like he believes he was Cleopatra in a previous life or likes to wear a diaper and be spanked in bed?"

Jack choked, then wiped his mouth with his handkerchief. "Would you buy it?"

"Nah. He's too down to earth, too neighbor-next-door." Bobby tilted his head back and swallowed the rest of the bottle's contents, sighing contentedly. "He'll win, you know."

"You think?"

"Yeah. I might even vote for the son-of-a-gun."

Jack laughed. "The only Republican journalist comes out of the closet!"

"Hey, I didn't say I'd change political parties." Bobby glanced at his watch. "No offense, big guy, but it's late. I haven't slept in a couple days. So why don't you just spill it."

Pacing across the room, Jack glanced at the door separating him from his problem. "It's about Annika." He ignored Bobby's cackle. "I just can't stop thinking…"

* * *

"…stop thinking about him. What he's been doing, it's noble and sincere."

"It would be great fodder for the spin mill," Shea said, her bluntness cutting through the bad connection.

Annika frowned. "No. I mean, yes, it would, but he would never allow it. You promised!"

"I know, I know. Go on."

"Anyway, he's incredibly angry with me—"

"Which is totally understandable."

"Thanks a lot."

"I'd be pissed, too. Don't get me wrong, professionally, I would have done the same thing. But, Nik, were you acting out of professional obligation or personal curiosity?"

Stumped, Annika fingered the telephone cord. Static flickered like thunder. "I wish I knew." Her cell phone began its shrill call. "Damn it, my cell's ringing. Talk to you soon?"

"Take care, Nik."

"You, too." She hung up quickly, then snapped her cell phone open. "Annika Andersen?"

"Darlin', the senator wants y'all to come over for a debriefing. I tried your hotel number, but it was busy."

"I was on the phone. Thanks, Gem. I'll be right over."

Shutting her phone, she glanced at the clock. Ten-thirty. Maybe she'd get some sleep tonight after all.

*   *   *

"Did you get it?"

He stubbed out his cigarette with his shoe, sparks settling in the snow. "No. We were in Washington all day."

"Why didn't you call, we could have done lunch." The vice president snickered. He winced.

"I'll get it tomorrow. I've got the morning off."

"You do that. And give your wife a call. I think she misses you."

He doubted that. "When do you want me to do it?"

The senator turned to her, grasping her cold hands in his own warm ones. "Annika, my dear, you are not fired. I love the job you're doing. Keep up the good work.

"Jack, work with Agent Bailey on the matter. I assume there will be all sorts of new security to be planned and implemented. I would appreciate daily updates."

Agent Bailey nodded, then excused himself. The senator waited until his footsteps had receded, the door shut gently. "Finally, since we are all being so up front and honest, I had a meeting with Vice President Martin today. It seems he has gotten copies of some of my private medical records." He sighed, rubbing his eyes.

"Not many people know this, but after Sandra's death I had a major bout of depression. I wished I were dead, and went about killing myself the slow way. With booze."

Lauren reached out, covering the senator's hand with her own. He turned his hand over, clutching hers. "After several months, I admitted I had a problem and voluntarily checked into a substance abuse clinic. I've been sober ever since.

"How Martin got those records is beyond me. But he has them, that son-of-a-bitch." Steven shook his head in anger.

"What did he want?" Jack asked, his prior fury threatening to rise.

Steven looked around the room. Annika shuddered when he met her eyes, wishing she could erase the pain etched in them. "He wanted me to appoint him to my Cabinet in return for his silence."

Axel huffed. "I hope you told him to stick those papers up his—"

The senator waved his hand. "Of course I refused. But now, we have to think about the possibility of these papers being leaked to the press."

Annika cleared her throat. "Unless we beat him to the punch."

Steven turned to her as if moving in slow motion. "How?"

"You could hold a press conference clarifying your prior addiction, but insisting you haven't had a drop since. We have already said you don't have a drug or alcohol problem." She smiled weakly, hoping to ease the shock of her words. "If someone else tells the public, it'll just look like you are lying."

Steven sighed. "That's what the vice president said."

"Annika's right," Richard agreed. "It may cause a setback in the New Hampshire Primary, but at least it will be addressed early."

"Then let's fix this." Steven looked around the room again, smiling. "Thank you. Thank you for your constant support." He beamed at Lauren, who blushed.

Annika allowed herself a deep breath before diving into work. The weight of Jack's gaze still scorched, but work was her balm.

Chapter 9

Damn him, she thought, dumping the entire box of hotel bath gel into the tub, vanilla vapors churning from the mounds of bubbles. Normally the patter of water would loosen the knots in her shoulders and quiet the buzz in her head. But each splash, each gurgle murmured his name—Jack, Jack, Jack.

Annika perched on the edge of the fiberglass tub, deeply inhaling the sweet steam and willing her heart to slow its mad rhythm.

Impatiently, she jumped to her feet and paced the short length of the hotel bathroom. Grabbing a hard-bristled brush on one absent-minded pass, she tugged it through her wild curls.

How dare he try to fire her, like one of the envelope-stuffers, in front of the rest of the staff. The fact that he shunned her apology hurt badly enough. She regretted her curiosity and imposition on his privacy. But her drive to know was an asset. How else could she stand in front of the greedy pack of reporters day after day?

And he damn well knew it.

Then why was this choking lump weighing in her chest? She paused mid-stroke, absently running her fingers through a tangled lock.

Untying her robe, she let it fall to the floor and stepped into the tub. She sank into the bubbles with a sigh.

As the hot water unknotted her kinks, she relaxed her head against the rim and allowed her thoughts to circle aimlessly. What was this feeling? Long-buried anger resurfacing? Or just dislike?

Hurt? Her mind hummed as if hitting the correct note on a tuning fork. She closed her eyes. She had vowed never to be hurt again. So why was it happening? He was held at arms length, he didn't enter her day to day thoughts.

Just her dreams.

The distant burr of her cell phone interrupted her analysis, bringing her back to a vanilla-scented world with her questions still circling like butterflies in the spring.

Annika twisted the faucet. Silence. Whoever, whatever it had been, she knew that if it was important enough she would be tracked down.

Bbrrriiiing! Annika groaned, squeezing her eyes shut. **Why did hotel phones have to be so damn loud**? she fumed. "Leave me alone for just a minute," she whispered to the water, the frothy remnants of her bubbles huddling at the edges of the tub. It wasn't as if she was out partying it up or—God forbid—meeting a reporter to leak a story.

The shrill ring disagreed. Its burst shattered the quiet like glass.

The lump in her chest dissolved in the heat of her rising temper. "I'm not here!" she shouted, then angrily slid down the tub's curve until she lay submerged, the scratchy slipguards rubbing her back.

Feeling like a champion oyster diver, she reined the urge to rise out of the water and mentally ticked off the seconds. Twenty-one, twenty-two, twenty-three…gasp! The silence that welcomed her surface felt almost as good as her calmed spirit.

She breathed more naturally, her calm, rational self netted the butterfly thoughts.

Of course she felt a bond with Jack; she felt close with everyone she worked with on this campaign. Just like every campaign. There's a goal. There's a challenge. It's a high-stress, high-adrenaline, high-power rush.

When meals, trips and risks are taken as a team, there has got to be some bonding as well.

The heaviness in her chest pressed her deeper into the water. Leaning her head against the tub, she sighed. Why was it that whenever she looked at Jack she saw the way his steely gray eyes darkened in concentration? Or how he stroked his hair into bristling quills when pondering a strategy? Or when he was arguing with her a smirk would wink from the corner of his mouth?

All he had to do was glance at her and her heart would race. He would brush against her and her skin would flush with heat. But in the next moment, he would say something so patronizing and self-righteous that she would grit her teeth in anger. Just like when they were children.

Annika sat up abruptly, lingering flecks of foam sticking to her back. **What a fool I am**, she thought, clenching her hands into fists. Of course he's patronizing. And why not, when the press secretary hired for the campaign is not only someone Jack knew as a child, but someone who was continuing to *act* as a child.

She hugged her knees to her chest, goosebumps beginning to pebble her skin in the cooling water. You're blowing it, she chastised herself, pressing her lips to her knees. She was taking her eye off the ball, disregarding her meal ticket. Choose whatever cliché, but she was forgetting who she was and what she was doing here. This wasn't some small-town bid for mayor, this was the big league. A shot at the Democratic Party candidacy, and then…well, and then who knew? Governor Carver had wooed and engaged her trust and respect. With her help, maybe he could spin all the way to the White House.

That was the job. Annika had not deprived herself of sleep, standards and a social life for second best. So any of the burning desire or passionate dreaming was going to stay in its rightful place…a romance novel, not a primary election.

Mind steeled with new resolve, she pulled the plug from the tub, feeling more sure of herself as she watched the water drain. The harsh ring of the hotel phone jumpstarted her heart. Scrambling out of the tub, Annika had enough time to sling her Japanese silk kimono-style robe around her before the phone reached its fourth ring.

"Annika? Where the hell have you been, I've been trying to get a hold of you?"

She sat at the edge of the bed. "Senator Carver. I apologize sir, I was—"

"Well, now, it's not important. I've caught you now." Carver's voice mellowed considerably. Always the mother hen looking out for his chicks, Annika thought with amusement.

"Is there something I can help you with, sir?"

"Actually, since you ask…"

"You called me, sir." The smile in her voice traveled across the phone line as clear as a northern Minnesota lake. Carver couldn't help but grin in return.

"Now that's why I hired you, Annika. Always keeping me on my toes."

"Quit trying to butter me up and spill it, would you Senator Carver?"

Carver cleared his throat, hoping to inject some seriousness into his tone. "It's about Jack and what happened today."

Silence.

"Now, I've already had a talk with Mr. Wiese about his behavior today. It was inappropriate and disrespectful. However…" he paused, glancing up as Lauren entered the room mouthing a question and waving a stack of papers. Nodding, he refocused on the telephone receiver. "However, I've heard enough rumors and seen you two bump heads enough times to know that this isn't a one-sided problem."

"Sir, with all due respect—"

"Now is not the time for my team to fall apart on me. Axel just sent me the polling numbers from Governor deMarco's speech. Seems we've lost credibility on social security and medicare, while his popularity is up three points from yesterday." Carver removed his reading glasses and rubbed the bridge of his nose. "Annika, I need you to help me win this thing. But I need Jack, too. You and Jack need to come to some kind of understanding so that we can all work together. Can you do that for me?"

The pause was half a second, but Carver sensed her frustration anyway. When she spoke, her voice was smooth as polished jade. "Of course, sir. And please accept my apologies for taking you away from your work for this trivial issue."

"Nonsense." Lauren sat on the edge of the bed, her dewy eyes warm with affection. He almost set the phone in its cradle before remembering he hadn't finished the conversation. "Oh, by the way, Jack should be there shortly to discuss all of this. See you bright and early at seven."

"But—" Annika stared dumbfounded at the burring receiver. Perfectly on cue, a harsh knock rattled the door against the deadbolt.

She slammed the phone down. Duly chastised by the senator's remarks, she still bristled at the thought of "making nice" with the class bully. **There you go again**, she seethed. Let's move on.

Maybe that's not your real problem, her inner voice whispered, and she remembered how it had felt to kiss him, their bodies molding together, feeling the power she held over him. And his hold on her.

"Don't be ridiculous," she muttered to herself, standing. Smoothing down her robe, she turned to the door. "Coming!" She was satisfied that her voice sounded calm, crisp. Professional.

Jack leaned his forehead against the door, willing the aspirin to take affect. He'd gulped it down with coffee after his chat with the senator. Now he couldn't remember if caffeine helped a headache or contributed to one.

Hearing the swish of movement beyond the door, he stepped back. Jack knew who contributed to most of his headaches. And she was fumbling with the lock right now.

With the fluid swing of the door, she was there. Jack sucked in his breath. Annika was leaning against the doorframe, coal-black hair tumbling over her shoulders in wet corkscrews, dampening the shoulders of her robe. If it was in fact a robe, he thought, staring at the flimsy covering. Pure silk, even its cherry red shade couldn't combat the backlight that filtered through, turning an ordinary robe into an alluring peepshow. The outline of her legs showed smooth curves and gentle slopes, the slit folded back allowing just a glimpse of ivory skin, a sight more teasing and tempting then if she had opened the door completely nude. The thumping of his headache dropped into his groin, a hot pulse of desire.

He again raised his eyes to Annika's cool blue ones. Ice water dumped over his head, he mused as he grinned at her scowl. "I take it the senator has already called you."

"Yes." She leaned a shoulder against the doorframe, crossing her arms. A flex of silk parted, showing the flush of the high arch of her breasts. "But obviously now is not a good time…"

Jack nudged the door open with his foot and strolled in. "Now works for me." Flopping down into a chair, he smirked at Annika, enjoying the flash of anger that creased her forehead. Just as quickly, her brow smoothed, and she smiled politely before turning to shut the door.

What was that? he wondered, narrowing his eyes. Familiar with her tricks, he mentally turned over the reasons for Annika's change in attitude. The senator's scolding? Hardly. She was more frightened of getting a piece of cork in her glass of wine than that old softie. True regret for her actions? Perhaps. Maybe he'd really frightened her when he'd tried to fire her.

Frightening Annika Andersen. The press secretary with steel nerves. Now that was a thought.

Annika sat on the edge of the bed, crossing her legs and causing Jack's heart to speed again. He wondered if she could hear the thrum of his heartbeat. It seemed as if a brass band was playing, knocking against his ribs.

"First of all, I'd like to thank you for meeting with me," he started, leaning backward and crossing his legs.

"Wait, stop!" She held a finger up. "Your posture is all wrong. To show submission and open communication, you need to change your body language. More like this." Uncrossing her legs, she leaned over, elbows on her knees. The gape in her robe widened, tantalizingly. Jack reminded himself to get his blood pressure checked.

Clearing his throat, he mimicked her posture. "Like this?"

"Much better," she said, sitting back. It took him only a millisecond before he realized why she had such a satisfied look on her face. His jaw clenched.

"Hey, I'm not showing submission here. That is the last thing you can expect to see from me." He resumed his former pose. "You see, there. That's why you're ruining this whole campaign!"

Annika jumped to her feet, eyes icy with anger. "Me! I'll let you know that Senator Carver would not have gotten this far without my attention to detail, something you seem to overlook. We actually have a chance in New Hampshire, damn it! And another thing…"

"Here we go again," Jack muttered.

"And another thing," she repeated even louder, stomping her foot. "You had no right to bring something personal into a campaign staff meeting. I have regretted my actions since the minute Agent Garcia drove away, leaving me at the foot of those stairs. Why can't you accept my apology?" Breathing heavily, she threaded her fingers through her fountain of curls, reminding Jack again of how he longed to do the same. Shaking her head, she met Jack's gaze. "I apologize. That outburst was completely unprofessional."

Jack choked on his laughter. "Since when do you act professionally with someone outside of the media?"

"I'm afraid I don't understand your meaning," she said, arranging the folds of her robe around her as she sat on the bed. Her face was devoid of expression, and her eyes were downcast. If only he could get a glimpse of her eyes, he'd know why she was acting this way.

"On second thought, since when have you acted courteous and professional to me?" he asked, tapping his thumb against his leg.

"I've always treated you with the utmost courtesy—"

"New Year's Eve."

Annika met his eyes with detached coolness. "That was a personal victory. This is strictly business."

"Strictly business, huh?" Jack leaned closer, watched her eyes flicker with heat before the mask dropped again. "See, I'm of the mind that our professional issues are becoming more of a personal nature."

She raised an eyebrow. "How so?"

"For one, you seem to bring out the tyrant in me." He shrugged. "I suppose I owe you an apology." Moving swiftly, like a panther, he squatted next to her. Enveloping her small hand in his, he began to lightly rub circles in her palm. "I'm not going to give you one."

Her eyes snapped with fire, much to his satisfaction. Recovering from the shock of his closeness, she tried to pull her hand away. Jack held on even more tightly, rubbed even more delicately.

"For two, while I find you arrogant, rude, obnoxious and aggressive, I must admire your personal qualities as well. You are creative and innovative, and know what the press corps is thinking before they do." Annika sat frozen, eyes decidedly focused on her lap.

"And finally," Jack leaned closer, his voice a husky whisper. "Whether in the flood of camera light or the dimness of the conference rooms, on an airplane or in a bus, seated at a governor's head table or laying on my hotel room bed, I can only think of one thing."

His strokes were hypnotic, sending warmth through her arms. Annika was barely aware of the flush that was spreading over her breasts, but the tingling sensation lingered, lowered, until her veins thrummed with desire and need.

"Do you know what it is?" Jack's voice sounded far away, as if from under water.

"I think so," she whispered, pulse racing as she met his eyes.

Jack pulled away abruptly and stood. "Great! I knew that getting the senator nominated was your top priority, too. So I'm confident we'll figure out a way to work out our minor differences." He shoved his hands into the pockets of his khakis. "Besides, I think we've learned a lot about each other since New Year's Eve."

She'd let down her guard and he'd sneaked right through the hole, slashing a gash in her already aching heart. Struggling to remain in control, she glared at him. "You're right. I've learned that you treat women like dirt, then to atone for your sins, you visit women in shelters. You expect to be respected, but you hold no respect for me, or the work I've done." Standing, she raised her eyes to his, only inches away. "And I've learned, after all this time, you are still the mean kid on the beach, only looking for pats on the back."

Jack stood impossibly still. She held her mouth tightly shut, her jaw grinding against the rise of tears. She held his gaze. Like twin statues, they stood for minutes, a contest of wills.

"Do you really believe that?" he asked, finally.

His eyes were the color of evergreens, and held hers steadily. Without a thought, she whispered, "No."

The thudding of her pulse echoed in her ears. As the seconds passed, it faded, like a retreating marching band. In the stillness, she could hear the faint chatter from a television set and the murmurs of the special agents.

Jack stood like a statue, his nerves nearly visible through his skin. His jaw flexed even as his eyes remained motionless, staring a hole right through her. She refused to look away, a primal instinct to fight.

Finally, he sighed, shut his eyes. Running a hand through his hair, he sank onto the bed. Cautiously, she sat next to him.

"Do you want to know why?" he asked. "No, don't answer. Of course you want to know why." He sighed, his body brushing against hers. She remained silent, studying the carpet. Maybe it would be easier for him that way.

"What did you see when you looked at twelve-year-old Jack Wiese?"

She wet her lips, buying time. Carefully, she said, "I saw a boy who had it all. Popularity. Intelligence. The ability to both win a girl's affection and break her heart in the same minute."

His shoulder shook as he laughed, a short, staccato bark. "The things that made me the man I am today, right? Well, no. You saw what I wanted you to see. What I wanted everyone to see." His voice dropped. "My reality was too frightening to share."

The puzzle pieces in her mind began to shift, falling into place, but she waited for Jack to confirm her thoughts. He took a deep breath, blowing it out through his mouth.

"My dad worked very hard. His job required him to travel quite a bit, which was considered a vacation for us. My sister and I never went to bed hungry or to school in non-designer labels." He picked at a spot on his pants. "He claimed that since he worked so hard, he deserved to play hard, too. Drinks at the country club, drinks at the downtown bars. He would come home so pickled that Jess and I swore we could smell him before he climbed the stairs."

Jack shook his head and folded his hands. "For years we never thought what happened in our home was wrong. So many years of listening to him stomp up the stairs, past my door. Hearing my mother beg for him to stop, then covering my ears to her screams."

Her heart ached for him, reliving the fear of a young boy, burying his head under comforters and pillows against sounds he didn't understand. She reached out, pressing her hand against his folded ones.

"We would pretend to not see the bruises the following mornings. Mom would pretend, too. 'Who moved the dresser again,' she would say. 'Bumped into it again last night.' Jess and I would play along. For years." He gently placed one hand on top of Annika's.

"Then one night, his feet stopped at Jess's door." He shuddered. "I was about sixteen. She was twelve. The minute I heard her first scream, I was in her room." Shaking his head, he gripped her hand more tightly. "I've always asked myself, how drunk do you have to be before you find your own daughter sexually appealing? I've never been able to answer that.

"Anyway, I pushed him off of Jessica and just started to punch him. Over and over. All the years of pent-up rage just was released in this huge rush. I remember my mom pulling me off, screaming my name. Jess sitting in her bed, the covers drawn up to her chin, sobbing." He released her hand and cradled his head. "And my father, blood covering his face. The bastard. He never touched either of them again. At least, not while I lived there."

Jack raised his head, his eyes dark gray as thunderheads. "But, his was the gift that kept on giving. You know how I told you Jessica went to Marquette?" Annika nodded, but he didn't seem to notice. "She never got her degree. Unless you want to call it her M.R.S. She met the jerk she's been with for years now. He beats her. It's been for so long now that she can't see a way out. She was pregnant, last year, and he beat her so badly she miscarried. The doctor doesn't think she can have children now. But she won't leave him." He met Annika's eyes. "Just like my mother."

Tears trickled down her cheeks, and she wiped at them, embarrassed. "Jack, I…I don't know what to say."

"Then don't say anything," he replied, voice husky. His breath tickled her neck. "All the words in the world won't change what happened to my family. But if I can help just one woman. If not for herself, for her kids."

Suddenly, he was standing, moving toward the door that adjoined their rooms. She shivered, already missing the heat beside her. Rising to her feet, she followed him.

Jack held his arms out, stopping her from reaching for him. "Don't," he choked. "Not now. Just listen to me."

He bent near her, his mouth brushing her hair. The rasp of his voice near her ear sent delicious shivers down her back. "I want you. But not right now."

Jack held her tightly with one hand and twisted a lock of her hair with the other, murmuring in her ear. "When I open my eyes in the morning, my first thought is of you. When I go to bed at night, the last thing I remember is you. When I wake up in the middle of the night, aching with want and need, it is your face, your body I dream of.

"You can try to resist. You can try to deny it. But when I look in your eyes, I see it. The desire. You feel it, too." He drew back, looking at her with green eyes blazing with fire.

Too shocked to resist, she simply stared at him. He released her, stepping back into his room. Disappointed, Annika crossed her arms over her chest.

"Come to me when you're ready," he whispered, then slowly shut his door.

Battered with emotions, she shut her own, clicking the lock into place by habit. She wasn't surprised when there was no answering click from the other side.

*   *   *

Restless, she punched her pillow, trying to shape it into a ship of dreams that would carry her off to sleep. It resisted, melting back into its marshmallow-like shape.

Glancing at the clock, she groaned. Four-thirty. It had been hours since Jack left, hours filled with blinding fantasies and dazzling wishes. Her body felt newly awakened, like a butterfly in the spring, every nerve exquisitely sensitive.

It had been a long time since she had been with a man. Even so, she had never felt this heightened urge, this impatient desire.

So go to him, she thought, a thrill running through her. The thin line of light still spread beneath the door. He was awake. He would welcome her to his bed. Perhaps, he was thinking of her right now, wishing and waiting for the doorknob to turn.

Stop it, an inner voice spoke. **The last thing you need is to complicate your life. Stay professional. Stick to the campaign. You don't want to end up getting hurt.**

Hurt. Jack knew of her kind of pain. Intimately. After his confession tonight, her heart reached for him, full of trust. His arms would be safe, his words would be truth.

But some fears have had lifetimes to permeate the soul, and hers was tainted was streaks of yellow. Lifting the mushy pillow, she buried her head, wishing for the peace that dreams would bring.

* * *

That bitch. It hadn't been enough to make him a fool once.

He turned off the television, fury edging his vision with crimson. No word on the dear senator. That son-of-a-bitch. Back stabbing weasel. Probably bonking her right now.

Don't you get it? He turned, cocking his head to hear the voices more clearly. Listening, he nodded. His pulse slowed. The world clicked into focus, like when he went to the eye doctor.

He walked into the bathroom, zipped open his shaving kit. His fingers touched plastic, and he grabbed. Standing over the toilet, he opened the bottle, spilling out a waterfall of pills. They danced a dizzy circle when he flushed the toilet, spinning, spinning.

As he walked back to his bed, he felt his thoughts spinning in the same way, individual pieces falling into his hands. He lay on the bed, waiting for enough pieces to create a plan.

Chapter 10

"Let's try using a firmer tone, Senator Carver." Richard snapped his fingers at the cameraman. "And keep a loose frame. I don't want to see his feet, but let's have a view of his crossed legs."

"Ultra-liberal body language, extra-conservative tone. I like it." Jack patted Richard on the back. He glowed appreciatively, his eyes specks behind his lenses.

"Hoover meets the Harvard Hasty Pudding drag queens," Steven mumbled, twisting his tie.

"And, don't forget, just be yourself," Jack said sarcastically, sitting down beside him.

"I can't forget, with all of you and every lobbyist in the world reminding me."

Jack laughed. "Back to your old self. You must have gotten some sleep last night."

"I think I banked six hours. Felt like twenty." Steven yanked his tie, trying to get it to lie flat.

"Here, let me do that." Lauren stepped forward and with deft fingers, straightened the tie with ease. Rebuttoning his collar, she smiled. "There, much better. Just needed a woman's touch."

She flushed, turning to resume her post next to Gem. Jack watched Steven follow her with his eyes. He seemed lit from within, like a candle. Why hadn't he noticed before?

Jack cleared his throat, causing the senator to jump self-consciously. "She's right, you know. Maybe this whole campaign needs more of a woman's touch."

With a quick glance, he could tell the senator read his thoughts. Steven shook his head. "Annika has been a real asset. Besides being able to steer the reporters, she is a woman and she is on the television every day, as a representative of my campaign."

"True enough," Jack said, lazily playing with a shoestring. "But maybe what the American public wants to see is their next president standing next to a woman. A woman who not only supports his campaign, but supports his needs as a man."

"Are you trying to tell me I need a wife to win this election?" Steven glowered beneath his dark eyebrows.

"No, what I'm trying to tell you is you need a wife. Period." He sighed. "I know you miss Sandra. There isn't a day that goes by that I wonder what she would think of all of this." He stood, facing his boss, his friend. "She would be so proud of you. You know that? But, she would want you to move on. Because no bill you pass, no office you hold is going to bring her back." He looked over his shoulder at Lauren, whose bright smile flashed at Gem's shared joke. "And sometimes your most vocal supporter can be your most committed companion."

He watched Steven, waiting for the flood of anger. Instead, the senator just sighed. "Is it that obvious?"

"Yes."

Steven laughed. "I wonder how she feels."

"I don't know for sure, Senator Carver, but if she ignores you when you call her names, that means she likes you."

"Jack, no wonder you haven't held on to a woman for more than a month."

"I'm learning, sir."

"Not fast enough." The senator's eyes shifted. Jack turned around and caught his breath.

Didn't they say that absence made the heart grow fonder? Then why, after seeing her day after day, sometimes for twelve-plus hours, did she appear more beautiful and desirable?

"Take some of your own advice, Jack," Steven whispered, before smiling widely. "Annika, dear, how many votes have you won for us today?"

"Not nearly enough in the west, it seems," she answered, barely acknowledging Jack. "You've dropped two points since yesterday."

"That's because Governor deMarco is already campaigning in California. What do you think, Jack?"

Jack paused. "Well, it would be wise to bulk up our advertising in the top five television markets: Sacramento area, San Francisco, Orange County, San Diego and Los Angeles."

"Let's talk to Axel and get the latest numbers before you finish taping these spots," Annika suggested.

Jack grinned at her. A brain for business. "Good thinking. I'll tell Richard to hold on for a few minutes."

"Do you want to consider running a spot announcing the senator's previous addiction?" she asked softly.

"I'll consider it." He smiled at her surprised look. "But you'll have to convince me."

Annika returned his smile. "I'll be right back."

"Great."

He watched her speed-walk, as at ease in her high heels as she would be in sneakers.

* * *

"I don't mean to keep bothering you, but –"

The New Hampshire polls were predicting a win. All the West Coast ads were completed, with Richard completing the demographic data. The reporters, well fed with the daily spin, were tucked in for the night.

Annika paced the length of her room. Mentally, she ticked off her to-do list, even though her computer schedule had already confirmed it. She had nothing to do. The New Hampshire Primary was tomorrow, and she had nothing to do but wait.

Restless, she flipped on the television on one of her passes. C-USN was covering the Republican candidates, their press secretaries weaving and threading together each individual statement. It was nerve-wracking work. She knew, since she'd already done her job that evening for the cameras.

She flopped on the bed, studying the candidates. One appeared to be straight from a police line-up, while the other looked like the old Charlie McCarthy ventriloquist doll. Yak, yak, yak.

In a country where good looks bought votes, sold products and granted favors, Senator Steven Carver had the edge over the other candidates. Even Axel's polls had shown that among women, eighteen to fifty, regardless of political persuasion, over seventy percent favored Senator Carver.

She could think of one woman in particular who favored the man. Lauren, with all her determination and persistence, had convinced the senator to bring her to the political dinner that night. She had also convinced him to allow everyone a night off. **Gem and Axel were probably still celebrating at the bar downstairs,** she mused.

While others, like her, were looking for work to complete. Her eyes were drawn to the light under the adjoining door. She wondered why Jack hadn't taken the opportunity to go out, but instinctively knew he would be tying up loose ends before the big day tomorrow.

Annika leaned over and turned off the television set. Straining her ears, she could pick up no sound from the other room. She repressed the urge to hold a hotel glass to the door, mainly because she suspected Jack would hear the clink of glass against the wood.

She lay back on the bed with a self-pitying groan. Staring at the ceiling, her mind began to wander, thinking of the way she and Jack had worked together that day. As if the two hands of a pianist, playing together to create a beautiful piece. They had accomplished more in one day than they had the past few weeks.

Smiling, she thought of his face, how he bit his lip while thinking and smiled broadly when something worked. Their hands had accidentally brushed every once in a while, and his nearness seemed to make her awareness more acute, as if she could feel each fold of fabric against her skin.

Expelling her breath in a frustrated burst, she sat up again. A bath. And a pint of ice cream. Then, some much needed sleep.

But her eyes moved to the door as if magnetized.

Her body began moving before her mind caught up. Surreally, she watched her hand unlock her door, then, without knocking, open Jack's.

As he had said, it was unlocked. As if he had been waiting for her.

But he wasn't there.

Disappointment froze her limbs. She tried to swallow its bitter taste. Scanning the room, she noticed the laptop next to the bed, the cursor blinking expectantly. There was an empty glass alongside it.

Her gaze drifted back to the computer. The screen was filled with icons. The automatic screen saver had not yet kicked in. **He must have just left**, she thought, feeling her heart, and hopes, drop.

"Spying again?"

She jumped, whirling around with arms raised to fight. In an instant, she tensed even more. Jack was standing outside of his bathroom, hair slicked down, bringing out the emerald in his eyes. She couldn't resist skimming over his muscled torso, the indents of his abdominal muscles a staircase for fingers to walk. The towel hung around his waist loosely, the hollow near his hipbone a teasing shadow.

Gulping, Annika tried to regain her composure. "I'm not spying." She tilted her chin up. "You said your door would always be open to me, so I came in."

Jack raised his eyebrows. "So you were going to seduce me?"

Heat flushed her cheeks even as she defiantly met his eyes. "Hardly. I was going to see if you wanted to…" Her eyes searched the room desperately, falling upon his empty glass. "Go have a drink."

"I've already had a cocktail this evening," he said, slowly walking up to her. The dizzying scent of soap and shaving cream and male made her arms fall to her sides, weak as a fledgling bird.

"Well, then, I'll just drink alone," she murmured. "I mean, I'll skip it. I've got to…"

His face was so close she could see the flecks of gray and blue in his eyes. His lips looked so soft, his face freshly shaved. As if pulled by a marionette's strings, she leaned into his body, still hot from the shower, but trembling against her.

"Annika," he whispered, then bent his head, smoothly pressing his lips against hers. Tenderly, he kissed her, with such care that she hungered for him to take her roughly. As if reading her mind, he swiftly parted her lips, plunging his tongue into her welcoming mouth. She moaned against him, clutching the back of his towel, feeling the flex of his shoulders as he gripped her in return.

They broke apart, each breathing heavily as if they had completed a marathon. Jack leaned his forehead against Annika's, tenderly stroking her hair. "I need to hear you say it."

She shivered under his touch. "What?"

"That you want this. That you want me."

"Jack…" She kissed him deeply, felt his fingers tighten against her scalp. She nuzzled his ear. "I want you. Now."

He groaned, taking her into his mouth, bringing pleasure with every kiss. She had never felt so powerful and yet so paralyzed, so wanted and yet so needy. His lips held every answer, but kept them out of her reach.

They bumped into the bed, tumbling into it like teenagers. Jack fumbled with the buttons on her blouse, and she reached for the table lamp.

"Don't," he said, eyes dark with passion. "I want to see you. All of you."

"No." Nervousness edged over her desire. "I...no, I just can't."

Jack's mouth separated her blouse, fingers flicking open the front clasp of her bra. His warm hands slowly pushed the cups to the sides. Annika stiffened, waiting for him to see.

She watched him look at her body, frigid with embarrassment. First the questions would come, then the awkwardness. She waited, eyes on the ceiling.

"Oh, God," he said, voice husky. She met his eyes, lip quivering. "You are the most incredibly beautiful woman I have ever seen."

He bent his head to nuzzle her breasts, sending sparks through her veins. He hadn't noticed, she mused, feeling as if her thoughts were helium balloons, drifting away.

Unbuttoning her pants, he slid them down over her hips. His mouth ran a trail of hot kisses along the waistband of her panties, initiating a pulse to throb between her legs. He paused, then with exquisite gentleness kissed the scar that ran from her right rib to her navel.

Before she could react, he yanked off her panties, kissed her inner thighs. The flame blossomed to full fire, as he parted her with his tongue, teasing and tasting. Blindly, she arched against him, the heat spreading throughout her belly, immersed only in his touch until fireworks exploded behind her closed lids. She shuddered against him, but he insistently buried himself further, igniting such raw desire she thought she would scream.

Just as she reached another peak of pleasure, he balanced above her, raining soft kisses on her breasts and neck. "I'll try to be as gentle as I can," he whispered, pressing against her experimentally.

The primal urge overcame her, and she grabbed his buttocks, urging him to drive deeper, faster. His moan echoed in her ear, his scent overwhelmed her thoughts. All she knew of was the need, the blind, desperate need that ached within her, wanting to be filled.

She climaxed again, arching against him, while he buried his face in her hair, whispering words that were as incomprehensible as the wind. Goosebumps pebbled his skin as he collapsed against her, his muscles taut under her hand. Drifting on a wave of bliss, she felt herself slipping away, Jack a safety net.

* * *

Someone had hurt her. The idea of it made him nearly shake with anger.

Annika slept, her wild black curls tumbling over the white pillowcase, dark lashes brushing flushed skin. It was the first time he had seen her forehead smooth, free of worry and strain. Life under the masks, he mused, wrapping a curl around his finger.

Protectively, he had tried to cover her, keep her warm as the sweat began to dry from their bodies. But she had kicked away some of the blankets as she slept, leaving a porcelain-perfect river of skin to her knees.

Except for the scar.

Puckered at the edges, it resembled the letter 'c', curving from under her ribcage toward her belly button. Years had leached the color from it, so it was only a shade pinker than her skin. Hardly noticeable, except for the way it brutally thickened toward the base of the 'c'.

She had tensed when he had touched it. He remembered her pliant flesh instantly stiffen, before melting again like wax under his persistent touch.

He hadn't asked. And he wouldn't. There were reasons why people wore so many different faces and had such different personas. He, of all people, could understand that. The masks he wore could outfit a block of trick-or-treaters.

And he, of all people, knew the value of privacy.

She stirred, restlessly kicking at the sheet. Jack leaned over to turn off the lamp. The room sank into semi-darkness, the streetlights casting a silky shine against the flimsy curtains. Light leaked from Annika's room, where she had probably spent her evening pacing, wondering what to do with herself.

He smiled, watching her sleep. He approved of her decision.

Her eyes fluttered, then slowly opened. She stared, her face a barrier to her thoughts.

"Hi." Leaning on his elbow, he was careful not to touch her. She blinked once, then her lips curved. Under the covers, he began to stir, the need tingling in his belly. How could he want her again, so soon and with the same passion?

Noticing her nakedness, she reached down and pulled up the blankets, snuggling down into its warmth. "So," she said, raising her eyebrow.

Jack smirked. "So."

"I should be feeling very awkward right now." She wiggled closer to him, her cold body invading his warm cocoon.

"Why?" He reached for her, hissing as her icy thighs pressed against his. "After all, you're the one who started this."

"Me?" Purposely, she ran her cold fingers down his belly. His testicles tightened, hiding in self-defense. "I just wanted to have a drink, maybe swap some stories."

"Or some spit."

She laughed, curling against him. How naturally she fit, nestled into his shoulder, her length of beautiful breast and stomach pressed against him. They lay together, each quietly breathing. Jack stroked her hair, waiting. The quiet rattle of doors being opened down the hall was the only interruption in the silence.

"Aren't you going to ask?" she whispered, finally.

He pressed a kiss to her forehead. "No."

"Why not?" She pulled back, the faint light glinting in her eyes.

"Do you want to tell me?"

She studied his face. "No."

He pulled her close again. "Then, I don't need to know."

Like a light breeze, she exhaled against his chest. It both tickled and aroused him, shadows of his need a reminder. In response, Annika pressed closer, her body now as warm as his, her hands stroking his thighs and buttocks.

Biting back a groan of pleasure, he savagely took her mouth, plunging desperately, wanting her taste, her touch to be forever imprinted on his memory. She returned his kisses with an urgency of her own, sucking on his lip, teasing him with her tongue.

With an elegant lift, she was atop him, kissing him more deeply. He ran his hands along her thighs, cupping her hips, rising over her belly. Gently stroking the underside of her breasts with his fingers, his thumbs brushed her nipples. The soft sigh she made only heightened his necessity, and he arched up to thrust into her.

She threw her head back, pinned to him like a butterfly to a mat. Slowly, she gained her rhythm, coaxing him down an endless tunnel of sensation. His hands fell to her hips, kneading her as she rocked against him.

Sex was familiar to him, a quick escape from stress, or a simple need rapidly fulfilled. But this molding of two bodies, each anticipating and reacting to each other's needs—this was unfamiliar ground. Each nerve vibrated under her touch, while he desperately sought out her sensitivities, wanting to further her pleasure.

She was nearing the edge, her body tightly convulsing around his. Matching her strokes, he thrust upward, rearing until they both collapsed, a tangle of arms and legs and emotions.

Chapter 11

He awoke, slowly at first, his fingers groping the empty sheet beside him. It was cool to the touch. Squinting against the dark, he read the clock and groaned. Another day, another dollar.

Or another vote. It was election day. He sat upright, urging his schedule to the front of his mind.

He was late.

Why hadn't Annika woken him? He brushed away the thought like a gnat. She didn't know his schedule, and she had enough projects on her plate this morning without worrying about him. He stretched, then walked to the bathroom, kicking last night's towel out of the way.

Unless…He ran the shower until the water was nearly scalding. Unless she was reluctant to see him now, in the blazing light of day. After all, last night was rather wild.

He whistled while he showered, scrubbed his body with hotel soap. Thoughts wandering, he wondered what kind of private celebration he could share with Annika after the senator won the New Hampshire Primary.

Twisting the faucet, he froze. Making plans? Already? And he hadn't even seen her yet this morning.

In previous affairs, he could wash away the sex, the faces, and the memories with his morning shower. But now, as he vigorously towel-dried his hair, he could not shake loose the images of last night. Or the desire to repeat them.

A knock at the door tore him from his thoughts. Quickly dressing, he pulled it open.

"Y'all are in the henhouse now," Gem drawled, festively dressed for the election day in a zebra-skin dress, each stripe dyed either red or blue instead of black. "The senator's waitin'."

"How late am I?" Jack asked, knotting a tie under his chin.

"Devilishly late."

"Damn, and I haven't even had breakfast yet." His stomach rumbled in sympathy.

"He's in the car already. But you are luckier than a two-headed nickel." Gem held his coat as he slid into it. "Why is that, Gem?"

She smiled, all capped teeth and cherry lipstick. "Y'all are going to a pancake breakfast at the Armory."

"Thank God for small favors."

* * *

Annika typed furiously, her fingers flying. In high school, she had been tested at eighty words per minute, but with experience and deadline pressure, she would bet a Benjamin Franklin that she could reach ninety.

At least I better today, she thought, glancing at the clock ticking away minutes faster than the cursor blinked. Her press corps had been given the customary send-off of dodged questions and listed destinations, then were bundled against the near-freezing temperatures and shuffled into the waiting buses.

In exactly thirteen minutes, Annika would be appearing on five television programs in succession. Her message needed to be varied to each particular program and target audience, while sticking to the senator's platform.

With a triumphant smile, she pressed the print command, then stood and straightened her skirt. **Like clockwork,** she thought.

The printer jammed.

Lauren cringed, waiting for her outburst. But Annika just smiled at her. "How's my makeup?"

"Fine," Lauren replied, caution slowing her words. "Maybe a little lipstick."

"Oh, I almost forgot." Annika whipped the tube from her purse and applied it without a mirror's aid. "There, how's that?"

"Wonderful." She paused, giving her boss the once-over. "Did you do something new to your hair?"

"No." Closing down her computer, she glanced up. "Why?"

"You just seem to, I don't know, glow today."

"Really?" She wanted to bite her lip but remembered the freshly applied lipstick. Her smile unfolded like rose petals. "Amazing what a good night's sleep will do for you." She buttoned her jacket, thumbed her briefcase strap over her shoulder. "Walk with me?"

"Of course." Lauren struggled to keep up as Annika walked out of the senator's suite.

"Did you have fun last night?"

"It was wonderful." They paused at the elevator doors, nodding to the stationed guard. "We danced together at least five times."

Annika raised her eyebrow. "Really? Is Steven a good dancer?"

"Wonderful. But then, he's a great leader."

"Mm-hmm." Annika entered the elevator and pressed the lobby button.

"It's a joke. Good 'leader.' As in dancing?" She stared blankly at Lauren. "Earth to Annika."

"Sorry, I'm just wrapped in my own thoughts. You were saying?"

Lauren shook her head. "It doesn't matter." She paged through the organizer. "OK, after your interviews, you will be meeting the **Concord**

Monitor reporter for lunch. Then it's back here to headquarters as we watch them tally the votes."

"Is Jack with the senator today?" She tried to keep her voice steady, nonchalant.

"Yes, I saw them leave earlier while you were in the pressroom." Lauren laughed. "Steven…I mean Senator Carver had gotten out of the car to come pull Jack out of bed. I guess he overslept."

"Really." She sucked on her lower lip, remembering how she had left him, hair tousled, blanket pulled over his chin. "Well, I can't blame him. We've all been working very hard. I'm surprised you're so chipper this morning, after working last night, too."

Lauren's cheeks pinkened. "That really wasn't work to me. Dressing up, eating wonderful food, getting to dance the night away. I'm surprised I haven't turned into a pumpkin by now."

The elevator doors opened to a quiet lobby, all reporters in pursuit of a new story, a new headline. A lone woman stood by the doorway, mysteriously talking into her collar. Heels clicking against the marble, Annika nodded to the desk clerk and turned to Lauren.

"New security agent? I don't recognize her."

Face tightening, Lauren looked pained, as if passing a kidney stone. "Promise not to get angry?"

She shut her eyes. "Oh, no."

"Steve—I mean the senator just wanted all members of his staff to have protection. With all the e-mails and everything."

Turning her back to the agent, Annika frowned at Lauren. "Does Richard have his own security guard?"

"Well, no, but—"

"And Axel? Does he?"

"Axel never leaves the room."

"Gem?"

Blowing her bangs off her forehead, Lauren tried to look stern. "Gem and I are under the general protection of the positioned officers."

"I don't need a bodyguard, Lauren."

"Her name is Brenda Bostitch, and she's very nice."

"I'm sure she is, and I look forward to getting to know her. Along with the other agents." She cast a glance over her shoulder and saw Brenda look away, pretending not to be listening even though their voices echoed in the empty lobby. She turned back to Lauren. "I don't need a bodyguard," she whispered. "Agent Garcia is my driver. Isn't that enough?"

"The senator gave specific orders."

"The threats aren't against me, they're against him." She rotated her wrist and swore. "I've got to go. Lauren, don't worry about it. I'll take it up with the senator later."

She spun on her heel and moved toward the door. Agent Bostitch stepped forward, hand outstretched.

"Nice to meet you, Agent Bostitch," Annika said hurriedly, giving her hand a vigorous shake. "It sounds like there has been a miscommunication. Why don't you ride along with me and I'll explain on the way."

* * *

"...so would you agree with the governor's statement?" The newscaster's face filled the television opposite where she sat. No wrinkles, no gray hair, even though he was over fifty. Uncharitably, she thought the doctors had put enough plastic on this man's face in order to hide his hateful thoughts.

"I think Senator Carver has reached more people with the current health care bill without closing down inner-city health clinics and hospitals, as had happened in Governor deMarco's state."

The anchor's eyes nearly glazed with disappointment. She smiled naturally.

"Ms. Andersen, another concern of the American public is the current war against drugs. What are Senator Carver's proposals?"

"Fighting the war has become increasingly difficult in recent years. Studies have shown that more than sixty-five percent of twelve-year-olds have tried alcohol, while thirty percent have dabbled in marijuana or other street drugs. Senator Carver has several plans to—"

"But don't you think that many will find it hypocritical for the senator to balance on his anti-drug platform, while still dodging questions regarding his own past use?" His snake eyes slitted. She almost expected him to lick his lips with a forked tongue.

"John, this issue has been dragged through more mud than a New England spring could offer. The senator has repeatedly denied all allegations of drug use during his campaign."

Triumph lit up his eyes, putting her on guard immediately. "We have Robert Bardikoff, former press secretary for Senator Carver, who disputes these claims. Good morning, Mr. Bardikoff."

"Good morning, John." The television screen split, one side filled with Bardikoff's weasel face, the other a reflection of Annika's surprise. Quickly, she relaxed her facial muscles and prepared her responses.

The camera switched back to the anchor. Even though he frowned, John's eyes gave away his excitement. "Sir, you were fired from your position as press secretary, correct?"

Bardikoff cleared his throat. "That's correct. Senator Carver fired me because I knew his cocaine use had become uncontrollable. After I recommended he withdraw from the campaign, I was suddenly ousted."

"Ms. Andersen?"

"These allegations are completely false. The senator has meetings from dawn until nearly midnight, day after day. If he used drugs, it would be obvious to those who have met with him, who have heard him speak—"

"Which is precisely why he takes cocaine," Bardikoff interrupted, his face reddening in anger. "How else could he keep up with his erratic schedule?"

Annika laughed politely. "Sir, I keep the same schedule."

"Then maybe all of his staff should be tested for drugs!"

"I'm sorry, but we're out of time for today." John, indeed, looked terribly remorseful. His rating points had been climbing by the minute. "This issue will, undoubtedly, be up for debate again. I'm John Wilshire for **LiveWire**."

Annika's smile lasted until she had pulled out her earpiece and stalked off the set. Ducking into the empty green room, she reached into her pocket for her cell phone. Punching an automatic dial, she paced the room while the phone rang.

"Answer, damn it," she growled. Five, six.

"Jack Wiese."

"We've got a major problem."

"Hold on." Muffled noises, like the crinkling of tissue paper, filled her ear. "Good morning, beautiful."

Her temperature dropped a degree. "Jack, this is serious."

"So am I. How'd you sleep, anyway? I slept like a rock, must have been the third time that knocked me out."

"Wiese, I just got done with an interview for **LiveWire**. John sprang Bardikoff on me."

Jack's swearing was much more colorful than her own. She listened, mildly impressed. "Are you finished yet? Because that's not the bad news."

"What happened?"

"He brought up the cocaine accusations, again. Except this time, he started to lose it, on the air. He accused the entire staff of being on drugs."

Silence. Sudden laughter echoed over the phone. "Is that it?"

Her temper refired like a well-loved car engine. "What do you mean, 'is that it?' Isn't that enough? And on an election day, too."

"Most of those who are going to vote are already out there. If not, the last thing they're doing is watching television at noon."

"Damn it, is it noon already?" She glanced at her watch. "I've got to go. I'm late."

"Hey, Annika?"

"Yes?" She shut the green room's door behind her, holding the phone in one hand while pushing her other hand through her parka arm.

"I don't have a single regret."

She stopped at the glass doors, looking at the darkening sky. Was he fishing? Or just being honest? Sighing, she gave in, reluctantly. "Neither do I. But, Jack…don't think this is going to become a habitual thing. Last night was last night. We have a lot of work left to be done."

Agent Garcia opened the Lincoln's back door and she hurried out, sliding into the warm interior, the leather seat heating her rear.

"When don't you think about work?" His voice sounded as smooth as his caresses. She involuntarily shivered.

"I always think about work."

"I don't think you were thinking about it last night when—"

"Jack, I'm serious," she said, trying to repress a smile. "I've got to go."

"Me too. And, Annika? Senator Carver will address the other issue after New Hampshire. Don't worry about Bardikoff. All he's doing is lighting himself on fire. You didn't pour the gasoline on him."

* * *

The results from the first precincts began to trickle in at 8:30, the votes mostly from small towns where Governor deMarco had dominated. By 8:45, the staff had gathered to watch the results play out on television, grim expressions etched on each face.

Senator Carver huddled with Axel in the corner, deciphering the endless polling data from the recent onslaught of the south. Richard whispered into his cell phone, leaning against the kitchenette countertop. Every few minutes, he pulled a ragged handkerchief from his pocket and dabbed at his thinning pate.

"What does that mean? What did they just say?" Lauren sat on the edge of the couch, squirming like a two-year-old. Annika put a hand on her knee, trying to settle her down.

"Governor deMarco holds fifty-five percent of the votes, with only fifteen percent of precincts reporting."

"It means that it'll be a long wait," Jack said, putting a reassuring arm around Lauren's shoulders. Annika felt a strange twinge pull at her stomach. Jealousy? Why, when she knew that Lauren adored the senator?

Jack met her eyes over Lauren's blonde head and winked. The twinge spread into an instant heat, glowing like an ember. She wished they had one more night in New Hampshire, just to replay last night's pleasure, then shunned the thoughts with shock. It was one night's release, not a commitment.

And definitely not a relationship.

"Y'all, I didn't get dressed up for nothing." Gem stood opposite Richard, spreading snacks on a tray. She picked up a celery swab with her All-American Red nails. "The senator has it in the bag. Y'all are just torturing yourselves." She bit off a chunk, then muttered something about dip before streaking for the door.

"I wish I had her confidence," Richard said, clicking his phone shut. "That was Michael O'Hara. His scouts have reported that Governor deMarco seems certain of a win, and is already celebrating. Even has all-you-can-eat crab leg dinners."

"I wonder how much he's charging the taxpayers for this shin-dig," Axel said.

Jack leaned back on the couch. Annika watched his arm drop from Lauren's shoulders with a heightened sense of relief. Angry at her thoughts, she turned to study the television.

"Hey, Ax, let's slip in and try some of the crab. We'll smuggle a ton back to share with everyone."

"I'm with you, Jack!" Axel was halfway standing before the senator dropped his hand on his shoulder.

"Have you forgotten what happened at the NRA charity dinner?"

Richard groaned, covering his eyes. Axel and Jack exchanged mischievous grins. Even Lauren pulled away from the TV, laughing.

"I thought they were going to pull their guns out on you guys," she said.

"You did! You're just lucky you got out the back door in time."

"Luck had nothing to do with it," Lauren scoffed. "I knew it was a bad idea from the minute it hatched in Jack's head."

Annika turned to Jack, eyebrow raised. "Jack?"

"Well, it happened one night, before Steven had even announced he was in the running," he began, settling in with legs outstretched, arms molding the sofa. It was a classic storyteller's position, and intrigued her. "We were in…where, Axel?"

"Godforsaken southern country."

"Spoken like a true redneck," Richard interjected.

Jack waved him off. "Anyway, it was a very small town where the men judged each other by the size of their shooters, and I'm not talking about the ones in their pants." Lauren giggled, while Annika just gave him a cool glance.

"The restaurant where they were holding the fundraiser was rumored to have the absolute best peel and eat shrimp. Unfortunately, that night they were closed for business, other than the fundraiser. So, we thought it would be fun to see how the other half lives and sneak in."

"Watch yourself. You may be talkin' about my kin." Gem sauntered into the kitchenette, hands full of snack reinforcements. "Is this the NRA thing, again? Boy, don't you ever learn?"

"Anyway," Jack said, winking at Gem. She pooh-poohed him with her hands. "Lauren, Axel and I sneaked in the side door. Richard wimped out and went to the car to act as our get-away driver."

"I did not wimp out. I just have a thing with guns."

"Whatever, Richard," Axel muttered.

"By the time we found a table, we realized that the entire room was completely sauced. And, completely armed. There were pistols on the tables, shotguns leaning against chairs."

"I swear I saw a grenade launcher," Axel interrupted, still typing rapidly on his computer.

"I've told you, that was an old-timer's fire extinguisher." Jack looked at Annika, green eyes dancing.

"So what happened?" she asked.

"Well, these fellows seemed to recognize right away that we weren't supposed to be there. I don't know what gave us away, our Yankee accents, our lack of weaponry…"

"The fact that we were all dressed like we were attending a New York City celebrity fashion show," Lauren said, then laughed.

"Well, they didn't include dress requirements with the invitations. And I'd forgotten to pack my duck waders." Jack accepted a cup of coffee from Gem with a smile, his dimple winking. "Thanks, ma'am. So, they pulled us to the front of the room—"

"Not me! I was long gone by then," Lauren said.

"Chicken. Between the moonshine fumes and the wavering gun barrels staring us down, I thought it was all over."

"Naw, it wasn't that bad," Axel said, swiveling his chair around. "Jack, here, he told them how we were representatives from Smith and Wesson. We left in a hurry, shaking hands all along the way."

"I wonder if they've figured it out by now," Senator Carver mused. "If so, we may have some hasty explaining to do." He shook his head. "Aw, who cares. They'd never vote for me anyway. My hands are already reaching for their guns."

"Hey, look!" Lauren's voice had raised a pitch, like a songbird. All the eyes turned to the television as Jack turned up the volume.

"…with sixty percent of precincts reporting, Governor deMarco holds thirty-six percent of the votes, while Senator Carver has jumped ahead with forty-five percent of the votes."

Stunned silence lasted a millisecond before they all leaped to their feet, screaming and cheering. Lauren leaped over the sofa into the senator's bearhug.

"Had you worried," a deep voice rumbled in Annika's ear, sending sinful vibrations through her body. Jack held her arms gently, his whiskered cheek scraping delicately, erotically against hers.

"Not for a minute," she breathed, pulse leaping in her throat.

He brushed her neck with his thumb, pressing against her throbbing heartbeat. "We'll celebrate later. Privately."

Pulling away, he addressed the chattering staff. "Well, what are we waiting for? We have a celebration to attend!"

"I told y'all. I wore my lucky dress," Gem sniffed.

Chapter 12

Come on, Annika thought, hands on hips. Her frown nearly sliced her forehead in half. The notes had to be around here somewhere.

Gazing across the room, scattered with red, white and blue streamers, she nearly exploded with frustration. Dim light filtered through the open doors, faintly reflected by the podium on the makeshift stage. The echoes of last night's victory rally still rang in her ears.

Was it last night? Her thoughts jumbled in her head, creating such an atmosphere of cotton that she wondered if she could even find her way to the airport, let alone her stupid notes. She blamed her condition on too much coffee, too little sleep and too many interviews given after last night's win.

Glancing at her watch, Annika could barely make out the hands. By squinting in the dimness, she saw that it was 3:12. **Damn**, she thought, rubbing her temples with her fingers. If she didn't hurry, the plane would leave without her.

Kneading gently, she allowed herself the luxury of shutting her gritty eyes. They had won, and they had done what was deemed impossible. It was a narrow victory, but with a couple more under his belt, Senator Carver could expect Governor deMarco to bow out of the race. Now, the nation was watching, and Annika planned to use the momentum of the New Hampshire Primary to carry them all the way through to the Democratic National Convention.

Her breathing slowed, facial muscles relaxing under her fingertips. Where to next? South Carolina? Florida? She couldn't remember. So tired, but so much more to do.

The heavy clank of metal roused her. Blinking rapidly to clear her blurred vision, Annika searched for the source of the noise. Her heart leapt to her throat, fluttering against her windpipe like a trapped bird. Swallowing hard, she saw the doors had closed, the only light was seeping through the miniature windows.

Who had shut the doors? She was certain she had propped them open against the magnetic backs, and knew it took a hard pull to dislodge them. Nausea made her nearly double over.

Calm down, she ordered herself. In the darkness of the auditorium, one of the hotel workers couldn't see her and had probably shut the doors. There was a reasonable explanation.

But the hairs on the back of her neck rose, along with the taste of bitter bile in her throat. Forcing her numb legs to walk, Annika moved toward the rectangle of light.

Almost there, she thought, perspiration dampening her blouse, making the back stick to her unpleasantly.

She barely had time to register the dark movement before she felt the rush of air empty her lungs, the hard concrete blocks chilling her back. Struggling to breathe, she forgot to fight, and instantly had her hands held behind her back.

"So, we finally meet."

The breath was sour on her face, a mixture of alcohol and vomit that made her gag reflexively. She turned away, pressing her cheek into the cold wall, carefully inhaling through her mouth.

"You have really messed things up for me, little lady." He tightened his grip on her wrists, making her wince with pain. "But I figure you're going to find a way to help pay back what you have done."

Breathing shallowly, Annika forced herself to relax against his grip. She turned to face him, hoping the light wouldn't reflect the fear on her face. "Robert, you nearly scared me to death!" She chuckled, thankful it sounded genuine, rather than the lunatic asylum laughter that echoed in her mind. "Let's go grab a cup of coffee and we can chat."

Bardikoff slammed her into the wall. Once, twice. The third time, Annika's head bounced off the concrete, causing tiny fireflies to buzz behind her closed lids. The pain exploded with such severity she bit back a sob. Limply, she sagged against the wall, willing herself to stay conscious.

"Who do you think you are? Coming out of nowhere to that son-of-a-bitch's rescue." His C-USN demeanor had dissolved into this drunk, bitter, raging skunk of a man. Even in his condition, he was dangerously strong. Annika's shoulders began to ache from being restrained, her wrists numb and fingertips tingled.

"Robert, I can see you're upset. Let's just—"

"Shut up!" With his free hand, he grabbed her hair, fisting it until her eyes watered. "You listen to me. He'll never make it. All it takes is one moment and blam…" His shout rang off the walls, making Annika wince.

Pacing her breaths, she glanced around frantically for anything that could be used as a weapon. With her arms pinned, she knew they would be too numb to come to her aid, even if released.

Feminine wiles. Distasteful even in a situation like this, but right now she would use any distraction to get this foul-smelling man away from her.

"Robert," she murmured. "Why don't we go upstairs and talk this over more." Pressing her breasts out, she felt them strain against the fabric, buttons gaping. Bardikoff's bleary gaze left her face and stared, lust twisting his mouth into a leer.

Annika shifted her weight and stomped down, hard. Her heel connected with a satisfying squish, breaking away from the sole with the impact. Bardikoff screeched like a barn owl, releasing her hair. Wiggling frantically, she tried to slam her knee into his groin, but he blocked her with a knee. In his fury he gripped her hands harder.

"You...bitch," he spat, twisting her wrists until the tiny bones ground together like sticks. "Whore." Wedging his knee between her legs, her skirt ripped up the back seam. "You're...gonna...pay."

Annika screamed as Bardikoff pressed his body against hers, turning her face away from his rancid mouth.

Suddenly, his weight was gone. She slid bonelessly to the floor, trembling and gasping, the cold of the concrete wall and floor seeping into her bones.

Muffled grunts and shuffling feet shifted inches in front of her. Squinting in the dim light, she could see the dark figures wrestling, dancing. With a final heave, one of the figures slumped to the floor. Annika shivered uncontrollably, turning her face to look at the rectangle of light.

"Did he hurt you? Oh my God, you're shaking like a leaf." Heavy wool settled around her like a blanket, smelling of snow and fresh air, with an underlying hint of musk. Her arms hung limply, wrists cradled together in her lap. The single act of kindness sent her reserve to the basement.

Sobs shook her like a tree in a storm, the pain welling up from a pit deep within. Uncontrollably, she moaned amid her tears, clutched her hands to her face in an effort to still them, but the tears poured through her fingers like a waterfall.

Warm arms surrounded her. Strong arms, secure arms. There was no fear in being held this way, gently as a piece of fragile crystal. Her hair was smoothed down by a tender hand, stroking, stroking. Soft words were whispered against her head, words she couldn't understand, yet comforted her anyway.

Between the rhythmic caresses and murmurs, her sobs mellowed to stray tears. Sleep reached for her with smooth fingertips. Secure in the arms of a safe man, she allowed herself to let go, relaxing into a cocoon of warmth.

For such a spitfire, she weighed no more than a child. Jack held her closely while winding his coat more securely around her ripped skirt. Face pale with shock, nearly gray against the raven's wing of hair, she looked like death's sister.

Pushing open the door with his shoulder, Jack looked over at the still, dark figure on the floor. With a violent curse, he kicked the door shut behind him, walking toward the front doors in his lengthy stride.

"Call the police," he said curtly to the night desk attendant, who nearly leapt out of her seat with surprise at the sight of him. "There's a man hurt in the auditorium."

The attendant stammered a reply, which Jack dismissed immediately. Backing into the front door, he gently maneuvered Annika into the waiting limo.

"Mr. Wiese! Sir!" Agent Barrington's mouth was agape, staring at Annika's limp body. "What happened?"

"Never mind. Take us to the airport. Hurry."

Obligingly, the agent floored the car, the back wheels spinning against the icy road. Jack raised the privacy window and settled Annika's head against his shoulder, his arm wrapped protectively around her waist. They were going to have to pry her away from him with the jaws of death after what nearly happened that night.

Slipping his hand into his coat pocket, he pulled out his cell phone and punched in several numbers. "It's Jack." He took a deep breath, controlling the tremor that threatened to cause his voice to quiver. "I've found Annika. She's hurt. It was Bardikoff."

Silence echoed on the line. "That bastard," Steven rumbled. "Is she all right?"

Jack glanced at her, still trembling in his arms. "No. I want to take her to Minneapolis."

"Jack, she needs to be treated by a doctor—"

"Not now. I don't think she could take it."

Steven's sigh cut through the silence. "Take her. Take all the time you need. I've got California State Representative Cleo Speros meeting me in Florida, and Lauren can manage some of the press secretary duties. We don't have anything major before the California primary."

"We can work with you from my home office. I just think she needs to be someplace safe right now."

"I'll have a plane ready for you. And, Jack?"

"Yeah?'

"We'll nail the bastard. Count on it."

*   *   *

Running, sprinting through a dark tunnel, the light at the end a pinprick. Her chest heaved from the exertion, lungs burning, legs trembling with fatigue. Her thighs screamed in pain, cramps threatening to slow her down. But she couldn't stop, couldn't even drag her pace.

She dared a glance over her shoulder. He was still there, his heavy steps matching hers, his lengthy stride decreasing the distance that divided them.

Pumping her arms, she ran, the wind drying the tears on her face. Her breath came out in panicked sobs, each inhalation nearly choking her. A belt tightened around her chest, but she pressed on.

The tunnel opened, its light reaching out with hazy welcome. She reached out, wanting to feel its heat, tangible against her skin.

Then, he stepped into the light.

"Wake up! Annika!" She fought the strong hands that held her down, gasping for air. Struggling, she kicked her legs in a final frantic fight.

"Annika, it's me, Jack. Wake up." Legs slowed, like running under water. The hum wasn't the from the tunnel's dim lighting. She stared above at the rounded cabin.

"What…where am I?"

"It's all right. You're safe." Jack slowly stroked her hair, patiently wiped her wet face. Her eyes still darted around, wild, but her muscles loosened under his touch.

"Oh my God," she sobbed, leaning forward and burrowing in his shirt. "It was Bardikoff. He said he wanted to pay me back."

"Sshhh. Don't worry about him." Jack bit back the anger, forcing his voice to remain smooth and steady. He gently pried her off his shirt, cupping her face in his hands. Searching her dewy eyes, he asked, "Are you hurt? How do you feel?"

Annika rubbed the back of her head and moaned. His fingers deftly followed hers, lightly gauging the goose egg. "Do you feel nauseous? Dizzy? Here, how many fingers am I holding up?"

Irritated, she swatted his hand away. "Twenty."

Jack chuckled. "You're going to be fine."

Like a thunderhead, lightening flashed across her face. "No, I'm not going to be fine. In fact, I haven't been fine for years." Her eyes squeezed shut, a feeble attempt to hold the tears back. Silent sobs wracked her body, and Jack felt instant remorse.

He pulled her against him, smoothing the hair from root to tip in mesmerizing strokes. Slowly, her sobs dissolved into sniffles. She pulled away, and Jack reluctantly let go.

Yanking a handkerchief from his pocket, he slid it across the armrest. She picked it up and gave a good blow. "Funny, the last time I was offered a handkerchief to blow my nose was when I fell down and scraped my knees bloody. My grandpa gave me his handkerchief."

"And they say chivalry is dead." Jack shook his head when she offered him the cloth. "Keep it. I have several others."

Annika tucked it into her coat pocket. With nothing else to put away or touch, her hands flitted like moths, looking for a distraction. She avoided Jack's eyes, instead perusing the small cabin.

"Do you want to talk?" he asked, gently reaching for her hand, stilling the drum of her fingers against the armrest.

She sighed. "No, but after what you did for me tonight, I feel like you need to know." Twisting in her seat, she leaned her head against the cushioned back. Her eyes stared vacantly past Jack, like silent, limpid pools.

"A friend in my media studies class introduced me to him. Chet Jedowski. He was a fellow Rocky Mountaineer in the strange land of college. By then, Shea and I had become roommates at Columbia and dreamed of making a difference in the world through the camera's eye." She blinked and looked at him. "Journalists make squat, so we had to have some ulterior motive."

Her eyes shifted back to the empty window. "Anyway, Chet seemed to want the same things. The passion for truth, the drive to get the story." She sighed, holding herself tightly. "But he also wanted to control me. He resented my friends, he hated my activities. And I bucked at being controlled, even back then. I broke up with him."

Eyes hard as turquoise, Annika stared directly at Jack. "So he made me his life's ambition. First, it started with drunken phone calls in the middle of the night. Hang-ups on my answering machine. Then, I started noticing his car following me to work. His messages became more violent, more…" Covering her mouth, she was trying to fight the tears.

Jack reached for her, drawing her to him. "It's OK. You don't have to tell me any more."

"But I do." Face pressed against his shirt, voice muffled, she continued. "He would sit outside my apartment, just waiting for me to go places. Finally, Shea convinced me to get a restraining order. The next day, I came home from work to find the apartment in shambles. He took my favorite photos and shredded them. He blacked out dates on my calendar, dates that had once been significant between us. With my makeup, he scrawled across the walls words like 'slut' and 'bitch.'"

Jack breathed in the scent of her hair, an oasis of sweetness in a desert of vulgarity. "Then, what happened?"

"The police helped me file a complaint. But the next day…" She took a deep, shuddering breath, her fingers tightening against his shirt, clinging. "I left from work planning to meet Shea at a local restaurant, so we could walk home together. I was running late and most of the other staff members had already left for the day. I thought they said they would lock the door behind them. They did, after letting Chet in." She sniffled, running her thumb against his shirt. "He said he wanted to help with the mayor's campaign. Of course, they believed him. I hadn't told anyone about him."

They sat still, the whirrs and grumbles of the plane blanketing the silence. Jack stroked her hair slowly, feeling her tremble faintly against him. Even as he wanted to know the truth behind the masks she wore, he found himself dreading the words that spilled from her like a freshwater spring.

"The scar. On your belly. He did that to you, didn't he." It wasn't even a question, just a statement delivered as flatly as he could manage. Inside, fury boiled like lava.

"He stabbed me with a knife he had stolen from my own kitchen." She laughed, a short, humorless bark. "My own kitchen! And told me that if he couldn't have me, then no one would.

"Luckily, no major organs were hit, but I lost a lot of blood. When he left, the door was unlocked, so Shea found me very quickly."

"Where is he now?" Images of slamming his fist into Chet's face, holding a knife under his chin began swirling through his mind. His muscles clenched in response.

"New York State Penitentiary. Attempted murder in the first degree. He drew a sympathetic judge who believed in counseling and Jesus as prisoners' saviors, so he was only given ten to fifteen."

Jack stiffened. "How long ago did this happen?"

"Eight years. Why?" She pulled away, worry wrinkling the corners of her eyes.

"Is he up for parole?"

"Not that I know of. And the prosecutor promised to let me know if and when that happens. So, he's still behind bars." Her face hardened, like a clay mask drying. "I hope he's experienced all the fun social experiences fellow prisoners can provide."

Jack laughed, easing the tension that surrounded them like mist. "I get the feeling you're not talking about shooting hoops or making license plates."

She smiled at him, still holding his shirt gently. "More along the lines of after hours parties."

Gently, he brushed the remnants of tears from her face. She was so exquisitely beautiful, with such strength beneath her beauty. It was a combination he had often dreamed of, but seldom saw in the real life world of politics.

"So, why politics? You could be rich and famous like Shea?"

Annika laughed. "She has had the whole act down since we were twelve." She nudged Jack. "Even you fell for it. Show the people what they want to see, but still hold true to your own heart. She still teaches me a trick or two."

"You didn't answer the question."

Rolling her eyes, she leaned back in her seat. "I had my own dream, too. Impossible, some would say."

Intrigued, he leaned toward her. "What was it?"

"I wanted to make politicians real. How many people sit at home and see these public servants, but they're wearing nicer clothes and going to fancy dinner parties. Mr. John Q. Public recognizes the dance, the courtship of politicians. I wanted to make politicians stop and speak from their hearts.

"And I finally found my candidate in Senator Carver." She looked at him, self-consciousness pushing her to defensiveness. "He's one in a million, but I truly believe that if a man like him gets elected, it will change the whole momentum of politics as we know it."

"But what about the public persona you exude every day? Isn't it hypocritical to expect higher standards from a politician?"

She bristled against him, the electricity nearly leaping from her body. "I'm not the one getting elected. I'm the one telling people why he should be elected. It's always the truth, with just an added spin to it."

"Then why the masks? Why do you hide your true feelings?"

"I don't know what you're talking about." Annika shifted to the far side of her seat. A bell sounded, the 'fasten your seat belts' sign blinking on.

"By the way, where is everyone?" she asked, clicking her belt into place. "Where are we going?"

Jack did the same, then smiled at her. "Home."

Chapter 13

The Hubert H. Humphrey terminal was eerily empty. No airline staff greeted them as they exited the small plane, and no people lounged in the waiting area. The fluorescent lights along the hall flickered. Annika relaxed more when she saw a janitor, mopping idle circles in a far corner of the corridor.

Somehow, Jack had retrieved their luggage from the senator's plane. She had been too exhausted to ask questions when he handed her a pair of sweatpants and sneakers. In the plane's cramped restroom, she had changed clothes quickly, avoiding her reflection in the mirror. When she'd pulled off her skirt, the back slitted to the waist, her hands shook. Moments later, she had been back in her seat, feeling calmer, the skirt wadded into the bottom of the restroom's trashcan.

They moved soundlessly down the airport hallway, sneakers cushioning their footsteps. Sliding glass doors opened mechanically, and a blast of frigid air froze the lining of her nose. She took no more than a breath or two, steam puffs floating from her mouth, before Jack shuttled her into the waiting limousine.

Shivering, she melted into the buttery soft leather. The events of the previous night seemed hazy, nightmarish. Definitely not real.

In the distance, a scattered batch of cars drove on 494. Annika felt a sense of déjà vu.

"Other than the New Year's Party, I haven't been back to Minnesota in years," she said.

"It's probably changed a lot. The Mall of America, the new interchange at 494 and 169. Not to mention all the new businesses that have popped up like mushrooms after a good rain."

The chauffeur piled their luggage into the trunk with a series of bumps. Squeezing his bulk behind the wheel, he puffed with exertion. "Where to?"

Annika lifted her eyebrow and looked at Jack. He grinned at her, his devilish dimple playing with her heart. "Just get to 694. I'll give you directions from there."

As they drove, the sky brightened, first into a luscious peach and coral that melted into pale pinks. A bright blue sky beckoned on her first day back home.

Home. Funny that she should consider it home. Since college, home had been a series of rest stops in different cities. Her mother kept most of her extra stuff packed away in the attic of her Colorado home. Stuff she never thought about and never needed.

But being back in Minnesota, she felt a sense of connection she had never felt any place else. Her exhaustion slipped away as she stared out the window, trying to connect landmarks with her memory.

"Didn't that used to be a pizza and video games place?" She pointed past Jack. "We went there on a class trip."

"That's right. I'd forgotten about that. It's been a strip mall for fifteen years now, at least."

She swiveled her head. "And that's La Casa Buena! I can't believe they haven't painted it, after all these years."

Jack laughed. "They have painted it. They just keep choosing the same Pepto Bismol pink."

"We used to go out to eat there all the time. My father…" She let the sentence trail off.

"Do you remember Happy Chef?" Jack asked.

Annika silently thanked him for his courtesy. "The big baker? You'd press a button and he would tell jokes or riddles. Why?"

"It's gone now."

"Oh, no! That was a child's fantasy, getting to touch someone who was thirty feet tall. And having him talk to you."

"I know. There are only a few left, I guess. One's outside of Mankato. I made Steven stop when we were doing our southern Minnesota campaign trip."

She was surprised to hear herself laugh. "What did he think?"

"He didn't get out of the van. Gem got to Happy Chef first and was posing rather provocatively while Axel took her picture."

She laughed harder, visualizing her colleagues. "Whatever happened to the pictures?"

"Oh, they're probably floating around on the Internet somewhere." He grinned at her. "Just kidding."

"You almost gave me a heart attack. First drug accusations, then e-mail threats. How much do you think I can take?" She meant it to sound like a joke, but her voice wavered.

Jack caught it instantly. Reaching for her hand, he met her eyes. "Don't worry about Bardikoff. We've got the entire government on our side against him." He squeezed her hand gently. "And I don't know how much you can take, but based on your past experience, I think you are the strongest, bravest woman I have ever met."

Her heart thudded as he raised her hand to his lips. "You amaze me, Annika," he murmured against her fingers. "Every day, you amaze me."

* * *

Annika wasn't sure what she had expected. Something regal, perhaps, a home encased in tan brick and ivory columns, with immaculate gardens and overwhelming windows. Or something gaudy, a rustic stucco and log monster atop a hill overlooking the highway and lake.

A home that reflected the Jack she thought she knew.

So she was surprised when, after winding along a two-lane highway, Jack ordered the driver to turn on to a gravel road. Trees stretched above them, offering their branches to the sapphire sky. Scattered leaves lined the road like orphans, wintered away from their parents. The woods were thick around them, without a glimpse of anything but trees and plants.

Then the trees surrendered, drawing back from a small clearing. In the center, a house stood, its Cape Cod style and painted shutters almost a fantasy gingerbread house. It was both welcoming and private at the same time. Annika loved it at once.

"Oh, Jack," she said. "How did you find this place?"

He held her hand as she stepped out of the car. "It used to be Steven's. After Sandra died, it held too many memories for him. He sold it to me at a very decent price." Jack gestured to the woods. "Want the dime tour?"

"Of course."

He paid the chauffeur, who tipped his hat respectfully before driving away. Jack unzipped a suitcase and rummaged, pulling out a pair of gloves. "Are you warm enough?"

"I'm fine," she answered. Breathing deeply, she could smell the spice of evergreen trees and the char of fireplace smoke. The air was still, her breath wisps of steam.

Jack tucked her hand in his arm. "Stick close. There may be some old traps still hidden."

"Traps? For what?"

"Steven's wife used to complain about rabbits eating everything in her garden. He set a few traps, then forgot how many he'd put out." He flashed her a smile. "Didn't matter anyway. The rabbits just kept coming."

He led her down a rough trail that ran behind the house. From the back, she could see a large sun deck with a trellis lining it. No garden was visible, but a line of bushes edged the far side of the backyard before the grass melted into the woods' wild.

"Are those rose bushes?" she asked.

"Yes." Jack looked embarrassed. "I don't have a green thumb, but I've always wanted a house with rose bushes."

Me, too, Annika thought, gaze lingering over the yard.

"Now, watch your step. Follow behind me, or it'll be a tight squeeze."

Dutifully, she followed, Jack still holding her hand. Eyes glued to the stone stairs, she didn't notice they had stepped out of the forest until she looked up.

"Oh!" she gasped, tightening her grip.

"It's not much to look at now," Jack said. "But in the summer, it's like Grand Central Station."

A cedar dock, anchored by the lake ice, spread out deeply, like a patio. Custom made wooden chairs stood with a dusting of snow crusted to the seats. Across the stretch of ice, another dock was visible, much smaller and less elaborate.

Jack nodded across the ice. "That's the only neighbor I've seen. The property is owned by a family of six."

"Six?"

"Yeah, two older boys, about ten and nine, and two girls, maybe seven and four. They float around on their rafts in the summer, waving at all the passing boats."

"Where does this lead?" Annika stretched her neck, trying to peer beyond the bend of trees.

"To Trista Bay, part of Lake Minnetonka. That way," he pointed in the opposite direction, "is a dead-end alcove. But the fishing is usually good, so the old-timers come through often."

"It's beautiful," she said, rubbing her hands together.

Jack grabbed her bare hands with his leather ones. "Weren't you brought up in Minnesota? Where are your gloves?"

"I don't remem—"

"Here, take mine." Before she could argue, he slipped them onto her hands. Since the heat was welcomed, she just murmured her thanks.

"Let's head back. Hopefully, the place isn't too cluttered." He started walking back up the stone steps. "Sara is going to come by later with some groceries, but I think I can find something to fix for breakfast."

The strange pang of jealousy nudged her throat. "Who's Sara?"

"An old friend. I met her through Steven and Sandra."

Walking more quickly, Annika felt her blood pumping warmth through her body. "Well, I hope you have coffee. Pretty soon I'm going to have to prop my eyelids open with toothpicks."

* * *

"What do you mean, he's gone?" Jack slammed the refrigerator door shut.

"Darlin', there's no sign of him," Gem answered, her drawl thick as honey over the phone line. "He musta left before the law got there. But don't y'all worry none, 'cause the senator has got all his connections plugged in."

He pressed the phone to his ear using his shoulder while his hands dug through the masses of icy blocks in his freezer. "He couldn't have gotten too far. I really pummeled him."

"Whatta man," she said sarcastically. "Any who, he left everything in his room. Wallet, luggage…"

"Was he staying at the same hotel?"

"No, he was in Franklin. It's about eighteen miles from Concord."

Jack found a package of frozen waffles and tossed them on the counter. "So he could have easily driven to the New Hampshire State Library on, say, the same day you received that e-mail?"

"Agent Bailey's way ahead of y'all. Seems Bardikoff was in Des Moines when we got that e-mail, too."

"That son-of-a-bitch." He paused to flip the frying bacon. "You know, I never did like him."

"Oh, honey, that's what they all say. Do you think people really admitted they were fond of Ted Bundy after the fact?" The line crackled. Jack could almost see her shift the phone to her other ear while she continued to work. "How's Annika?"

"Other than a nasty bump, she's doing just fine. Do you need us to meet up with you?"

"No, we're going to be traveling so much the next few weeks will be a blur anyways. Senator Carver thinks you can stay connected and work from home for a little while. As long as Annika is up for it."

Jack laughed, pressing the toaster button down. "It's a good thing she has a hard head, then."

They said their goodbye's quickly, knowing they would be speaking often throughout the next few days. As the waffles popped up, Jack turned off the gas stove.

"Hard-headed, am I?" Pouring syrup on the waffles, Jack glanced up, then did a double take. Annika leaned against the door frame, wet hair curling over her shoulders, wearing the robe he hung over the back of the bathroom door. It was his robe, a ratty old thing that had once been green and blue plaid, but had faded to a pleasant woodsy look. He suddenly remembered the gaping hole in the back, and dropped his jaw.

"Don't you think that's enough?" she asked, moving toward him. He blinked, confused. Smiling, she took the syrup bottle from his hand. "You don't need to drown them. They're already dead."

He looked at the waffles, the plate filled with syrup, and chuckled. "I thought a little extra sweetness would do you good."

"Mm-hmm." She moved to the oak table and slid into a chair. "It's a good thing you fixed food, or I wouldn't be able to be held accountable for my actions."

He handed her a mug of hot coffee, instant cream and sugar, just as he knew she liked. Then he sat across from her, sliding a plate of bacon and waffles her way. He tried not to stare as she ate, but it was nearly impossible. She ate the way she did everything else, with a heady passion that drove him wild inside. Tasting the bacon, she opened her mouth wide to take a larger bite. His body began to stir. A drop of syrup clung to her lower lip and she licked it off hungrily.

Jack wanted to take her on the table right then, tasting her natural sweetness as well as the syrup.

She was saying something, but he held up his hand. "What? I can't understand you with your mouth full."

Swallowing, she wiped her mouth on a napkin. "Sorry, I was just starving. So whom were you talking to? Steven?"

"No, Gem." He took a bite and chewed slowly, giving himself time to think. "Everyone is worried about you."

"I'm fine, now. Just tired." She leaned her elbows on the table, sipping her coffee. "What else did she say?"

"That we can work from my home office for now. There's a lot we can do from the Minneapolis headquarters."

Annika frowned. "But won't the press become suspicious?"

"No. Lauren has filled in for you before. She'll do it again." He kept his eyes on his plate.

"Jack." She started to reach across the table, then hesitated. "Don't start playing games with me again," she whispered, eyes dewy. "Please."

Swallowing the bacon felt like shards of glass. He reached out and held her hand. "They can't find Bardikoff."

Blood emptied from her face, making her skin seem almost translucent. "What? But, I thought…you. He wasn't moving."

"No. And I thought he was badly hurt, too." He stroked her fingers with his thumb. "So he can't get too far, right?"

Annika nodded, her chin set with determination. "I just hope they catch him soon. For the senator's sake." She gasped suddenly, as if bitten.

"The senator! Bardikoff said he would never make it. That all it takes is one moment." She clutched Jack's hand with her other one. "Don't you see? Just like the e-mail threat. 'All it takes is one bullet, and one perfect moment.' It's him. It's Bardikoff."

Grimly, Jack pulled away. "I need to call him. The security needs to be tightened. No more crowd walk-throughs or unscheduled stops. At least, not until Bardikoff is found."

He dialed from memory, never glancing at the notes he'd written while talking to Gem. When she answered, his voice was curt. "It's me. Get Agent Bailey."

*   *   *

With Jack's flash of ego, Annika knew the trophy room was in existence. She just hadn't found it, yet.

The house surprised her with its obvious femininity. Lacy curtains in the front windows, rose and cream striped wallpaper in the foyer. Sandra's taste had been impeccable. Annika was willing to bet that Jack hadn't changed anything because he didn't know how. A mass of dead flowers were crammed into a smelly, mold-lined vase and given the seat of honor on top of an antique settee. Movie posters provided wall hangings. A doormat with the inscription, "Here's mud in your eye" lay at the doorway.

In contrast, the guestroom held no aura. The blue bedspread was plain, the sheets simple white cotton. The closet was completely empty, as was the dime-store dresser. White walls glared brightly with no adornments.

Following the low murmurs of Jack's voice, she discovered a door hidden behind an opened closet. She twisted the knob then pulled the door open and Jack's voice became clearer.

"…want to hold a press conference at the downtown headquarters. I think the media list is in the computer files."

Descending the oak stairs carefully, she inhaled the sharp smell of smoke with undercurrents of leather. As she stepped off the last stair, she smiled smugly.

Jack had transformed the entire basement into a political consultant's dreamscape. While a fire crackled homily in the corner fireplace, a line of four televisions flickered noiselessly, each screen filled with a different reporter's face mouthing silent words. The programming for the hearing impaired was activated, so lines of sentences rolled across the bottom of the screen. Leather couches the color of caramel matched Jack's desk chair on the opposite side of the room.

He waved her in, the phone clutched in his other hand. "No, the local news crews will be there. I'm sure the national news will have backups available."

As she walked over to his desk, she perused the 'wall of fame.' There were photos of Jack with a variety of congressmen, the president, and a famous supermodel. She almost laughed out loud, but instead turned around and lifted her eyebrow. Jack rolled his eyes in response.

Turning back, she looked at the other momentos that lined the wall. A framed crayon drawing of a lopsided house, with the words, "Thank you Jak 4 hellping my mom." Pictures of Bobby and Jack, the boys she remembered with a mixture of fondness and distaste. A gold certificate awarded to Jack Wiese, winner of the longest putt contest, signed by Bob Hope.

The wall spoke volumes about this man who sat before her. The man who had saved her life, the man who had driven her mad. The man who could melt her with a glance, torch her with a touch.

And now she was staying in his house, would be sleeping in a bedroom next to his. She was both relieved and regretful that he hadn't put her luggage in his master bedroom. The passion they had shared seemed weeks past, instead of only a couple nights. As she watched him finish his conversation, she felt her soul relax, as if she had found a safe haven.

And, in a sense, she knew she had.

Just as Jack hung up the phone, a door slammed upstairs. "Hello?" a voice called.

"It's Sara," Jack told her, then yelled, "We're down here!"

Annika turned to face her opponent, the 'dear, sweet' woman who held so much of Jack's admiration.

Chapter 14

She was seventy if not to the day. Her hair was highlighted with blonde streaks, the undertone of hazel perfectly matching her wide eyes. Laugh lines ringed her mouth as she smiled widely. "Annika Andersen, I feel like we've already met. I've watched you with our Jack on TV. I'm Sara Johannson."

Annika took her hand gently, but was surprised by the woman's firm grip. "Nice to meet you. Jack has told me you used to work for the senator."

Sara beamed like a sunny window. "Such a nice man. With such wonderful taste in friends." She turned her smile to Jack, who had risen from his chair and rounded his desk.

"It's so good of you to come by," he said, pulling her into a bear hug.

Sara laughed, pushing him away with a smack to the chest. "You think I'd let you starve? Well, maybe I'd let you, but not your poor guest." She turned back to Annika, eyes wide with concern and smile tucked away. "And how are you doing, dear? It's been all over the television. What a brave girl you are."

Worry curdled into an icy ball in the pit of her stomach. She stared at Jack. "What has been reported? Is it affecting the campaign?" Mind working rapidly, she paced to catch up. "When are we going back? We'll need to set up a press conference and talk to—"

"Slow down, it's being taken care of." Jack reached out and put his hands on her shoulders. Oddly enough, it melted away the worry and she felt reassured. She looked up in his gray eyes. "I've already scheduled a press conference at the downtown headquarters. And," he spun her around, "I've set up an office for you."

In her examination of his office, she hadn't noticed the cleared desk adjacent to his, or the matching leather chair that fit snugly under it. She had a job to do, and a place to work. At that point, it was all that mattered.

"Great. I'll go get my laptop."

Jack listened as her bare feet patted against the wood staircase, the top step creaking as it always did.

"She's a nice girl," Sara said, pinning him with her hazel eyes. Eyes that he knew missed little.

He sighed. "Yes, she is."

"You love her." It was spoken so matter-of-fact that Jack was immediately on the defensive.

"No, I don't." When confronted with Sara's grin, he just shook his head. "What you just witnessed was Annika in a good mood. She's been under tremendous strain, so she hasn't had the energy to be her usual, nasty self."

"Mm-hmm. Well, I'll just go put away those groceries I brought over."

"Don't give me that," Jack said. He ran his hand through his hair, blowing out a frustrated breath. "I want to protect her. I respect her work. Does that mean I'm in love with her?"

Sara pursed her lips, thinking. "First of all, that woman doesn't need anyone to protect her. She needs someone to love her for who she is. And secondly," she went on, ignoring Jack's wave of disagreement, "You better respect more than just her work. She is the type of lady who can get whatever she wants, in however means."

"I know firsthand," he grumbled, but Sara ignored him.

"And third of all, you both are denying feelings that nature gave you on purpose. Do you both need to be slapped on the head?"

He glared at her. "What do you mean?"

"I mean it's obvious to everyone but the two of you." She put one foot on the steps before looking over her shoulder at Jack. "Honey, when God puts a gift in front of you, it's just plain bad manners to refuse it."

*   *   *

"...and while Minnesota Senator Steven Carver continues his campaign march across the nation, he took time in Ohio today to respond to questions."

Steven's face filled the screen. "He looks like hell," Annika murmured.

"He worries," Jack replied simply.

She quieted, watching the senator address the crowd. "Last night, a night that should have been filled with victory and joy, a tragedy occurred. Annika Andersen, my press secretary and a close friend, was attacked while leaving our hotel." His eyes scanned his audience, which had fallen silent as if at a funeral. "It has been reported the attacker was Robert Bardikoff, my former press secretary. However, he has not been brought in for questioning, nor has he appeared to defend himself.

"I am making a plea for the safety of my staff." Senator Carver stared directly into the camera, the sun glinting off his silver temples. "Robert, please. Turn yourself in. For your own sake, as well as that of others."

Tears filled Annika's eyes unbidden. She blinked them back rapidly before Jack could see.

The dark-haired reporter filled the screen with her serious expression. "Meanwhile, security in the Carver camp has been tightened. Besides more secret service agents being put on duty, the senator has agreed to only stop at scheduled meetings. This is Susan Carlyle for C-USN."

Jack turned the volume down. "At least there hasn't been a leak about the threats. That's all that we would need is a bunch of lunatic copy-cats."

Leaning back into her new office chair, Annika asked, "What about the alcohol rehabilitation?"

"Steven's going to call us later to discuss our strategy for that. What are your thoughts?" He sat in his chair, spinning it around so they were face to face.

She shut her eyes for a moment, then opened them. "I don't know, Jack. Personally, I think we should have had a press conference before New Hampshire. But now…"

"I know. It would almost seem as if he were playing the sympathy card. First a member of his staff is attacked, now he's admitting to an alcohol addiction."

"But he has to admit it soon."

"The timing just seems a little off."

Annika blew a curl from her forehead. "I can't even think straight anymore. Caffeine isn't even helping."

Jack rolled his chair over, reaching for her hands. "Are you OK? How's the lump? Do you think you need to see a doctor?" The worry made his forehead crease. Annika smiled.

"I'm fine. Just tired. Have you counted how much sleep you've gotten in the past few days?"

"Well, I know I got an average of three hours the night before you came to my room…" His eyes twinkled, like sunlight through summer green leaves. Her mouth was responding before her mind stopped her, leaning into his security. Their lips brushed gently, soft as cashmere.

She abruptly pulled away. "Jack, I—"

"It's all right. Take your time." He released her hands, rolling his chair farther away. "I'll still be here."

The words gave her back the power. She could stop it, or she could start something. It was up to her.

Then why did she feel even more helpless near him? He was allowing her to set the pace. And she knew she didn't want to become involved with anyone. There was too much pain, too much hurt. It didn't balance out the long nights of sweet seduction.

Sleep. That was what she needed. Then she would be able to think more clearly about everything. Senator Carver, Jack. Her own feelings.

"I asked Sara to grab some luncheon meat for quick sandwiches. There should also be dessert in the freezer."

He was trying so hard to turn away, even when she could see the desire in his eyes. "Thanks, Jack. Can I bring you anything?"

"No, I'm just going to get started on a few things."

She nodded. "I'll probably catch up on some sleep so I can be more useful."

He waved a hand, not even looking up from his desk. "Take all the time you need. You'll know where to find me."

Annika walked up the stairs slowly, feeling as if the farther she got from Jack, the weaker she felt. **Like Superman and kryptonite**, she thought. Or did kryptonite disarm him? She could never keep that straight.

I must be tired, she mused, opening the fridge. Three different kinds of deli meat were stacked neatly beside a package of Swiss cheese. She chose ham, then shut the door. Putting the ham and cheese on the countertop, she remembered Jack saying something about dessert.

Just a peek, she thought, then opened the freezer.

The happy faces of Ben and Jerry smiled at her from the container of Chunky Monkey ice cream.

* * *

The chirping noise dragged him from his thoughts. Its high pitch warned him it was something electronic, but damned if he could find out where it was coming from.

After pressing several buttons on the fax machine and copier, he turned to Annika's makeshift desk. She had left her cell phone out next to her laptop computer. It blinked a ghastly green with each increasingly louder call.

He flipped it open, its shrillness silenced. "Hello?"

A pause. "Who the hell is this?"

He frowned. "Who is this?"

"I asked first. I know whom I was trying to call, and you are not that person. So speak up." The woman's voice was nearly as ear piercing as the phone's ring. Jack wondered if he'd made the wrong choice by answering the phone.

"This is Jack Wiese. Now why don't you tell me who this is."

There was an audible sigh. "Jack. Jesus Christ, you scared me to death." Her voice mellowed until it was recognizable. "This is Shea Sheldon. How are you?"

Jack grinned. "Not **the** Shea Sheldon! Homecoming queen, goddess of Minneapolis North High?"

"The one and only. You forgot to mention goddess extraordinaire."

He laughed. "Nice to see your modesty hasn't kept you from success."

"The only thing that hasn't kept me from success is a man. You know of any that would be my type?"

"And what type would that be?"

"Handsome, horny and highly trainable."

Jack nearly choked on his laughter. "Shea, it's been too long. And the day you come to me looking for a blind date is the day the devil sells ice cubes for a living."

Shea's voice became instantly serious. "Jack, how is Annika?"

"She could be a lot better, but she was lucky. Only a bump on the head, no thanks to that bastard."

"What the hell happened?"

"Now, Shea, you know I can't talk about it."

Her breath whistled in his ear. "I'm her best friend. You damn well better tell me about it."

Jack ruffled his hair with one hand. "Let's just say that the man was certifiable. And if Bardikoff didn't have a screw loose before, I helped him along."

"If Annika's OK, why aren't you with the senator?"

He paused, thinking. "We will be joining him shortly." His eyes flickered over the television screens, watching for the latest news. "Shea, she told me about what happened. About Chet."

The line was silent for a long time. "Shea?"

"I'm still here. I was just surprised."

"I just thought she might feel better being someplace safe."

"Where are you?"

"My house in Minnesota. It's hidden, it's anonymous. Hardly anyone knows where I live."

"Hmmm." Strange how he felt nervous over Shea's opinion. "Can I speak with her, please?"

"She's sleeping right now."

"Where?"

Jack snorted. "What do you mean, 'where'? In a bed. I'm not a complete Neanderthal."

"No, I meant where as in, the bed you sleep in or the couch?"

Jack rolled his eyes. "Are you her guardian or something? She's sleeping in my spare bedroom. Alone."

"All right, I just had to ask. Jack?"

"Yes?"

"Be good to her." Shea's voice became tender, soft. "She hasn't had much goodness in her life."

"I will."

"And have her call me when she gets her lazy ass up."

* * *

It was dark when she awoke, confused and disoriented. She looked for the digital clock where she always stuck a post-it note telling her where she was, but only blackness stared back. Panic threatened to overwhelm her, winding up her throat like ivy. Her chest tightened.

The clang of metal against metal gave her something to grasp. Someone was cooking, the faint scent of oregano and basil perfuming the air. Her heart quit trying to leap from her chest and she sat up in bed.

She was at Jack's. She was safe. Nothing else really mattered.

Her stomach grumbled. Except, maybe, food.

Yawning, she rubbed under her eyes, hoping her makeup hadn't run down to make her look like a raccoon. As she opened the bedroom door, her senses were assaulted with delicious smells.

Following her nose, she walked down the staircase, her feet sinking into the soft carpet. At the bottom of the steps, she stopped.

Jack stood over the stove, sticking his tongue out tentatively to test the red sauce. He dabbed at the spoon, then recoiled. "Aahh! Dammit!"

Annika laughed out loud, covering her mouth with her hands. Jack looked up at her, glowering, sauce clinging to his lip. "You think that's funny, do you? I slave away here, making my specialty so that you don't starve, while you sleep away the day like a socialite."

He picked up a wineglass and sipped its burgundy contents. "Then you laugh at me while I stand here, injured. Perhaps permanently. I may never have full use of my tongue again."

"We should all be so lucky," Annika smirked, walking up to him. "Then you wouldn't jabber at us all the time."

"I was rather hoping you'd miss its other positive attributes."

She held her eyes to his dimple. "You have sauce on your lip."

He wiped one side of his mouth with his thumb, then raised his eyebrows.

"No, the other side." His movements mesmerized her, as if watching a magic show.

Jack thumbed the other side, inspected it, and then sucked the sauce off. Annika's belly tightened with heat.

"Did I get it?"

She nodded, not trusting her voice. Turning around, she asked, "What can I do to help?"

"Nothing. Everything is ready. Just sit down and I'll pour some wine."

Following his lead, as well as the rumblings of her stomach, she scooted her chair up to the table. Matching china and bright silverware adorned the forest green tablecloth, a bowl filled with cinnamon-scented pinecones the only decoration.

"Sara's doing," Jack said, sitting across from her. "Now, let's eat."

"It smells delicious." Annika used a pasta spoon to scoop spaghetti onto her plate, then smothered it with the chunky red sauce. After twirling a forkful, she took a hearty bite. "Mmmm."

"You like it?" Jack stopped dishing his sauce and waited, spoon held high.

"Mm-hmm."

"It's not the Des Moines Harmony Hotel, but I thought it would do."

She laughed. "We could always drink the wine from styrofoam cups."

Jack grinned. "Or use our lips instead of napkins to get the sauce off our mouths."

Annika looked at him sternly. "Is this your idea of not pushing me?"

"Sorry. I've never been good at being patient." Pushing her the plate of garlic bread, he changed the subject. "How are you feeling? I didn't know if I should try and wake you up. If you had suffered a concussion, aren't you supposed to stay awake for a certain number of hours?"

"I think so, but I feel fine. Even the lump seems to have gone down." She sipped her wine. "What did you do?"

He shrugged, chewing slowly. "Not much. Set up the press conference for you, which will be held tomorrow morning. Arranged a work schedule with the senator. Between now and Super Tuesday, he's got to woo thirteen states, so the group will be traveling constantly.

"Other than that, Shea called. She wants you to call her back."

Annika dropped her fork. "What did she say?"

"Not much. She was surprised that I answered." He picked at his bread crust, then met her eyes. "I told her I knew about Chet."

"Oh." Annika picked up her fork again and twirled her spaghetti. "She was probably surprised to hear that, too."

"She cares about you a lot and was worried when she heard what happened. You're lucky to have such a caring friend."

She nodded, mouth full. After she swallowed, she asked, "What about you and Bobby? I never asked you about your friendship?"

Jack wiped his mouth with a green cloth napkin. "It's like almost every man you meet. We grew up together, so we've stayed close. Men don't usually make a lot of close friends after college outside of work."

Annika scrunched up her face. "You know, I've never thought about it, but you're right. Why is that?"

"I don't know. Probably another reason why we're the inferior species." He laughed with her. "We don't get to see each other much, but we talk a lot on the phone. Our jobs have made it hard to stay connected, too, without feeling like I'm cheating on the senator. But I guess you feel that way with Shea, too."

"Yes. We have to lay down ground rules before we talk. Otherwise something that I slip could be on 'Good Evening, San Francisco' before I could jump."

Jack pushed back his plate and they sat in companionable silence, sipping the dry red wine.

"It was nice talking to Shea," he said, so suddenly it made her guard rise.

"Hmm?"

"Why hasn't she gotten married? I'm sure there are a lot of men who are falling over themselves for her attention."

Annika ignored the bite of jealousy that gnawed at her chest. "Why haven't any of us gotten married?"

Jack stared at her directly, his eyes mixing into that queer shade of grayish blue-green. "Maybe we haven't met the right person, yet."

Her heart flip-flopped, but she let her eyes drop, her hand fidgeting with the tablecloth. "Or we are all just tied up with our careers right now."

Jack leaned over and grabbed her hand. "Or maybe we're just learning that work isn't everything and that when you find someone special, you want to share a lot more with them then just your opinions."

She pulled her hand away quickly. "That reminds me, I haven't checked on the political opinion polls after what has happened in the last twenty-four hours." Standing, she looked down at him. "Thanks for dinner. I'll clean up."

As she made her escape, Annika thought of Jack's dreamy eyes, his warm touch. She had to get back on the senator's travel schedule, or she may lose the remainder of her willpower.

* * *

"God damn Bardikoff. The senator is appearing free of sin."

"Yes, sir." He knew by now that arguing with the vice president was like trying to drink by catching snowflakes on his tongue.

Vice President Martin inhaled sharply before coughing loudly into the receiver. "You still got it?"

He breathed deeply, looking over his shoulder. "Yes, sir. In my bag."

"Good. Just hang on to it. Hmm, now that I think of it, this could actually work in our favor. Give Senator Carver enough rope to hang himself, as the phrase goes. We'll let him get nice and comfortable in his role as martyr, then—"

"Sir, is there anything else?" He was itching to leave, to remove himself from the hotel's telephone booth where anyone walking past could see him.

"No. But my next call will be a go."

Chapter 15

The next weeks blended into a haze of public relations and political strategies. Annika could no longer remember where the senator was on a day to day basis, or even on an hourly basis. It seemed he flew someplace else as often during the day as she took potty breaks.

She depended on the row of televisions to keep her informed, as well as the constant calls from Gem, Axel, Lauren and Richard. Gem's concerns about the campaign faded with each stop, since she couldn't believe the 'Changeling' could follow their breakneck speed. Axel and Richard were breaking in the 'new guy,' Cleo Speros, the California State Representative who was filling in for Jack. And Lauren, well, Lauren seemed to gush, blush and flush all in the same sentence. It was nearly enough to make her want to vomit, if her jealousy didn't clog her throat like a drain.

Between the paper overflowing from the fax machine and the constant ringing of the phones, Annika felt as if she were actually on the campaign trail. In fact, she felt even more productive since she wasn't babysitting the press corps at the same time as she was developing spin.

"Have you seen this, yet?" Jack spun in his chair, holding out a sheet of fax paper.

She grabbed it and glanced through the text. "'Connecticut Governor deMarco announces a plan to cut taxes.' Well, where is it?"

"It's a teaser. Anything to get some media coverage. The exit polls from New Hampshire showed that if he won the Democratic nomination, he would get his butt whipped by Grayson Marshall."

"Well of course. He's getting his butt whipped by Senator Carver." Annika rubbed the bridge of her nose. "Isn't this a bit conservative? I mean, Democrats don't usually cut taxes."

Jack's eyes lit up. "I'll talk to Richard and see if we can work that into the next advertising."

"Also, what do we know about Marshall?"

"Why?"

"Well, shouldn't we be planning ahead? After Super Tuesday, deMarco may drop out. I'd hate to be caught with our pants down, figuratively speaking of course."

"Call O'Hara. He's the dirt digger."

And before she knew it, another day had passed. She and Jack would share dinner before climbing the stairs and retreating to their respective rooms. As she listened to him wash up before bed, she would remember the night they had spent together; Jack damp and bare in a hotel towel, the heat that burned her like no other. In the dark, she would ache silently, wanting to tiptoe into his room and slip under the comforter, seeking his warmth and love.

But she didn't want love. Love brought pain and complications. She had loved Jack once. Even if it had been puppy love, she had still felt the quick pain like a paper cut under a fingernail. And she had adored her father, until she and her mother had found him caressing her babysitter's blonde curls, kissing her deeply.

Chet didn't even deserve explaining. She traced her scar in the dark, wondering why the skin seemed ultra-sensitive at its puckered peaks. Remembering the hot tickle as Jack had pressed kisses against it.

No, love was not meant to be a part of her life. She imagined herself settling down someday, but she was always alone in her daydreams. No husband, no children. Maybe a dog. But no pain, no hurt.

Just a haunting, aching loneliness.

Annika punched her pillow. Strange, how she had never felt lonely before. She had always considered herself good company and enjoyed going out to dinner and to movies alone. But sitting at the kitchen table sharing coffee and after-dinner conversation with Jack felt blissfully peaceful.

As the house settled, its creaks and groans already familiar and homey, Annika lay awake refereeing the battle between her hidden desires and her blatant fears.

*   *   *

She was running down the tunnel, the light at the end so faint as to appear nonexistent. His growls of anger echoed off the curved walls, ricochets of oaths. She didn't know how far behind he was, but she was afraid, oh, so afraid of what would happen when he caught her.

Her lungs screamed for oxygen and her leg muscles burned. But the light grew larger with each step, widening its oval form until she could see a way out.

Then someone stepped into the light.

She choked back a scream, knowing she was caught. Slowing to a stop, she clutched her stomach, the crescent shape of her scar throbbing against her touch.

Then, a feeling of peace washed over her. She peered at the shadowy figure.

It was Jack.

He reached out to her, his hand open and welcoming. She could be safe. She could enter that circle of light with him.

But then, she looked over her shoulder.

*   *   *

"Annika! Wake up!"

He flipped the bedroom light on and was taken aback by her appearance. Her eyes were the wide open depths of the ocean, tears streamed down her face. Legs tangled in the sheets, she kicked furiously.

He crossed the room in giant steps. "Annika!" Holding her shoulders was like touching a live wire. She shook with barely suppressed heat, quaking under his touch. "You're all right. I'm here."

"Jack?" The words were dry, choked.

He pulled her to his bare chest. "It's OK. You just had a bad dream." He stroked her wild hair, fingers tugging through the tangles. She shuddered against him, the wetness from her face soaking his skin.

He held her for a long time, listening to the sounds of the house. The refrigerator kicked on, its low hum vibrating against the wall. Trees rattled their branches with the sudden gusts of wind that made the house creak in its foundation. He reminded himself to check the plastic sheets that protected his roses in the morning.

After a long time, her trembling ceased. He kept stroking her hair, more for his own gratification than to soothe her. Coiled so tightly, yet each curl as soft as a kitten's fur. It was the perfect metaphor for the woman he held so tightly against his chest.

"How did you know?" she whispered.

"You called my name." He nuzzled her hair, breathing in the deep scent of vanilla and almonds. "Screamed it, actually."

She chuckled against his chest, making the hairs rise in response. "I'm sorry."

"What for?"

"For waking you up."

"Annika." He pulled away, cupping her face with his hands. "Haven't you figured out by now that sleep is overrated?"

He was awarded with a smile. Her tears had dried, and she looked more like herself.

"Now, can I get you anything?" he asked.

She hesitated, picking at the sheet with her fingernails. Long lashes brushed against the apples of her cheeks.

"Would you stay with me?" She looked up, meeting his eyes with a look of combined defiance and fright. "Sleep with me?"

He brushed back a strand of hair gently, trailing his hand along her jaw. "Of course."

After flicking off the light, he moved with infinite care into the bed next to her and gathered her into his arms. She shivered, and he wrapped his arms around her more tightly.

They lay, listening to the wind. He wondered if she heard it like he did, a song of nature. He suspected she found it malicious and mean.

Her breath had lost its ragged edge and was now a sensual whisper against his skin. She wiggled closer, stray hairs tickling his face, until her face was sheltered between his pectoral muscles.

A soft, wet line was drawn across his skin. The shock of it took him by surprise, even as his body stirred and hardened against her. Moist lips pressed against him, making him shudder feverishly.

With deliberate care, he squirmed low under the covers until he could rest his forehead against hers. "Annika," he whispered.

She lay, silent. He wished the wind would blow away the cloud cover, so the moonlight would light up the room. Then he would be able to read her face, her true feelings, with no mask blocking the emotions.

Instead, the night embraced them, and Annika, without a word, fell into the heavy breathing of a much needed sleep. Relaxing against the pillows and the touch of the woman beside him, Jack listened to the wind and dreamed.

*   *   *

He knew she was gone before he opened his eyes. Rolling over, he clutched her pillow, inhaling her sweet scent. The sheets were still warm from her body.

Cracking open his eyes, Jack blinked away his dreams and stared at the pebbled ceiling. Before he had awakened, Annika had been whispering in his ear, telling him her secrets, but he couldn't understand the language she was speaking. In his dream he had irritably told her to repeat herself, but only foreign babble tickled his ear.

Jack followed the trail of a slender crack in the ceiling as it wound across to the far wall. The house was quiet, the welcoming aroma of coffee drifting into the room. When he strained his ears, he couldn't hear any sounds coming from the basement office, either.

She was gone.

He swung his legs out of bed and stood. Rubbing his head, he walked into the bathroom to pee before heading down to the kitchen.

The coffee pot was full to the seven cup line. Toast crumbs littered the countertop. Jack pressed his hand against the toaster. It was still warm.

OK, Sherlock, he mused. Reaching up into the cabinet, he pulled down his favorite coffee mug, etched with "I'M the boss, who the hell are you?". He poured slowly, then replaced the pot.

Leaves skittered across the deck, sounding like the dry rattle of a poisonous snake. Jack walked to the sliding glass door and looked outside. The wind had done some minor damage. A few branches had fallen off the trees and leaves piled into neat bundles against the rose bushes. Unfortunately, it had also blown off the protective plastic.

Jack set his coffee mug down on the counter and started for the stairs. **May as well do a little yard work before hitting the phones**, he thought. The senator was in New York and scheduled until late afternoon, so he wasn't expecting any urgent calls.

The phone rang.

He paused halfway up the stairs and stumbled back down. Picking it up on the third ring, his tone was short. "Jack Wiese."

"Please hold for Governor Sheraton."

Jack straightened his spine reflexively. The Minnesota governor was not a lady that gave second chances.

"Jack, how are you?"

He cleared his throat. "Fantastic, Governor Sheraton, and you?"

Her throaty laugh rumbled over the phone line. "Well, I wish I could get out and enjoy this springlike weather that blew in last night, but I'm stuck in meetings all day."

Jack laughed, hoping his nerves didn't change the pitch of his voice. "What can I do for you today, ma'am?"

"First of all, you can cut the crap."

He tried not to choke. "Governor Sheraton?"

"I am tired of the senator passing over his home state while on the campaign trail. Minnesota may not give him more than 10 votes, but we are still his most outspoken and vital supporters. Let's not forget that, even with your eye on Super Tuesday."

"Of course. I know Senator Carver has planned on a statewide visit—"

"I'm hosting a party for him on Saturday night. Make sure he's in attendance, would you, Jack?"

Her sarcasm rang in his ear even louder than the dial tone. He hung up the phone and paused only a second before picking it back up again. As he punched in the numbers to Gem's cellular, he pushed his thoughts of Annika out of his head.

* * *

An hour later and he was immersed in plans. It was Thursday. Flights could be arranged, meetings rescheduled. Axel's numbers showed Governor deMarco holding a strong lead in New York, so the senator didn't want to waste any more time there anyway.

The televisions blared in the background, the mix of four different channels creating a comfortable buzz. Jack's fingers flew across his keyboard as he wrote an apologetic speech for the senator to give at the governor's party.

Annika's scent drew him from his self-induced hypnosis. Without turning around, he knew she was sitting behind him.

He coughed noisily. "Do you have your schedule out?"

Pause. "Yes."

"Good. Governor Sheraton is hosting a party for the senator on Saturday. The headquarters manager is arranging some meetings during the day, but with it being so close to Super Tuesday, you'll want to keep marketing your p.r. to the west."

"Jack—"

"Also, Lauren wanted you to call her when you got a chance. Something about an exclusive with the **New York Times**." He kept typing, even though the sentences were now unstructured and personal. *Annika, why are you holding yourself back? Why do I even care?*.

She didn't seem to notice. Her own steady typing was the only answer. He erased the words on his screen, pressing the backspace button in Morse code-like pauses to make it sound like he was still working.

"I'll call her now," she said.

Jack whirled around in his chair. Annika stared at him, her hand reaching for the phone, but then her eyes wavered and she let her hand drop away.

His frustration melted away like the lake ice. "Are you all right?" he asked.

At first, she hesitated, biting her lip. He expected lies and fabrications to spill out and waited.

Finally, she shook her head, her curls tumbling over her shoulders. "No. I mean, yes." She paused, then rolled her chair closer to him. "God, this is hard to say," she said, shutting her eyes.

Jack reached for her hand and she grasped his tightly. "Just pretend I'm not even here. Pretend you're talking to Shea."

Annika smiled. "No. What I want to say, I only want you to hear."

He stroked her hand with his thumb. "Then, say it."

Her eyes were liquid sapphire and pulled at his soul. "Thank you. For last night." She took a deep breath. "There, I said it. Thanks."

"See, that wasn't so hard."

"Maybe not for you," she joked, squeezing his hand. Her face became serious. "Jack, we've needed to talk ever since… Well, you know."

"Since we made love?"

She colored, her cheeks flaming bright pink. "Well, yes."

"What do we need to talk about?" Her skin was so smooth under his fingertips, like caressing a polished stone. "Look, Annika, I'm not going to hide my feelings for you." He raised his eyebrows. "There, now I said it."

"Yes, but—"

"But nothing. I know you are afraid. I can't blame you, with everything you've been through." He ran his thumb along her palm and watched her shiver. "But I will still be here when you're ready."

She watched him from under her eyelashes. But she didn't pull her hand away. **That was progress,** he thought.

"Don't you want to know where I was?"

"Only if you want to tell me. I figure either way, it's your business."

She sighed and squeezed his hand. "I walked down to the dock. I sat in the cedar chair and watched the ice melt." Her gaze became dreamy. "I imagined what it must be like in the summer, with the sound of children's laughter filling the air. Warm sun on your face and a fishing pole between your knees." Smiling, she pulled away and sat back in her chair. "But instead of making me feel relaxed and at peace, it made me sad."

"Sad? Why?"

She shrugged her shoulders, but her eyes shifted. Whatever it was, it was staying close to her heart.

He rolled his chair over by hers, bumping it playfully. "Did you notice that there are two chairs on the dock?"

She bumped him. "Yes."

"When you imagined me fishing off the dock, who was sitting in the other chair?" He kept his voice low, as if talking to an easily spooked horse.

Annika spun in her chair so the tall back nearly swept him away. Conveniently, it also hid her face.

"Oh, I don't know." But her voice trembled, giving away her thoughts.

Jack grabbed the arms of the chair and slowly turned it around. Annika's face was neutral, but her fingers drummed restlessly against her jeans.

"That second chair has been waiting for someone for many years. All they have to do is just sit still long enough to realize it."

Before she could react, he stood up and held a hand out. "Now, I'm bored. Let's go on an adventure."

Chapter 16

She recognized the old houses first. Stately Victorian homes rising regally next door to uniquely modern glass blocks.

"Do they still hold the Uptown Art Fair?" she asked.

"Yes, only it's huge now. The streets are smothered with pompous people." Jack took his eyes off the road for a moment to wink at her. "Makes our political obligations seem like cake."

Annika laughed. "Don't remind me about Saturday. I have to find a dress to wear. Almost everything I have is packed away."

"Wear that cream-colored dress you have."

She glanced over at him, heart thumping. "You remember that dress?"

"Of course." He turned the steering wheel to the left, then slid the gear into park. Flipping the ignition key, he looked over at her. "It was the first time I saw you. How could I forget?"

While Annika thought desperately for a glib reply, Jack rescued her.

"Anyway, it's hard to forget a dress when you're down on the floor, gasping for breath, and that's all you've got to look at." He grinned at her, his eyes green with mischief.

Her mouth hurt from smiling. The entire winding drive was filled with jokes and political anecdotes. The wind blew off Lake Minnetonka in warm waves and they had opened their windows to welcome it.

Relaxed, she had shared some funny stories of her own, and they had laughed together like old friends.

Her face wasn't used to it.

A tall, brick building towered above them, strangely ordinary in the eclectic neighborhood. Mental pictures clicked into focus like the lens of a camera.

"Jack, why are we at the firehouse?"

"You'll see." He opened his car door and rushed to her side before she could even get her own door halfway open. "Allow me," he said, gallantly.

"I can open my own door, thank you," she scoffed, brushing past him.

"Thank God. We can finally send out a press release stating that chivalry can indeed be dead."

When she reached the sidewalk, she turned around, raising an eyebrow. "So?"

"So, what are you waiting for? I thought you were looking for an adventure." Jack opened the door, pushing in front of her rudely. Sighing, she grabbed at the door before it swung shut.

"I almost got my fingers caught in the door, Jack."

"Sorry, modern woman. You can't have it both ways."

Feeling more comfortable on familiar fighting ground, Annika began her argument. Before a single word could come out, her mouth dropped open in awe.

It was the fire station, but stunningly redone. As she raised her head to stare up at the high ceiling, she marveled at the change. Where the firefighters had originally slept on a second floor balcony, diners now sat at simple tables. The far wall still supported the brass pole the firefighters had once descended. A round window interrupted the jagged brick pattern, casting the afternoon light over the room. Brass sparkled under its glow.

The smell of chicken and fresh bread made her stomach call out greedily. Perusing the crowd, she hoped they could get a table quickly.

"Jack!" A woman with skin as creamy as cappuccino walked toward him, arms outstretched. They embraced, she kissing him on both cheeks in the European fashion. "We've missed you! No one can charm our servers out of extras like you."

"Are you kidding? Your staff is so well trained they are supplying extra napkins or more beverages before the thoughts even crossed my mind." He stepped back and wrapped his arm around Annika. His scent reached her senses, and without thinking she leaned into him.

"Monique, this is Annika Andersen. Annika, this is the owner of the best restaurant in the Midwest."

Monique's coal-black eyes seemed to glow like embers with welcome. "Welcome to Firebrick. It's an honor to have you here."

Annika shook her tiny hand. "The honor is mine. What you've done here is stunning!"

"Well, when the city proposed its demolition, I told my husband that we couldn't let them destroy this beautiful historical landmark." Monique smiled. "Luckily, they agreed with me. After some persuasion." Her eyes darted to Jack.

"Don't look at me. Your proposal is what won them over."

"That and the support of Senator Carver." She beamed. "Such a fantastic man. I would love to hear your take on the campaign, but first, let's get you some lunch."

A hostess appeared at Monique's side as if by magic.

"Follow me, please," she said, shyly glancing at Jack.

"Enjoy your lunch!" Monique waved, then disappeared in a swirl of crimson and tangerine skirts.

Annika noticed several of the female patrons glancing up from their plates as they walked by. Each watched Jack appreciatively. If he noticed, he didn't let it show.

Holding her chair out, he waited until she was seated before taking his place across the table. "Was that allowed?"

"Yes, that was very gentlemanly. Thank you."

He shook his head, his dimple deepening. "You're going to have to write a rule book so I can keep everything straight," he said, opening the menu.

"It's very easy, really." Annika pretended to study the specials. "If I'm right, I'm right. If I'm wrong, I'm right."

Jack laughed and folded his menu. "When did you get so stubborn? I don't remember you having this attitude in middle school."

"I wasn't like this," she replied. She shrugged, feigning nonchalance. "I guess I started being more assertive after my parents got divorced."

"Trying to gain some sense of lost control?" Jack leaned his elbows against the table.

"I guess." She was relieved when the waitress approached their table.

"Have you made up your minds?" she asked.

Jack raised his eyebrows at Annika and she nodded. "I'll have the lemon pepper chicken salad, please."

"And for you, sir?"

"The roasted pepper pizza."

The waitress nodded and took their menus without writing down their order. It always made Annika nervous when servers did that. "Anything to drink?"

They both shook their heads and she walked away.

"So." Jack sipped his water, then folded his hands. "You moved to Colorado and found a new attitude."

"Not really. I'm sure it had been there all along." She tried not to fidget in her chair and unfolded the red cloth napkin. "Kind of like what you said before. You never really know what is going on with a person. Only what they present to you."

Jack shrugged, batting aside her comment without any outward appearance of annoyance. "That makes sense, then."

"What do you mean?"

"Well, I've been trying to figure out why you would have ever gotten involved with someone violent. You being so 'assertive' and all." He poked at the silverware with one finger. "You must have been looking for it."

The hairs on the back of her neck stood up in prickly rage. "Looking for it? You think I was looking for that kind of relationship?"

Jack raised his shoulders while sipping his water, his eyes empty of emotion.

She leaned forward until the table pressed under her breasts. "I thought I loved him. But I was naïve and uncertain of what was involved in a good relationship. I didn't have any to compare mine to." Her teeth clenched together as she controlled the level of her voice. "How dare you imply that I wanted it."

Jack reached across the table for her hand, but she pulled away angrily.

"Here you go," the waitress chirped merrily, plunking their plates down heavily. "Watch out, the plates are hot. Enjoy."

Annika picked up her fork and mechanically began cutting her chicken.

"Feel better?" Jack shoved a large chunk of pizza into his mouth and chewed slowly.

"No. I'm pissed at you."

He swallowed and wiped his mouth. "I don't blame you. I was purposely baiting you and being cruel." He speared another piece and held it just near his mouth. "But didn't it feel good to be honest for once?"

Tears rushed to her eyes. The stone that weighed down in her belly seemed to lighten, as if transforming into feathers. She was not to blame. She was never to blame.

She choked down her bite of salad. Dabbing at her mouth with a napkin, she regained her composure. "Since when are you an armchair shrink?"

"It doesn't take a psychotherapist to figure out that you're in pain. Or a dream analyst, either."

She looked up, but he kept his eyes on his plate, sawing away with knife and fork. "I guess that's why I keep having the nightmares then."

He shrugged and popped a bite into his mouth.

"You know, I always wondered what I did to deserve it. Losing my family, losing friends, nearly losing my life." She sat back in her chair and folded her hands in her lap thoughtfully. "But I never allowed myself to think about it. I would just push away the pain, and if there was someone else in the way they got shoved, too."

She stared into Jack's dark green-gray eyes. "But it wasn't me. The things that happened to me were not my fault."

"No, they weren't." Jack wiped his mouth and pushed back his plate. He smiled, eyes twinkling. "So, how do you feel now?"

"Fantastic!" Annika laughed. She did, too. Her arms felt buoyant and her head light.

"Great. Because there's nothing like taking a walk after a bout of self-discovery."

*   *   *

"We're flying to Minneapolis tonight."

A husky chuckle roared over the line, making him pull the phone away from his ear. "Perfect. Let's see what the hometown thinks of him now."

As he hung up the phone, he wondered if he could still ask for a transfer to the White House. He'd like to watch the vice president every day and watch his discomfort grow.

*   *   *

Small waves lapped against the sand, whipped up by the stiff southwestern wind. They walked against it, feeling the warmth of the sun on their backs as the breeze heated their faces.

"This hasn't changed," Annika said, gesturing to the water. Lake Calhoun was just as she remembered, with the exception of a newly paved walking trail.

"Not much changes with nature," Jack replied, kicking a rock along the path. It skittered down the bank, landing with a small plop in the water.

"Look at those crazy people." She nodded toward the middle of the lake at the island of ice. A duo of fishermen were crouched over their poles, staring down into a possible icy death. "How can they take such a risk with their lives?"

Jack grabbed her hand and tucked it into his warm pocket. She snuggled closer and he put his arm around her. "Everyone has to take risks. Some just choose unwisely."

A rush of heat warmed her. She shook it off, thinking it was the closeness of their bodies.

"Anyway," Jack said, "What would any of us do if we didn't take risks?"

"I'm not much of a risk-taker."

Jack laughed.

"What?" she demanded.

"Oh, you were serious?" He squeezed her closer as she tried to squirm away. "Really, Annika. You've taken more risks than a lot of people are comfortable with. Like the MENSA t-shirt at the beginning of the campaign. That could have completely backfired."

"Hardly," she replied haughtily.

"That's what I mean. You make intelligent gambles. Like me, for instance."

"You."

He squinted at the lake as he strolled. "Yes, me. It's very smart to take a chance on me. I'm young, talented, entertaining, handsome…"

"Modest," she said sarcastically.

"That, too. A fine specimen of a man."

"You're making it sound like I'm looking for a breed of dog." Annika shook her head. "And, besides, I'm not looking. For anything."

"Suit yourself." Jack dropped his hand from her shoulders, putting it into his pocket as he whistled. Annika withdrew her own hand and put some space between them.

After they had walked a few minutes in silence, she crossed her arms. "Why do you keep pushing it, Jack?"

"Look," he said, ignoring her. "Is that familiar?"

She strained to see where he was pointing. A stretch of sandy beach seemed pinned under a tall, red lifeguard tower. The air suddenly smelled of tropical oil and lakeweed, memories of a far away summer.

"Do people still swim here?"

"It's not as popular as when we would come out, but some still come to swim. Especially when it gets really hot."

Jack stopped in front of the lifeguard tower. "Ever been up in one of these?"

"No." Annika glanced around, but only saw a few people strolling along the path. A rollerblader sped by on squeaky wheels. "Isn't it off limits?"

"Annika, we're adults now. Nothing's off limits." With that, Jack stepped up on the first rung and began to climb. Once he was halfway up he turned around. "Well?"

"Well, what?"

"Aren't you coming? It's not like you have to stand guard."

"I was just waiting until you got to the top," she lied, grabbing the wood.

"Uh-huh." Jack resumed his climbing. Looking up, she had to admit the view was breathtaking.

With a final glance over her shoulder, she began to climb. The tower stood about fifteen feet high, but the rungs were spaced far apart, so each step was gigantic. Her thigh muscles began to burn in protest.

By the time she reached the top, her breath was escaping in huffs. Jack reached down to help her swing her leg on to the wooden platform.

"Well, that was fun," she panted.

"Come here," he said, pulling her beside him. Without resisting, she leaned back into his warm, solid chest, feeling her body mold against his naturally. He held a hand out to the water. "Look."

From their high perch, they could see across Lake Calhoun to Lake Harriet, which was across the highway. The Minneapolis skyline reflected the sun, each building a giant mirror. The wind even seemed to be blowing more briskly.

Jack reached around her, enveloping her with his warmth. "Do you remember the time Bobby and I got kicked off the beach for climbing this during a lifeguard break?"

Annika laughed. "Which time? You guys were always getting into trouble."

"True, but Bobby was the instigator. I just followed."

She wiped at her nose with a gloved hand. "You've never been a follower. And I'd be willing to bet that it was your idea half the time."

"I wonder where those lifeguards are now," he mused, releasing her so she could slide beside him. The wind whistled through the wood slats. "I sure had a crush on one of them."

"Which one?"

"Betsy."

Annika strained to draw from her memory banks but came up empty. "I don't remember her."

Jack stretched out his legs. "She was my first love. I would stare at her for hours, and then go home with a blistering sunburn." He laughed. "I would imagine climbing this tower, and when she protested I would just lean over and kiss her." He looked at Annika with such self-mockery that she laughed. "Of course she would immediately fall in love and be the first to take a sixth grader to the prom."

"But instead?'

He squinted down the beach. "Instead, I followed her to the ice cream stand and made a really bad joke. She looked at me as if I was a slimy frog." He turned back to Annika, the early spring sun making his eyes appear to be translucent emerald. "So I became one. And hurt quite a few feelings in the process."

Annika let him pull her hand into his lap, a silent apology. His face was close enough that she could see where he'd nicked himself shaving that morning, a thin scab along his jaw. Although it was only early afternoon, a slight stubble was already sprouting. Staring hypnotically, she wondered what it would feel like to have him gently rub his cheeks along her bare thighs.

His mouth was slightly parted, sensual lips ripe for a kiss. She felt drawn in, powerless to resist.

He cleared his throat. The spell was broken.

Shivering, Jack rubbed his hands across his arms briskly. "It would be a nice day if it weren't for the wind. Are you cold?"

She nodded. "Yes, we should probably head back."

He hesitated, looking at her for the briefest of seconds. She had just decided that she was going to kiss him when he pushed himself off the wood platform.

"You're right. Wouldn't want the taxpayers to hear about these three-hour lunches." He began to climb down the ladder.

Annika followed, the taste of disappointment and desire still tart on her tongue.

* * *

The faxes overflowed the tray, leaving a small snowstorm on the floor of the office. Annika swiped one, then stood and read.

"What is it?" Jack asked, when she frowned.

"It's updated information from Agent Bailey," she answered. She glanced up. "The senator has received another threat."

His chest tightened. The afternoon's joy was diminished, like a dark cloud crossing over the sun. "What does it say?"

She read out loud. "Are you afraid of death? We all die at some point. You are fortunate to know the date of your death. See you in San Francisco."

"San Francisco?" Then, he remembered. "The rally in Union Square. We'll have to cancel."

Annika squatted down and sat yoga-style on the floor, paging through the rest of the paper. "Agent Bailey says he's already talked to the senator, and he has refused to change his schedule."

"Damn it," Jack said, dropping into his chair. "What else?"

Her eyes moved rapidly over the pages, skimming their contents. "This last letter was sent from a cyber-café in New York. Agent Bailey thinks the perpetrator knows we're looking for him in libraries."

"They're flying in from New York tomorrow," Jack murmured.

Annika looked up. "So he's still following Senator Carver."

They stared at each other, their worry mirrored.

"What do we do now?" Jack asked.

Annika stood up. "We work."

Chapter 17

A sea of candle flames flickered throughout the ballroom. The governor had ordered the caterers to decorate with a feeling of renewal. According to their interpretation, that meant gold branches woven into long garlands and table decorations of budding flowers.

The flower arrangements, though pretty, contained lavender, which made Jack sneeze. The candlelight was so dim he could hardly see through his watery eyes. And the guests were such prominent figures that his mouth already hurt from smiling so widely.

It was going to be another long night. Seeing the senator would be rewarding, but the only saving grace was Annika.

Excusing himself from the governor of New Hampshire, Jack walked to his table. He wiped at his dripping eyes with a soaked handkerchief and looked around the room.

She stood, talking to Governor Sheraton and a state representative. Although she had chosen to leave the cream dress in the closet, her selection left him breathless. Simple in design, it clung with sensual ease over her body like red paint. Her bold choice of color lit up the monotone room like a cardinal in the winter.

"She stunning."

Jack turned and saw Cleo Speros, a waifish dark-haired woman who always reminded him of an Irish elf. In fact, Cleo was of Greek descent and treated the staff to freshly made baklava every Saturday.

He glanced back to Annika. "Yes, she is."

Cleo gestured to his face. "And you decided to come color-coordinated."

Jack laughed ruefully. "Damn lavender does this to me every time. I'm going to ask Annika if she has any antihistamines in her purse. Excuse me."

Sneezing, he wiped his nose and started to walk over to her. A hand on his arm stopped him.

"Jack."

He turned around. Axel Gallo, with blue jeans on and a leather thong holding back his hair stood there, shuffling his feet back and forth. His face was pale to the point of being ashy.

Jack felt his stomach roll over. "Axel. What is it?"

He stared at the floor. "You need to go to the hotel. Annika, too."

*   *   *

The elevator ride to the twentieth floor passed as slowly as a kidney stone. Jack tapped his foot impatiently, one hand tucked in his tuxedo pants pocket, the other furiously rubbing his head.

Annika reached out to stop his movements, breaking him from his thoughts. She smiled and threaded her fingers through his. "What's the worst it could be?"

"Bomb threat. Or the 'changeling' managed to get past security."

She squeezed his hand. "What are you really worried about?"

Jack turned to her and was about to speak when the elevator pinged and the doors slid open. She dropped his hand like a burning coal and swept ahead of him, nodding to the secret service agent on post. Jack's hurt expression was shoved to the back of her mind.

There was a place for their relationship, and it wasn't in the middle of the crisis room.

She tapped lightly on the door to the senator's suite, then twisted the knob. It was locked. Warning bells rang in her mind. Never in the campaign had the senator locked his suite door before. He had always welcomed impromptu meetings and was too lazy to keep locking and reopening the door with each visitor.

She looked at Jack with alarm. He held a finger to his lips. Footsteps sounded from behind the closed door.

Annika stared at the glass peephole, wondering who was peering out of its magnified eye. The door unlatched and swung open.

"Oh, Jack!" A blur of crimson and black rushed past Annika and splashed against Jack. Gem was sobbing, her mascara running down her face in black rivulets. Stunned, Annika found herself marveling that she'd never seen Gem without lipstick applied with perfection.

Shaking herself out of her daze, she stepped forward and grabbed Gem's arm. "What is it? Where's the senator?"

Gem only sobbed harder, clinging to Jack with red fingernails curled into talons. A smear of black stained his white shirt.

His jaw clenched, the muscles as hard as marble. Carefully, he pried Gem off and held her at arms distance. Bending low to meet her eye to eye, he asked, "What is going on?"

Gem sniffled and wiped her face with wet hands, spreading the mascara to the edges of her auburn hair. "The Minneapolis police are here. They're sayin' they found drugs in the senator's suitcase." She grabbed at his lapels. "Are they gonna put him in jail?"

"Drugs? Impossible." Jack started for the door, then stopped, pulling Gem into an enormous hug. He cupped her face in his hands. "Go get Cleo and Richard from downstairs. Or send someone for them. And don't worry." He glanced up at Annika. "We'll take care of this."

Gulping back her own doubts, Annika forced a smile to her face. Jack nodded his encouragement. Like tying a slipknot on a sail, her smile secured its place. She met Gem's raccoon-eyes. "Go back to your room, Gem, and call down from there. Then, get Pam to help you with your makeup." She reached out and squeezed Gem's bony arm. "We know there will be cameras. We've got to look good."

Her personal appearance took precedence over any scandal. Her lacquered fingernails flitted like butterflies over her face. "I must look a mess. You're right, darlin', can't be seen lookin' like death. They'll think he's guilty for sure."

Flaming head held higher, Gem marched off as easily on her six-inch heels as she would barefoot. Annika's smile melted away.

"Drugs?" she hissed.

Jack shushed her and grabbed her arm, pulling her inside the door. "I don't believe it," he whispered, his voice husky with repressed fury. "The senator would never—"

"But he did, once." Jack's grip tightened reflexively, then dropped. They stood in the doorway, staring at each other. His foot propped open the door like a brick, his arms held stiffly at his sides. Even his eyes became remote, the distant gray of thunderheads. The only thing that gave away his feelings were his hands, which clenched and unclenched methodically.

"You don't believe he's been using drugs on the campaign trail," he said, voice flat. She wanted to pull him into her arms, whisper encouraging words. But her head was whirling with accusations, her world evaporating into the unknown.

She couldn't risk her heart any more.

"I don't want to believe that," she said, picking her words carefully. "But the senator has a history of alcohol abuse. And he's been extremely resistant to the ads we want to place on his recovery. I think we need to analyze all the information before we—"

"Damn it, I'm not a member of your press corps! Tell me what you think!"

She lifted her chin, forcing herself to meet his steely glare. "I think it's possible."

With a muffled oath, Jack spun around, slamming his hand against the door. Annika raced in behind him, ready to argue her case, the words streaming through her mind.

When Jack stopped abruptly, she walked right into his back. Still fuming, she swore, then snapped her mouth shut.

Senator Carver sat on the couch, flanked on each side by a uniformed police officer. His face looked like it had been carved from ivory wax, every wrinkle and every crease deeper than she remembered. The silver that graced his temples seemed to have extended past his forehead over the past hour. Across from him in the soft leather wing chair, the Minneapolis police chief sat scribbling on a pad of paper, seemingly oblivious to Jack and Annika's entry.

"Jack," Senator Carver whispered. "Tell them it's not true."

Without even glancing at Jack, Annika felt her world break apart from reality.

*   *   *

"…and the damn cat threw up all over Tabbitha's dance uniform so I gotta go buy a new one. Do you know how much those things cost? Of course, the other moms can all afford to have their own seamstresses sew them. Not us, oh no. I can't even buy the new leather pumps that were on clearance at Neiman Marcus."

He sighed, leaning his forehead against the payphone. The frigid metal made him shiver. "Honey, didn't you get it?"

She was already revved up for a good whine. "Do you know how much I spent at the grocery store yesterday? Three. Hundred. Dollars. Do you know how long it'll last? One. Week."

"Honey—"

"And the twins just grew out of their sneakers again, so I've gotta pay for them." Finally, when he thought she had used her last breath, her groan pierced through the receiver. "It's bad enough that I've got to take care of these g.d. kids by myself most of the time, but to have no money to show for it—"

"Didn't you get the money?" He spoke so loudly that the pimple-faced clerk behind the gas station counter cranked his head up from the girly magazine he was paging through under the counter. Smiling widely, he swore through gritted teeth.

"Don't use that language around me, mister. I won't have that. And, no, I haven't gotten the money."

"You didn't go pick it up like they told you to?"

"No, I went to the bus station and opened up the same locker they put the first payment into. It was empty. I thought I might of mixed up the times, so I went back today and it was still empty. Are you sure you got it right…"

Her nagging voice rang through his ear like a neighbor's annoying wind chime. No matter how he tried to tune it out, he couldn't.

Damn it, he had fulfilled his end of the bargain. The deal that made him lose sleep, made him wake up dripping in an icy sweat that stank of rotten lemons. His Catholic soul had warned him; now his religious hell was catching up to his living one.

"I'll call you back," he said abruptly, hanging the phone up on her wailing pleas. Time to meet with the devil, he thought, nodding at the clerk as he swung the door open.

*   *   *

The car drifted around the twisted corners like a silkworm, the darkness reflecting the faces of its occupants. Neither spoke, but just stared out their respective windows, drowning in their own thoughts.

Annika felt like she had just given blood. Once, at a Red Cross blood drive, she had sat up to quickly, the room spinning in a slow, dizzy circle around her. When she had awakened to the pinched face of a nurse, she had pretended she felt better. Choking down a graham cracker and some juice, her head had felt like it was floating above her shoulders, while her arms and legs were as heavy as coin-filled socks.

The heaviness now pressed her into the car's leather interior, her thoughts floating like a cartoon balloon above her.

Seeing the senator's face, pale as a death mask, had been enough to convince her of his innocence. But it was the other questions, the whys and the whos that distracted her while she and Jack frantically put together a press statement.

She glanced away from the window and pulled her hair away from her face, dropping the handful behind her collar. Jack didn't twitch, but just stared out into the night.

He was still angry with her. Well, to hell with him, then. If he can't understand why she was hesitant to believe everything at face value, after all she had told him and entrusted with him, then he can sit and pout like a child.

Blowing out a frustrated breath, she crossed her arms over her chest. The car slowed, taking the turn into the driveway with exaggerated caution. The spring-like day had thawed most of the snow, leaving scattered puddles along the streets. She checked her watch. Two a.m. The temperature had probably dropped enough to film the lake with a thin layer of ice. She wished she could walk through the woods to the dock, where she could just sit and wait while Jack stewed. But it was too dark, and she didn't trust her instincts enough to keep her on the path, away from the hidden rabbit traps.

Agent Bostitch flipped the gearshift into park, then stepped out of the car. Annika waited until her door was opened before slipping out into air that crinkled the inside of her nose.

"Agent Bostitch," she said, holding a hand on her arm. "Thank you for being there tonight."

She blinked, surprised. "Ma'am, it's my job."

Annika shook her head. "It's not your job to protect the senator from criminal action. You knew something wasn't right as soon as you and

Agents Garcia and Hamilton found the marijuana. You kept the crime scene clean. Because of that, we may be able to find out who did this."

The porch light struck Agent Bostitch's smile. "Thank you, ma'am." She stepped back and began to round the car to open Jack's door. Before she reached the rear of the car, his door was already open and he was walking with an inflated pace toward the house without a backward look.

"Good night, ma'am," Agent Bostitch said.

"Good night." Annika knew it was anything but, and hesitated, watching the car circle around and pull away into the night. Once she couldn't see the rear taillights, she sighed and stepped toward the door.

The house was so silent it seemed unoccupied, but Annika knew Jack was lurking somewhere. Damned if she was going to let him ruin what was left of a good night's sleep. She draped her coat haphazardly over the back of a chair then stomped up the stairs.

* * *

Jack's shoes tapped on the floors as he walked into the kitchen. Pulling out a bottle of Scotch from the highest shelf, he blew the dust off it. The upstairs bathroom sink turned on, and he imagined Annika getting herself ready for bed, donning the crimson silk robe he had wanted to tear off the first time he'd seen her in it.

Sighing, he replaced the bottle. Alcohol would only further ignite his anger, his frustration.

She hadn't said one word of apology. Not when they'd worked together on the morning's press releases, not when the senator had grasped her hand in both of his with thanks. And not a whisper in the car.

Leaning against the countertop, he felt the cold marble through the thin fabric of his tuxedo shirt. He pressed his forehead against his hands, trying to push away the thoughts and the eddy of confused emotions. The rhythmic beat of his pulse thudded inside his head, so he released the pressure.

He had no right to be angry with Annika. But even knowing that made him all the more furious. She had the right to her own feelings, her own beliefs. What made him think that the past few weeks had changed that? And why would he want to change her?

Because he always had. The sudden inspiration made him push away from the countertop to sink into the kitchen chair. "Oh, come on. She's exotic, she's intelligent, she's beautiful. All the requirements for a one-on-one with Jack Wiese." Steven had been right, all those months ago.

Except for one simple, beautiful thing. He was hopelessly in love with her. And no amount of fear or fury was going to change that.

The staircase was carpeted, muffling his footsteps. Just as he reached the top, the bathroom door opened. Annika looked at him in surprise, her face bared of makeup, skin glowing like the moonlight.

The bathroom light shone through the crimson robe, and he felt the last notch of control slip its gear.

He was at her side in two steps, surprising her with his quickness. She knew she still wanted him despite their disagreement that night, but she didn't anticipate the lightening-quick flash of her desire in that instant.

"Do you want me?" he asked quietly, his words a whisper against her neck.

"It's late, Wiese," she murmured, willing herself to pull away while her body betrayed her, pressing closer to his heat.

He leaned down and kissed her, roughly and hungrily, making her arch against him in response. She felt devoured, desired like she had never been with any man. His tongue flicked against hers and she drove against his wetness eagerly. With the ease of a shower's rainfall, he slipped his hand through her robe, caressing her bare skin.

Annika jolted. "Is this how you're going to solve all of our problems," she said haughtily, trying to pull away from his molten grasp. "Tumble into bed and when the last drops of sweat dry, you're over it?"

"No." The word, whispered throatily against her neck, only fanned the flame of desire burning within her. "But I thought it was worth a shot."

"Jack, please…Jack, stop." He released her reluctantly, eyes cloudy like a Minnesota thunderhead. They stood only inches apart, but the pull of their magnetism only made Annika want to lean back farther.

"I'm sorry," she said firmly, forcing herself to maintain eye contact. "I can't give you what you need, or feel for you the way you want." Backing up slowly, she bumped into the wall. "I understand how you feel. The excitement, the passion of the campaign…it just goes to your head, gets in your blood. Your feelings for Senator Carver go way back and are more entrenched than mine. I'm just an employee, here. What you are feeling is normal. But it's not true feelings."

Silence. She forbade herself to flinch under his scrutinizing gaze. Lifting her chin high, she returned his stare.

In a blink he was at her side, pinning her arms in his embrace. Her world exploded in a swirl of senses, the lingering smell of coffee on his skin, the musky taste of his mouth, the smoothness of his hands as they skimmed through the gap in her robe. Her carefree words meant nothing, and she grabbed at him like a lifeline.

He bent, lifting her against him. She wound her legs around his body, melded like their mouths. He carried her into his bedroom and slowly set her down among the mounds of pillows.

Jack thought he would go crazy with need. He wanted to possess her, yet he wanted to be enslaved by her. He wanted to punish her for making him feel so out of control, while making love to her would be his own punishment.

With deft fingers, he loosened the knot of her sash and she stood before him, ivory skin a stark contrast to the crimson robe. Sliding down from her mouth, he nuzzled her neck, licking and nibbling until she gripped the back of his head, forcing him to return to her mouth.

With a swish of silk, her robe fell to the floor. Jack leaned into her, completing the assault on her balance and she tumbled on to the bed.

"You know, for a press secretary, you're a terrible liar," he said, then covered her mouth with his own before she could protest. Dizzy and flushed, she gave in to her hunger, cursing her fingers for not unbuttoning his shirt or loosening his belt quickly enough.

Jack leaned over her, muscled shoulders flexed as an animal's. "Look at me, Annika."

She refused by grabbing his head and pulling him down on her, slick skin pressing together. A myriad of sensations were awakened as he cupped her breasts gently, teasing first one, then the other with his mouth, before sliding wetly down her belly. Tormenting her with his hands and tongue, he touched her inner heat, slowly stroking and caressing until a thousand butterflies beat their flaming wings within her.

Biting back a cry of delight, Annika arched against him, wanting the wild pulse to never end. His absence surprised her, and she opened her eyes. Jack was leaning over her, slate eyes savage in their need.

"Look at me," he demanded.

Still reeling from the pleasure shocks jolting her body, she tried to turn her head away. "No," he said, running his fingers through her corkscrew curls, holding her head still. "Look in my eyes. Don't ever tell me how or what I'm feeling. See for yourself."

Driving deeply into her, she gasped in stunned rapture. The gentleness of his recent loving had transformed into something primal, furious. Each thrust pushed her closer to the brink of ecstasy, a chasm of safety she yearned for. Raw emotion welled from her soul, and she tried to turn away so he wouldn't read it in her face.

"No. Watch." His words were gruff, his voice was hoarse. Standing before the edge, she stared into the depths, seeing a mirror of her wants and needs, hopes and fears. With one stroke she fell, crying out his name, embracing the pulsing heat that enveloped her body. She felt the power of his release, heard him murmur her name.

"I love you, Annika. Oh, honey, I love you so much."

Shutting her eyes, she turned away, brimming with the bittersweet emotion that beckoned to her to stay.

* * *

"It's done."

"So soon?"

He ignored the vice president's sarcasm. It wasn't as if he was the one calling from a phone booth in the middle of Siberia. Or that he had kids to clothe and collegiate. He probably sent his kids to Harvard, writing out the check right after paying for his new Mercedes Benz. "Look, you wanted it done right. I waited until the perfect moment and slipped it in his suitcase. One call tipped off the cops."

"Airport security?"

He snorted. "Are you kidding? You told me to go all out."

"Interesting. You didn't happen to get him smoking a joint during the middle of the governor's dinner?"

He forced himself to laugh. It sounded like a seal's bark. "Is that what you want?"

"No, no, you're doing fine." A breeze flipped up the ends of his hair, reaching its cold fingers down the neck of his coat. If this was spring in Minnesota, he can claim he did see hell freeze over.

"What now, President Martin?"

Hoarse coughing nearly masked the laughter. "President Martin. It has a certain, shall I say, distinguished sound to it." His voice rumbled through the phone line. "For now, keep close tabs on what the advisors are doing. And watch that Andersen woman. She's a feminazi if I ever saw one."

"All right. And, sir?"

"What?" The vice president sounded tired, frazzled. It was as if planning the attack on the senator was the only thing that kept him alive, and now he was wasted.

"What about the money, sir?"

"The money?"

Nice try, you bastard. "Yeah, the money. You owe me thirty K."

The vice president's chuckle rolled fluidly, then hit a speedbump, sending him into a fit of coughing. "Mo...money?" he gasped.

"Thirty thousand dollars payable on completion of the job, sir. I've completed, now I'm payable." He shrugged further down into his jacket, searching for a hidden layer of heat.

"Well, you have been paid. Quite well, in fact." He chuckled again. "I think I'd double-check with your wife."

Click. The phone dropped into silence.

Click. He pressed the off button of his mini tape recorder. Thumbing the rewind button with his gloved hand, he waited a second, then pressed play.

"...double-check with your wife."

Perfect.

Chapter 18

He made a copy of the tape then, painstakingly writing in feminine loops and whorls, addressed the FedEx envelope to Vice President Martin. The standard blue ballpoint pen kept slipping from his gloved hand, but that only amplified the dips in his artificial handwriting.

As he sneaked out into the night like a mischievous teenager, a sour taste coated the back of his throat. He reminded himself that it was nothing personal and imagined the number of zeroes it would take to put all six kids through college. But, still, as he huddled close to buildings and scurried through alleys, his stomach kneaded like a bread machine.

The FedEx delivery box was directly under a streetlamp, the logo's colors rich under the light. His eyes darted left and right before he passed under the glare. Other than a drunk who had stumbled into an alley to sleep off his Boone's oblivion, he had seen no one else on the streets.

Pulling the metal door open, he hesitated a millisecond before dropping the envelope. It was nothing personal.

His stomach gurgled. He dug into his hip pocket and thumbed a Tums into his mouth…

* * *

"Arrgh."

Jack rolled over and punched the alarm. His eyes felt pasted shut with super glue, the kind where in the old commercials the construction worker would hang from the underside of a metal crossbar with only the protection of his super glued helmet keeping him from certain death.

It was good that his imagination was already flipped on, since that day was going to require several creative twists to get the senator's ass out of a sling. Of all things to happen, just three…no, make that two days before Super Tuesday. The cops had promised confidentiality, but who wouldn't take that opportunity of a lifetime to leak to the press?

"Mmmm, good morning." The shock of a husky female voice and cold limbs pried Jack's eyes open. He blinked several times, letting his eyes adjust to the dim morning light. Hair swept over his chest, tickling gently. A kiss pressed to his skin. "What time is it?"

"Six." Cautiously, he curled against her, throwing one warm leg over her freezing hip. "Don't you ever use a blanket?"

Annika snickered against his chest. "I get too hot. Don't you ever get tired?"

"Not last night." The memory of their lovemaking made him stir unconsciously. He stroked her hair. "Too bad we have a million fires to put out this morning."

"And I forgot my firefighter gear in Colorado." She snuggled closer, the sweet scent of her rising from her curly locks.

"Don't worry. All you have to do is smile and the reporters won't even remember their own names." He tilted her head up until he could see her sleepy blue eyes. "That's what happened to me."

In only a few seconds, she was wriggling free, eyes downcast. "First dibs on the shower. The senator will have a nervous breakdown if we're not there on time."

He grabbed her hand before she slipped away and pulled her back down on the bed. Her obvious reluctance twisted his chest in achy knots. "Don't," he said softly, rubbing her knuckles with his thumb.

"Don't, what?" Annika stared at the sheets, tangled into an artistic pose.

"Don't pretend last night was just sex." Jack took a deep breath. "If you didn't hear me say it last night, I'm going to say it again. I love you."

"Jack." Her shoulders sagged, locks of hair falling over her face. "Please, don't."

He hadn't expected her to claim her unfailing adoration, but this was too much. Anger flickered helplessly. "What? Don't love you? Or don't say it?" He dropped her hand and bounced off the bed, the carpet thick under his feet. Standing in the path to the bathroom, he fisted his hands to his hips.

"Well, which is it?"

Annika's head whipped up, her eyes filled with unshed tears. She chewed her lip uncertainly.

He waited, aware of each goosebump that rose on his skin. He raised his eyebrows. She looked away.

"Fine, you may not want to hear it, but I will shout it to everyone. I love you, Annika. You may not want me to feel it, but I can't **not** feel it. That would be like asking me to change the color of my eyes or my hair. I love you. I am in love with you. I want to be with you, always.

"And if that scares you, great! It scares the hell out of me, too. But at least I'm being honest about my feelings, instead of running from them."

Her face paled as she stared at him, fury setting sparks in her eyes. "Damn you to hell, Jack Wiese."

He shook his head, crossing his arms across his broad chest, every muscle flexed for the fight. "Maybe I am damned, but living like this is already hell." Without another glance, he scooped up his boxers from the floor and headed for the bathroom.

* * *

The shower upstairs ran, but the tears on her face fell faster than rain. She lay her head on the kitchen table, sobbing with the freedom of a child. The thoughts tried to collect into a coherent bubble, only to twist and turn whenever they were probed.

How could she not want him? He was every woman's dream of perfection with his dark hair and flashing eyes, complete with the devilish dimple in his cheek. Success reeked from every pore on his body.

But so did arrogance. Or was that just playacting for the politicians and the cameras. She lifted her head, smudging her robe sleeve across her eyes. No. She knew the real Jack, the one who cared for women. Who said he loved her.

And she believed him. She believed, as she knew the truth about the color of the sky. But how she could believe with such natural grace, yet still shun the thought of her own feelings was impossible to understand.

Her tears had dried, the remnants of salt lining her lips as she sipped from her coffee mug. The water stopped with the now familiar squeal from the pipes.

She half-smiled as she looked around the cozy kitchen. How could she not want this? A home so like the one she held close to her heart. A place where she smelled coffee brewing when she awoke, where the hardwood floors always chilled her toes. A freezer that always held Ben and Jerry's ice cream.

And a bed that would always be warm and full of love.

"Shower's free." As she looked up, her insides turned over again. Jack leaned against the doorframe, impossibly handsome in his suit and tie, dew-like flecks still glinting in his hair.

She took a deep breath and held it. They stared across the room at each other, the only sound was the incessant drip of the sink faucet. Slowly, she blew out.

"I'm sorry."

He frowned. "For what specifically? Not loving me? Or pushing me away?" He crossed the room and yanked out a kitchen chair, its legs squeaking as they scraped over the floor. "Or are you just sorry you even got involved with me?" He sat down with a heavy thud.

Annika reached for his hand, but he pulled them off the table. Sighing, she said, "Give me a chance, Jack. I'm sorry for not knowing what to say. I'm sorry for not knowing how I feel. And I'm sorry that I'm hurting you right now." She slid her hand through the coffee cup's handle. "Just give me a little time. To think. I need to be sure, Jack. For my own sake."

His eyes were boring a hole through the table. Finally, he nodded. She scooted her chair back and walked around the table, setting a hand gently on his shoulder before heading for the staircase.

* * *

"If it's gonna be Super Tuesday, then today must be Sucky Sunday."

Richard rolled his eyes. "Axel, just get the numbers."

Axel swung around in his chair, nearly flying into the wall. "If you give me one more order, I'm outta here. Got it, pinhead?"

"Boys, boys," clucked Gem. "Pull it together. We're all under strain."

"He started it," Axel said sulkily, turning back to answer his phone.

"As if refereeing the cops and the press weren't enough," Annika mumbled, pressing the down arrow on her computer and glancing over the morning's copy.

"You just worry about the press. That will be more than enough." Jack's voice was unmistakably sharp. Gem and Richard glanced up from their work, looking first at Jack, then Annika. Her cheeks burned.

He was still hurt. Well, fine. At least she wasn't leading him on. When they went to bed together, they both knew it was only physical attraction. She never promised to call him in the morning or murmured loving words.

The pages continued to scroll down her computer. Then why did she call for him in the middle of the night? Why was he the first thing she thought of when she woke up? And why did she daydream about a summer snoozing on the dock, watching the children play in the lake?

"They've caught wind of something." Cleo Speros, the newest member of the team, rushed into the room. Papers flew off the countertops in her wake.

"Who?" Jack asked.

"The press. C-USN crews are setting up outside the hotel. I was stopped on my way in."

"That's to be expected," Annika said. "It's two days before Super Tuesday and I'm about to give the morning spin."

State Representative Speros put her hands on her boyish hips. "With Gregory Donahue?"

Jack swore loudly and jumped out of his chair, knocking it to the ground. "Turn on the TV."

Richard obliged and they gathered around it, silent. Annika crossed her arms over her chest and stood behind Jack. A commercial for auto insurance echoed throughout the room.

The screen dimmed to black then filled with the face of the most highly paid anchor in newscasting history. "Good morning. I'm Gregory Donahue, outside of the Minneapolis Radisson hotel. While Minnesota is experiencing a stretch of unseasonably warm weather, Senator Steven Carver's campaign may be cooling off.

"C-USN has recently learned the senator, who has won several primary elections since January, has been issued an arrest warrant for possession of an illegal substance. According to our sources, when Minneapolis airport security conducted a routine search on the plane's luggage, ten ounces of marijuana was found in the senator's suitcase."

Axel hung up the phone and walked over to the group. "That was the senator," he whispered to Annika. "The cops are in his room."

"Thanks." Stomach knotted, she turned back to the television.

"…after recent accusations by Robert Bardikoff, Senator Carver's former press secretary. Bardikoff has been unavailable for comment."

"Why dontcha tell them why!" Gem demanded.

"Shh," Jack hushed.

"Meanwhile, there has been no word from the Carver camp." Donahue looked appropriately grim. "Stay tuned with C-USN as we bring you more on this breaking story."

Jack slammed his hand down on the television's power button. "Fix this," he growled at Annika as he strode past her. "I'm going to see the senator."

"But, what should I say?"

He stopped at the doorway and fixed her with a steely stare. "It won't matter anyway."

* * *

"Annika, is it true the senator has waived his rights?"

"How long has he had a drug problem?"

"Ms. Andersen, will Senator Carver be incarcerated?"

She choked back the panic that threatened to seize her vocal cords. The press corps was frenzied, like a wolf pack that smelled blood. One had even grabbed her blazer as she walked in, trying to shove a microphone under her nose.

Suddenly, her fear dissolved into fury. How dare they? She knew they had a job to do, but this was not a journalistic endeavor. It was simply kicking someone who was down.

"I will answer all your questions, but first I need you to sit down." She glared at the reporters in the front row. "Now."

Like reluctant grade-schoolers, they pouted and sat.

Annika glanced over at Lauren, whose face was pale as a sheet. She took a deep breath and faced the cameras.

"Senator Steven Carver has been mistakenly accused of possessing marijuana. I say 'mistakenly' because it's true. Contrary to other beliefs, the senator has not used drugs during this campaign.

"However, now would be a good time to clear up some matters regarding the senator's past." She paused, taking the time to organize her thoughts. "Fourteen years ago, Sandra Carver died from ovarian cancer, leaving behind a stunned and grief-stricken husband."

Annika inhaled deeply, making eye contact with each of the most prominent journalists in the room. "Steven Carver was extremely distraught over his wife's passing and vowed to battle legislature until every woman and every woman's husband could be assured of excellent health care. He started his mission only one week after Sandra's funeral. As many of you remember, he stood before the Minnesota House of Representatives with tears streaming down his face." A female reporter broke eye contact and stared at the floor. Annika continued. "Was he a public figure at that point? No. He was simply a 28-year-old grieving husband."

She swallowed, crossing her fingers under the podium. "He couldn't sleep. He couldn't eat. He was hurting with a pain many of us can not even imagine.

"Steven Carver used alcohol to help him sleep. Once he realized it had become an addiction, he sought help. He was a 28-year-old man." She paused.

"Senator Carver has been sober for over ten years."

She glared at the reporters. "For those of you who understand alcoholism, you know this is a feat that should be admired, not shamed."

"Regarding the other matter, it is under police investigation." She stared deep into the camera's eye. "But I believe they will find out the senator has been framed."

The reporters tried to stay glued to their seats, but some couldn't help waving their arms.

Annika held out her hands to silence them. "What evidence to I have supporting this claim? First, the senator is a very busy man. He has assistants who pack his luggage." She cast an apologetic glance at Lauren, who bent her head in silent acknowledgement.

"Second, all of the staff's luggage is transported by numerous people. Between hotel and plane, it has gone through several hands."

"And, finally, I know of his innocence the way I know my heart will keep beating. Senator Steven Carver is a man who has brought honesty back to politics. He is a man who has renewed the people's faith in their leaders."

Meeting the eyes that stared back at her, Annika felt a sense of calm. Her gaze was drawn to the back of the room.

Jack leaned against the far wall, arms crossed in front of his chest. His hair stood up in porcupine quills, his white shirt sleeves rolled up to his forearms. The crimson tie blazed among the sea of muted grays and blues.

Goosebumps pebbled her arms. She tried to break eye contact, but couldn't. Finally, Jack nodded his head.

Victorious, she smiled into the camera lens. "Americans know a true, sincere candidate. And they will demonstrate their support by voting for Senator Steven Carver on Super Tuesday."

She turned away from the flashing bulbs and shouted questions. Gliding down the steps, she felt Lauren press against her side.

"Thank you," she whispered, her voice husky with unshed tears.

"Don't thank me yet. We still have to find out who did this to the senator." Annika rushed through the back door, Agent Bailey clearing a path through the waiting journalists.

"Where's Jack?" she asked suddenly.

Agent Bailey took her elbow. "Waiting for you."

*   *   *

The cops made him nervous. Even though officially he could snap away any one of their badges, they still made his bowels cramp and his brow sweat.

They were asking too many questions. This was not the way he had planned it. Especially now, after Annika's press conference. They were going to be looking at each and every person who came in contact with the luggage.

And they were going to find out.

"Coffee?"

He jumped nearly a foot before trying to appear relaxed. "Yes, thanks."

Gem poured into his empty cup. His stomach clenched in response. "Glory, everyone is so jumpy today," she drawled.

He shrugged casually. "Well, you know. Drugs, death threats. All in a day's work."

Gem laughed nervously and walked back into the hotel room. He wiped his shirt sleeve across his forehead, staining it with perspiration. He had to get a hold of the vice president. Fast.

*   *   *

Annika slid into the waiting Lincoln. Jack watched her from his corner of the car.

"Well?" she asked.

Jack measured her with a long look. She tried to calm the tingles that ran through her body as he stared, but each second seemed to last for an hour. Her breaths came in ragged gulps.

Finally, he leaned back. "The police have agreed to allow Steven to remain out of jail, pending an investigation." He grinned, his dimple deepening. "They want to talk to you, of course."

"Of course." The car began to move and she reached to buckle her seat belt.

They rode in silence. Annika embraced it after the tornado of noise in the press room. She watched as the Minneapolis skyscrapers passed by and the neighborhood became more residential. She didn't care where they were going, as long as it was away from the hotel, full of all its questions and anxiety.

"Annika." Jack rubbed his hair, carefully choosing his words. "Thanks. You may have just saved the campaign. Again."

"It's my job," she replied coolly.

"Not to be so personally convincing." Jack folded his hands. "By the way, what changed your mind?"

She shook her head. "My mind was never set to begin with. I just wanted to have some more answers."

"I'm afraid we've just gotten more questions to answer." Reaching down, Jack pulled a single sheet of paper from his briefcase.

She knew what it was before she even held it. Breathing deeply, she scanned the page.

'You have ignored my power for long enough. You will now pay. No one can protect you. You are lucky to know the day, place and time of your death. San Francisco, Union Square, Monday.' The e-mail address was the same: changeling.

Annika leaned back into the seat, trying to smother the icy chills that ran up and down her spine. Cold sweat broke out on her forehead. "We have to cancel the speech, Jack."

He shook his head, face grim. "I've already talked to the senator about it. He refuses to allow some 'crazy nut' to alter his schedule."

"But, this isn't just a crazy person. This is a certifiably insane maniac. It's the second e-mail referring to the Union Square speech. Doesn't he understa—"

"Yes, he does," Jack snapped. He raked his hand through his hair and blew out frustrated air. He looked at her with sad eyes. "I'm sorry. I didn't mean to yell at you. I just don't want him to waste his life on one stupid campaign stop."

Annika nodded, the pit of her stomach hollow with fear. "Who...who wrote this?"

"We're still searching. The e-mail was sent from the Minneapolis Public Library." He sighed. "I can't imagine who would want to do this to the senator, but it seems like it has to be someone on staff."

"I know," Annika murmured. The car speeded up, merging on to the highway. "But I feel like one person may have the answer to this mystery, as well as the question of the e-mailed threats."

"Bardikoff."

She glanced at him in surprise. "Yes. How did you know?"

"Because he called me this morning." Annika stared at him in shock. "He wants to talk."

"Wh- where is he?" she stuttered.

"Not in Minnesota." He hesitated. "I'm going to see him. I wanted to know if you would come with me."

Her blood chilled. See the man who had attacked her so brutally. The man who brought back all of the painful memories of her past.

The man who may have all the answers to their questions.

She stared out the window. "I have meetings all day."

"I took the liberty of clearing your schedule." She whipped her head around, and Jack's lips curved slightly. "I thought I may need you to help the senator more. But, it just makes it easier for you to get away now."

He reached out and pulled her hand into his lap. The fingertips were numb, as if frostbitten. "I know how much this scares you, Annika. You don't have to…but he may talk more if he sees you."

She shut her eyes, remembering Bardikoff's putrid smell, his pinched grip. When she opened them, she saw Jack's blue-green eyes.

He would keep her safe.

"All right," she said. "But I get to ask the first question."

Chapter 19

Thunder shook the small airplane with its roar. The plane dropped, losing several feet in altitude. Annika's stomach rushed to meet her throat, and her fingers tightened their death grip on the armrests.

The storm was a bad omen, she thought. Lightening flickered outside the window and an echoing boom instantly surrounded them.

Why had she agreed to go with Jack to meet Bardikoff in California? Her heart still pounded in fear when she remembered him pressing against her, his foul breath against her cheek. She shuddered.

Jack reached for her hand, probably assuming the storm caused her trembling. He gathered it inside his own warm, smooth palm and began rubbing her with his thumb. It was now such a familiar, intimate gesture that she immediately felt calmer.

She knew why she was going. The senator's life depended upon it.

The plane bounced like a carnival ride, the pounding of hailstones cracking against the windows. Annika gripped Jack's hand more tightly.

"We're safer here than riding in the back of one of those Lincolns," he said.

"We were never driving through the middle of a thunderstorm." She reached over with her free hand and snapped the window shade shut.

"Though Agent Garcia's overly cautious driving is looking very sensible right now."

"But we couldn't sensibly get to San Francisco by tonight if he drove us."

A sudden jolt made Annika clamp her mouth shut. She imagined herself storming into the cockpit and taking control of the plane, steering them back to Minnesota. **So much for letting go of her control issues,** she thought, shutting her eyes. She began to count her breaths.

Jack slipped his arm around her shoulders. "Ever play 'snap'?"

"Snap?" She kept her eyes tightly screwed shut. "What the hell are you talking about, Jack?"

"Snap. It's a game. My sister and I would play it when we were tired of listening to Mom and Pop argue."

Nestled against his shoulder, the airplane's bumps seemed less threatening. Annika leaned her head against him. "How do you play?"

"It's a lot like a word association test a shrink might give. I say something, and you tell me your answer as fast as you can. Ready?"

Thunder shook the airplane. She curled her face against Jack's shirt, burying her face into his musky scent. Opening her eyes, she stared at the smooth, white fabric of his button-down Oxford. A small thread had worked its way loose from one of the buttons. "Ready."

"Color."

She hesitated. "Red."

"No, you have to respond as fast as you can. Don't even think about what you want to say." The rumble of Jack's chuckle hummed against her cheek. "I know that's hard for someone in your profession."

"Well, it's saved your ass a few times—"

"I'm not arguing with you there." He caressed her hair. "Just try. City."

"Minneapolis." She was surprised the word was out of her mouth before the thought entered her mind. She smiled.

"Good," he said. "Movie."

"Gone with the Wind." She laughed. A fitting title for their present situation.

"Favorite memory."

"Eating ice cream on the porch of my parents' house." She waited, but sensed he wanted more. "I'd help my mom make homemade ice cream. We would take turns winding the crank, and just when I thought my arm would break off, my dad would walk up the sidewalk, home from work. My mom would say we couldn't let all our work go to waste, so we would get spoons and bowls and eat ice cream for dinner."

"Mmm." Jack pressed a kiss on her head. "President."

"Carver."

"Good answer. Song."

"Um…"

"Don't think…"

"…'Get Off of My Cloud' by the Rolling Stones."

"Pet."

"Siberian husky." The rhythm of their murmured words made her drowsy, with Jack's warmth only amplifying the effect. She closed her eyes.

"Wine."

"Johannasberg Riesling."

"Vacation."

"Caribbean." She felt herself drift. The beat of hail became the wash of waves against the beach. She lay in the soft, bleached white sand, watching how the water drifted into deeper and darker shades of blue the farther out she gazed. She leaned back into Jack's arms and smelled the salty ocean, felt the wind glide against her skin.

"Holiday."

His words were whispered in her ear. Flecks of foam bubbled on the beach, only to be washed away with the next wave. "Fourth of July."

He chuckled. "Always the patriot." When she didn't respond, he knew she had fallen asleep. The weight of her head against his chest felt natural, like destiny.

"Mr. Wiese?" A flight attendant bent over, whispering. "The pilot wanted you to know she has changed our flight pattern, allowing us to avoid more inclement weather."

"Thanks," he whispered.

"Is there anything I can get for you?" Her eyes drifted over to Annika.

Jack shook his head. "I'm perfectly happy." As the flight attendant walked away, he brushed his lips across the wild tangle of curls, relishing the ticklish sensation. "Perfectly happy," he whispered into Annika's hair.

*   *   *

"More coffee?" Gem dangled the pot at her side, her other hand on her hip. She looked like a waitress at a truck stop. All she needed was a short skirt and a wad of chewing gum.

She stepped out from behind the kitchenette countertop. Wait, now all she needed was the gum. He averted his eyes from her thigh high hem.

He forced a smile. "No, thanks. I'd really like to get some sleep tonight."

"Y'all taking the night off, huh?" Her eyes skimmed over him with unveiled interest. Nervously, he twisted the gold wedding band on his left hand, hoping she'd take the hint.

"It's been a long forty-eight hours," he replied.

"Tell me about it." She thunked the coffee pot on the counter and leaned against it. "I buzz around here like the busiest of bees and can't sleep at night 'cause of all this." She waved her hand expansively, seeming to include the long executive table, the kitchenette and the hotel hallway in her wide sweep.

He nodded, hoping to appear understanding but not too interested. Too further his point, he stood up. "Is there anything else you need tonight, ma'am?"

"Naw." She flapped her fingernails at him like she was shooing a pesky mosquito. "With Jack and Annika gone, I already am feelin' my nerves settle."

He laughed. "Were they getting to you?"

"Oh, no, darlin', that's not what I meant." She rounded the countertop, picking up the coffee pot and pouring its remaining contents down the sink. "They're off figurin' out our mystery."

Acid bubbled up his throat. He swallowed, hard. "Mystery?"

"Not that y'all don't know beans, but someone wanted to talk to Jack personally." She rinsed out the coffeepot, then turned off the tap. Turning around, she pursed her lips thoughtfully. "I wonder if they'll have the answers."

"Where are they?" His voice sounded high-pitched, fearful. Gem must have sensed it, because she tilted her head and gave him a strange look.

"Why?"

He backtracked, shrugging his shoulders casually. "No reason, really. Just wondering if they needed secret service protection, with everything going on."

Gem smiled, her poppy red lips parting to show the slight gap in her front teeth. "Jack can take care of himself."

Better get while the getting's good, he thought. "I'm sure he can," he said, walking toward the hallway. "Have a good evening, Gem."

"You, too." She shut the door behind him.

He stood in the hallway, his palms clammy. It was unlikely that Vice President Martin had received his Fed-Ex.

But he had to talk to him. Now.

* * *

The sun was low in the sky, a runny egg yolk dripping into the horizon. Annika rubbed underneath her eyes, hoping to erase any smeared mascara.

She had slept for the remainder of the trip, through thunder and turbulence. When she had awakened, she first been conscious of the smooth surface her face was pressed against. Then, the familiar scent of Jack. As she had sat up, she'd been embarrassed, hoping she hadn't snored or drooled or anything else similarly humiliating.

As they walked together toward the waiting car, she noticed that Jack kept rolling his right shoulder, shaking his arm and flexing his fingers. She may not have said poetic verses in her sleep, but she had definitely secured her nest against Jack's shoulder. And he was paying for his compassion now with pins and needles.

He held the door open for her and she slid in. Although the car was air conditioned, she shrugged out of her blazer. Seventy degrees felt like one hundred when her Minnesota winter blood was as thick as honey.

"Would you like a tour or would you prefer driving directly to your hotel?" the chauffeur asked.

"Hotel, please." Jack stretched his arms in front of him, twisting his wrists so his hands spun in concentric circles. "The San Francisco Embassy Towers."

"Yes, sir." He rolled up the privacy glass and the car began to roll.

The sunset was engulfed by a murky gray, the fog already beginning to tumble in from the bay. Annika remembered Shea's stories about sailboating during such weather. The fog would be so dense and impenetrable she would not be able to see any other boats. She shivered at the thought of feeling the waves slap at the boat, the eerie quiet that sheltered the noise of other boats.

"Cold?" Jack asked. He scooted closer to her side.

"No, just getting caught up in my thoughts," she replied. "I wonder if Shea would be able to help us out."

"How?"

"I don't know. Privately film our meeting with Bardikoff in case something goes wrong."

Jack took her hand and squeezed. "Nothing is going to go wrong. He just wants to talk to me."

"Does he know I'm coming?"

Jack hesitated. "No."

She blew out a frustrated breath. "Jack—"

"I know you're not comfortable with this." He ran his free hand through his hair. "The more I thought about it on the plane, the more uncomfortable I became, too. So, when I go to meet with him, I want you to stay at the hotel."

"No chance." She pulled her hand away. "You dragged me all the way out here. I'm not going to hide in the hotel like some mistress."

Jack raised his eyebrows, and she blushed. "Well, when you put it that way, I definitely want you to stay in the hotel."

She glared at him, trying to use the power she held over the media. He just smiled at her, his dimple winking mockingly.

"You never told me why he contacted you."

"You never asked."

"I'm asking now."

"Really? That didn't seem like a question to me."

Annika swore, then gritted her teeth. Jack looked mockingly offended. "My dear, I did not know they taught such language at Columbia."

"Are you going to tell me? Or do I have to tell the driver to take me back to the airport?"

"I don't know why he contacted me. When I answered the phone, I didn't believe it was him at first. But he has this upper-East accent that is unmistakable." He stared out the window. "And, he's the only person that ever called me 'Jacko.' Man, I hated that. I don't even know how many times I told him to stop."

"So, you're absolutely sure it was him."

"Positive."

"OK." Annika pushed her hair away from her face, holding it away in a casual ponytail. She fished in the pocket of her briefcase for a pencil or pen. "So, what did he say?"

"He said, 'Hey, Jacko, you've really fallen in it this time. Can you smell the stink?'"

"What the hell does that mean?"

Jack shook his head. "He always had a weird sense of humor. Obviously, he's been keeping track of the senator's campaign, wherever he is."

Annika felt the smooth plastic of a pen and grabbed it. Grunting, she sat up. Putting the pen in her mouth, she rolled and twisted her hair until it was tightly bound. The cool air felt refreshing on the nape of her neck. She took the pen out of her mouth and with an expert shove, pushed it through the bun, securing it in place.

Looking up, she saw Jack's dazed expression, mouth agape.

"What's the matter…haven't you ever seen me with my hair up?"

"Where did you learn to do that?"

"My hair? I started doing this in college to keep it out of my face while I was studying…"

"No." Jack leaned forward, drawing the tips of his fingers along her cheekbone, lining her jawline, before tracing the outline of her lips. "Where did you learn to drive a man so wild without even trying?"

She trembled, then chewed on her lips to erase the tickle Jack's fingers had drawn. His own mouth was so close, she could see the slight dent in his lower lip. An enormous pressure began to build in her chest, blooming into a heat that limited the amount of air she could inhale. Her heart pounded so hard, she thought it's beat must be visible on her white blouse.

Suddenly, Jack quickly slid away. "Is there a seatbelt law in California?" He clicked his into place.

Her own hands shook, so she folded them together in her lap. "Are there any laws in California? I thought this was the land where rules were meant to be broken."

Jack smiled. "Maybe not broken. Just bent a little."

She sighed, the frustrating heat still flaming in her belly. **Avoid it, ignore it**, she thought.

"You're doing far more than bending the rules by agreeing to meet with Bardikoff," she said.

"If I didn't, we may never know the truth." His eyes were nearly as gray as the imminent darkness.

The car slowly pulled into a circular driveway and stopped. Jack continued to hold her gaze while the chauffeur walked around to open the door.

"Can you understand that it's a chance I've got to take? For the senator's sake?" He stared at her, serious and assessing.

The door opened, light from the hotel flooding the car's interior. Annika nodded, slowly. She did understand. It didn't make her fear any less, but she understood.

*   *   *

The suite was on the top floor of the San Francisco Embassy Towers in downtown San Francisco. Down the hall, the enormous brass door of the presidential suite gleamed in the dim light. Rich, gold carpet lay luxuriously like fallen autumn leaves. A potted ficus tree stood in the corner near their room's door, not a yellow leaf in sight.

Jack was wondering their secret to plant success when he noticed Annika standing in the doorway, a look of hesitance on her face.

"Something wrong?" he asked, brushing past her into the room. It was the only executive suite the hotel offered, but it had everything he'd required. Three televisions, already in place at the head of the long conference table. The jet black of the furniture didn't even reflect in the floor to ceiling tinted windows. Several desks had been created from smaller wooden tables, phones and embossed pads of paper tidily arranged upon each one. The porter appeared from the far hallway.

Everything looked in order to Jack. He reached in his pocket and pressed a twenty-dollar bill into the porter's outstretched palm. Turning, he noticed Annika still lingering by the doorway.

"Are you sleeping in the hall?"

She jumped slightly and her protective mask fell. Any atom of angst had disintegrated. She stalked in, shoulders back and chin high. "Where am I sleeping, Jack?"

"In the bedroom, of course."

She glared at him, her eyes darkening. He always got a thrill out of teasing her. Once the shade of blue had heated into midnight, he knew she was at her boiling point.

Right now, she was getting close to sapphire.

"The couch looks comfortable." She leaned her hip against the sofa back, crossing her arms over her chest and shooting him a defiant glance.

"We could order a movie and cuddle down on it, if you like," he said, deliberately crossing his own arms and widening his stance. He bit the inside of his cheek to keep his grin in check. "But it'll have to wait until after my meeting with Bardikoff."

She uncrossed her arms and slid around the sofa, where she pressed the cushions, testing their firmness. "Comfortable enough to bed down on."

"Why, Annika, are you suggesting I take you right here?" The huskiness that crept into his voice was real, although his teasing was not. He had a sudden image of her nodding, and bending her sweet, soft body over the plush pillows. The blood rushed to his groin.

Annika's blood rushed to her face. Her eyes narrowed, nearly hiding their midnight blue hue. "Damn it, Jack. If you think that this is giving me some space, you had better flip the channel switch in your brain."

"The channel switch?"

She was in front of him in a blink. Her finger jabbed at his chest. "Yes, the one that turns on and off your hormones. Haven't I been clear enough for you? I need time to think about you and me." She poked him one last time. "I am not going to sleep with you!"

A discreet cough interrupted her tirade. She whirled toward the doorway, which had remained open. The porter stood, his eyes shining with merriment, his heavy jowls trembling with suppressed laughter. "Pardon me, but I had forgotten to ask if I should arrange dinner reservations for you or…" He glanced at Annika, "If you'll be dining in the suite this evening."

Annika's color turned from tomato to plum. "I…we…Jack?"

"We won't be needed dinner accommodations this evening, thank you." He smiled at the porter.

"Very well, sir. Er…enjoy your evening." His glance drifted to Annika again, then he bowed and left, firmly shutting the door behind himself.

Annika groaned and covered her face with one hand. Jack reached for her other hand and resisted when she tried to pull away. Finally, she relented, but made her fingers as limp and yielding as overcooked spaghetti.

"Please tell me you didn't register us under the guise of the senator's campaign."

"I didn't register us under the guise of the senator's campaign."

She peeked out between her fingers. "Really?"

"I registered as Jack Wiese, election manager for Senator Steven Carver. And I'll need rooms on the entire floor, please."

Annika sank back into the sofa, her legs hanging off the arms. She grabbed a pillow and put it over her face.

"What's the worst thing that could happen?" Jack edged in next to her.

"More shame, more embarrassment in the papers."

"Because the porter saw you yelling that you weren't going to have sex with me? Come on, honey, you've got to do better than that. This is California, for goodness' sake."

One turquoise eye peeked out from behind the pillow. "Really?"

"Really." He brushed the thin wispy curls off her temple. "And, another thing…"

"What?"

"You get first dibs on which bedroom you want." He stood and stretched his arms lazily to the ceiling. "There are two, you know."

Chapter 20

"What are you doing here? It's only Sunday."

"Jack and I came ahead to do some preliminary work." Annika stretched out on the king-sized bed, reveling in the luxurious way the satin caressed her bare legs. After a quick shower, she'd donned her Japanese robe and called Shea.

"Hmm, just you and Jack. Where is the valiant soldier now?"

"In the other room." The minute the words were out, she regretted them.

"The other room. As in, you and Jack are sharing the same sleeping quarters?" Shea laughed, her musical peals ringing over the line.

"No, we're not," Annika replied huffily. "It's a two bedroom suite."

"Um-hmm." Shea didn't sound convinced. "What, you need both beds?"

"Shea…"

"So, why didn't you call me? We could have had dinner. By now, all the decent places are booked."

"That's all right. We'll be working anyway."

"Are we going to get a chance to see each other? This may be our last chance for a while."

Annika rubbed her forehead. "Why? The senator's being accused of smuggling dope, our poll ratings are dropping faster than the Dow Jones. I'm going to have plenty of time on my hands once I'm out of a job."

"It's not that bad." Annika laughed. "Really. Let me do an exclusive interview to straighten the record."

"I don't know…"

"Think about it. Shows Monday night, right before Super Tuesday. Gets picked up and reported on C-USN by Tuesday morning, right as the voters are heading to the booths."

"You're forgetting about the equality of airtime issue, or do you already have an interview set up with Governor deMarco?"

"No, that moron is staying in New York. He has really downplayed his California agenda." Her voice became muffled. Annika checked her watch. It was getting close to Shea's on-air time.

"Listen, I've got to get in the makeup chair or my assistant is going to break her arm off waving at me. Promise to think about it?"

"All right." Annika started to hang up when she remembered the senator's schedule for Monday. "Hey, Shea."

"Yes?"

"Senator Carver is giving a speech in Union Square tomorrow at one. Can you make it? I'll try to get you some one-on-one time with the senator afterward."

"Ya, sure, ya betcha! I'll see you there." Shea hung up without saying goodbye.

"Ya, sure," Annika said out loud, replacing the receiver. If only she felt as confident.

*   *   *

Jack was talking on the phone when she strolled into the work area. She had changed into black wool slacks and a gray cashmere turtleneck. It made her feel like an undercover cop, but with her hair tied back into a low braid and minimal makeup, she was barely recognizable. Like it or not, she was going with Jack to meet Bardikoff.

"Yes...I see." Jack checked his watch and nodded. "That's what I wanted to hear. Keep me informed. Thank you." He hung up. "That was Agent Bailey. He has already increased the security surrounding Union Square tomorrow. Local FBI agents are sweeping the site for bombs, and all area businesses will be closed from ten until three. Their property will be searched before the senator arrives."

"It sounds like all preventative measures are being taken care of," she said.

"As much as we can do." He rubbed his temples between his fingers. "Agent Bailey is very nervous about the residential buildings facing the park."

"Can't we clear them out?"

"Just the ones that face the park. It's already being taken care of. Sharpshooters will be placed on the rooftops."

Annika shuddered. "This is not what I imagined."

"Welcome to the big leagues," Jack said. He glanced at his watch again, then paced the room distractedly.

"So, what do we do now?" Annika asked.

"Hmm?" Jack stood in the corner where the floor to ceiling windows met. A cloud of fog obscured the view of the Golden Gate Bridge.

She walked over to him and gently placed her hand on his shoulder. "I asked what we should do now. Are you OK?"

Jack stood in silence, staring out the window at the hazy rings that produced halos around the streetlamps. His shoulder muscles relaxed under her hand. "Bardikoff was supposed to call an hour ago. I don't know what to do now." His stomach rumbled loudly, pinging like pennies dropping to the bottom of a well.

"Well, we'll go crazy if we just sit around and wait. Let me order up some dinner. It's past seven-thirty."

"All right." Jack continued to look out the window, staring but not seeing.

She squeezed his shoulder, then turned to make the call.

*   *   *

She was ordering a feast, from the sounds of it. Italian food, his favorite. She even ordered a bottle of wine.

He wondered if he would be able to eat or drink anything. Bardikoff's voice on the phone had sounded anxious, urgent. Jack scoffed at himself. Of course Bardikoff had sounded nervous. He was a hunted man. He was probably just showing a little extra precaution.

Annika dropped the phone into its cradle with a clatter. He turned away from the window and walked over to her.

"Ordering for ten?" He kissed her cheek.

She shrugged. "I'm starving." Unconsciously, she smoothed a hand over his hair, then slid past him, eluding his embrace, and turned on the television. "Besides, stress makes me eat."

"Really. I don't get stressed out."

She glanced over at him, face neutral. "Uh-huh." A deaf man could have heard the sarcasm.

"I'm just going to check with Gem and see if she's heard anything." He picked up the phone and dialed 'nine' to get an outside line. Eleven digits later and Gem's drawl filled the receiver.

"Gem of the south, jewel of the senator's campaign, how may I be of service?"

"What happened to those professional seminars we spent good money sending you to?" Jack scolded half-teasingly.

"Honey, I knew it was you. Our darlin' Agent Bailey set up a caller I.D. on our phones."

"Tell him great work. How's everything else?"

Gem sighed loudly, then he could hear the shuffle of papers in the background. "Y'all got so many messages I'll have to pack an extra suitcase to carry them all. Let's see, Bobby, Bobby, Bobby, Axel, Bobby, Steven, Bobby, Nick Brady…"

"Who the hell is that?"

"Some law-yer from D.C. He's meetin' with the senator right now."

"Great." Jack ran a hand through his hair, rubbing along his temples. "So, what's going on? Are they going to let him keep campaigning?"

"This Brady says that until they can prove his luggage wasn't tampered with, the senator can be kept on a loose leash. So make sure you two lovebirds clean up the suite. We'll be there by five tomorrow."

"Five?" Jack ignored the 'lovebirds' comment. "But the rally starts at one."

"Five a.m. Damned if I'm not packin' as we speak."

"Better you than me. Say, anything else?"

"Um, let's see. Bobby, Bobby and Bobby. Dang, that child wanted to talk to you. Finally I gave him your hotel number to get him off my back."

"I haven't checked for messages here yet," he said. He hesitated. "Nothing else?"

"No, sugar, that's it. You lookin' for somethin' else?"

"Always. Never seem to find it, though. Safe travels, Gem. Try to get some beauty sleep on the plane."

"Honey, I've got my cool cucumber eye mask all ready to go. I don't know why the senator won't let me apply it to him…"

"Good night, Gem."

Just as he was hanging up, there was a firm knock at the door. Annika pressed the power button on the remote to turn the television off. "That must be dinner. I'll get it."

Without glancing through the peephole, she unlocked and opened the door. The door swung widely, banging against the wall. For a moment, all he could see was Annika, her hands held up, the thin gold band reflecting the light as she backed away from the door.

Bardikoff slammed the door. He was almost unrecognizable. The once bare face now sprouted a bushlike beard and moustache. His dark hair curled greasily around his ears. Once thin and wiry, he now appeared gaunt, the edges of his cheekbones sharp above his beard.

But, Jack thought, these physical changes were not as frightening as the dead glaze that covered Bardikoff's eyes like glaucoma.

Casually, he pressed "0" on the keypad, then set the phone in the cradle haphazardly. The receiver balanced on the ridges of the cradle, pressing against the hang-up button, but not depressing it.

He moved quickly to place himself between Annika and Bardikoff. She pressed herself against his back, her heavy breathing loud in his ear.

"Robert, you said you wanted to see me?" He tried to engage eye contact, but Bardikoff just glanced around the room.

"Where's your secret service agents?" His eyes were bloodshot.

"There are no—"

"Shut up!" Bardikoff screamed at the ceiling. "I said I would handle it." He looked at Jack with a wry smile. "Sorry."

Jack glanced at the ceiling quickly. There was nothing there. "That's all right," he said. Annika's nails began to dig into the skin of his back. He reached back and pressed his hand against her hip.

Bardikoff sneered. "No, it's not all right. You broke the rules, Jacko. Why'd you bring her?"

"I thought you may want to talk to both of us."

He snorted, but his eyes remained as flat and dark as lava rock. "You wanted to rub my face in it. One more time. She's got your balls in her fist, along with the senator's." He walked closer, the reek of urine and filth rising with each step. "Who do you think is smoking the weed now, Jacko?"

Confusion overrode Jack's fear. He had hired Robert Bardikoff a year ago, had worked with him on campaign strategies and media plans. This grimy, hippy-fied man bore no resemblance to his old colleague.

But then, Bardikoff's actions over the past few months had also been erratic and strange.

A clatter of plastic pieces made Bardikoff startle. He yanked a knife from the pocket of his long trenchcoat, its blade reflecting the lamp light. The phone had slipped into the cradle, cutting off any communication to the front desk.

He waved the knife in front of him, from the phone to Jack. "No tricks, Jacko. No goddamn tricks."

"Schizophrenic," Annika whispered in his ear. Her fingers loosened, and she stepped away before Jack could pull her back into his sheltered safety. What was she doing?

"Did you hear that?" She stepped toward Bardikoff cautiously, tilting her head to the ceiling. "What?"

Bardikoff looked at her with contempt. "They're not talking right now. And they're not talking to you."

"But they just said my name." She tiptoed closer to the hallway. Bardikoff slowly brought the knife down, holding the blade outward. Jack stared at the dull glint.

Bardikoff shook his head. "No tricks. You can't hear them. You don't know what they're saying."

"Shh." Annika placed a finger to her lips. "Listen. They're trying to tell us. What are they saying, Robert?"

The blade turned inward slightly. Jack felt his muscles tense, ready to spring.

"You hear them?" he asked doubtfully, a lone, wishful tremor marking his tone. He palmed the knife, holding it flat against his thigh.

Jack charged. He aimed low, hoping that if the knife stabbed him, it would be in the shoulder. His aim was slightly off, and he felt his shoulder grind into Bardikoff's knee with a popping noise.

With a high-pitched squeal, Bardikoff fell, arms outstretched. The knife fell to the floor, silently bouncing off the thick pile carpet. Scrambling to his knees, Jack cocked his fist and punched Bardikoff in the face. The squealing stopped.

The door burst open. "Police! Everyone put your hands up!"

"It's about time," Jack panted, rising to his feet. A freckle-faced young man who seemed too small for his uniform frisked him.

"Um, did you order dinner?" A waiter stood in the doorway, eyes round as the moon.

Annika brushed her hair back from her face and shot Jack a shaky smile. "Hungry, now?"

*   *   *

After a glass of wine, her hands stopped shaking. It was a delayed response to her absolute terror.

But now, sitting with Jack and watching the waves of fog break around the lights of the Golden Gate Bridge, she felt at peace. For the first time since she could remember, her thoughts didn't chatter incessantly in her head, battling over right and wrong, wants and needs.

Bardikoff was in police custody. The senator was safe, and tomorrow he would rejoice in front of the hundreds of people in Union Square. Soon, the California secret service agents would call and tell them that Bardikoff was behind the smuggled marijuana.

She sighed with contentment.

Jack's arms slipped around her shoulders, and she comfortably settled into his warmth. The way she fit into the curve his body made seemed...

Coincidental.

She chuckled low in her throat.

"Hmm?" Jack nuzzled her hair, the vibration making her scalp tingle.

"Just thinking."

"About me?"

She laughed outright. "No, about Gem."

"That's what I thought." His lips dropped lower, the words caressing her ear. The tingle gave way to heat, which swelled in her veins, tracing a path to her belly. "Because when you're thinking of me, you are usually frowning and muttering curses."

"You are the only man I know who could get so aroused by such blatant dislike," she replied sarcastically.

He nibbled along the side of her neck, and her breath caught in her chest. "Tell me how much you hate me," he murmured, sending a fresh wave of desire through her body.

"Words can't describe it." Her voice trembled.

"Try."

"Well, first, you are incredibly arrogant." His mouth pressed hotly against the hyper-sensitive spot behind her ear. She gasped.

"What else?" he said, breaking away for only an instant before assaulting her senses again.

She was twisting around to face him, wanting the delicious heat to swarm over every inch of her. "You're pushy." In jest, he pushed against her, just long enough for her to feel his taut thigh muscles against her body. The flames licked hungrily as he kissed along her jaw.

"And...and..."

"You love me," he whispered, then covered her lips with slow, melting kisses. She locked her arms around him, pulling him down on top of her.

The phone rang.

She groaned, feeling like the child who had dropped her only piece of candy in the mud. "Don't answer it."

But Jack was already pulling away. "It's probably the police. They said they would get back to us tonight." He rolled slowly off the couch, still raining sweet kisses on her face. "Don't move. I'll be right back."

With one last peck, he sprinted to the phone. "Jack Wiese." He wiggled his fingers at her, making her giggle. Suddenly, his eyebrows drew together.

"Wait, slow down...uh-huh." His eyes became steely gray with seriousness. He covered the receiver with one hand and whispered, "Paper."

Annika stood and walked over to the executive table. After digging in her briefcase, she brought Jack a yellow legal pad and a pen.

"Who?" Jack frowned, then nodded. "When are you... OK, that'll give us enough time to talk to our agents. How did you...?"

She stood, impatiently shifting her weight from one foot to the other. Finally, Jack hung up.

"What?" she asked.

He swept a hand across his face. "That was Bobby. And we've got more trouble."

Chapter 21

Their faces were solemn. No one reached for the fresh pastries and rolls, but the coffeepot was passed around the executive table silently.

"We have to tell Agent Bailey," Senator Carver said, finally.

Jack shook his head. "But, what if—"

He held a hand up. "It's not him." He turned to Gem. "Could you go find him, please?"

"Yes, sir." Cucumber mask or not, her eyes sheltered big bags like the rest of the staff. Her muted demeanor only stirred Annika's fear more.

Waiting for Agent Bailey, she stirred another packet of sugar into her lukewarm coffee. Another sleepless night, and the aching tremors that rocked her stomach were back. Each muscle felt sore, as if she had overdone a workout, when in fact each just automatically tensed every time someone shifted position or spoke.

She glanced at Jack. He looked worse than she felt. A forgotten fleck of toilet paper still stuck to the razor nick on his throat. The dark shade under his eyes was nearly as gray as his irises. He met her eyes, determination imprinted on his face.

The door opened, and Gem walked in, mysteriously silent. She wore sneakers, another first. Agent Bailey followed behind, his face registering his confusion at the sober people surrounding the table.

"Thank you for coming, Agent Bailey," Senator Carver said. He gestured to his right. "Please, have a seat."

Cautiously, Agent Bailey sat, his eyes darting from face to face. Annika smiled weakly, and his trademark twinkle eased her fears.

Jack cleared his throat. "You're probably wondering what is going on." He ran his hand through his hair. "Damned if we can figure it out."

"I'll help however I can," Agent Bailey said, his deep voice as thick as the hotel coffee.

"I'm confident you will," Senator Carver said.

Jack took a sip of coffee, then placed the mug on the table and folded his hands. "First, have you spoken with the San Francisco Police Department about Bardikoff?"

"Yes. After searching him, they found a hotel key in his pocket."

Jack nodded. "Have they found where he was staying yet?"

"Not only that, but they've already searched the room." Agent Bailey looked directly at Senator Carver. "They found several newspaper clippings about your campaign, as well as half a dozen notebooks filled with incomprehensible scribbling."

"Scribbling?" Annika frowned. "What do you mean?"

"The chief detective described them as being similar to speeches or notes. Except they were barely legible. The words were jumbled, disordered." He paused. "They also found empty prescription bottles. Zyprexa."

"What's that?" Lauren asked quietly.

"A medication that controls the symptoms of schizophrenia," Jack said, his eyes on Annika.

Agent Bailey turned in his seat, his dark eyes serious. "It seems you were right, Ms. Andersen. Robert Bardikoff wasn't taking his medication." He glanced at Jack. "In fact, the prescription bottle showed only one more refill, which most likely means he's been on medication for at least eleven months."

Senator Carver rubbed his chin. "That means he was ill during the beginning of our campaign."

"He's been ill for a lot longer than that," Jack said. "But the medication was controlling it for him. Why did he stop taking it?"

Agent Bailey lifted his beefy shoulders. "The investigator I spoke with said that if a person with schizophrenia isn't monitored by a physician, their symptoms can escalate. Especially when under stress." He nodded his thanks as Gem passed him a cup of coffee. "They suspect that Bardikoff began exhibiting symptoms, and decided he didn't need medication. Then his symptoms spiraled out of control."

"Which explains why he thought the senator was using drugs," Lauren said. She flashed a bright smile. "That means he's the one who planted the marijuana in your suitcase."

Agent Bailey shook his head. "Unfortunately, Bardikoff was already staying in the hotel at that time. So we can't pin that on him."

Annika stared at Jack until he met her eyes. She nodded slightly. "We may be able to pin it on someone else, though," he said.

Agent Bailey frowned and leaned forward. "Really? Like who?"

Jack leaned forward on his elbows, palms flat against the table. "How well do you know your agents?"

He visibly bristled. "I believe I know them well enough to trust them with my own life."

"What about the senator's life?"

"Why don't you cut the games and tell me what's going on?" Agent Bailey's voice raised. "Are you telling me that one of my team is responsible for the pot?"

Annika signaled to Jack to stay silent. "Agent Bailey, we're not sure." She pleaded with her eyes. "That's why we asked you to join us. We have some new information."

"You know Bobby Lansky from the **Washington Post**?" Jack asked.

He frowned. "Yes. He came in midway through the campaign."

"He's back in D.C." Jack leaned back in his chair. "He gave me a call last night.

"A Ms. Jeffries called him, saying she had some information on the Carver campaign. Does the name sound familiar?"

Agent Bailey shut his eyes and thought for a few moments. When he opened them, he smiled. "Yes. She's Vice President Martin's secretary. Very nice lady." He nodded at Senator Carver. "Gave me coffee when you and he were meeting that one day in Washington."

Jack nodded. "That's the same woman. Anyway, she met with Bobby. And gave him this." He bent down and reached into his briefcase, pulling out a single photocopy. He slid it across the table.

Picking it up, Agent Bailey scanned it. When he finished, he looked up with surprise. "I don't understand."

"Maybe this will help." Jack reached behind to the entertainment console and pressed the tape recorder's play button.

Raspy static filled the air. "It's done."

"So soon?"

"Look, you wanted it done right. I waited until the perfect moment and slipped it in his suitcase. One call tipped off the cops."

"Airport security?"

There was a muffled noise. "Are you kidding? You told me to go all out."

"Interesting. You didn't happen to get him smoking a joint during the middle of the governor's dinner?"

The sound of a cough. "Is that what you want?"

"No, no, you're doing fine"

"What now, President Martin?"

Hoarse coughing. "President Martin. It has a certain, shall I say, distinguished sound to it. For now, keep close tabs on what the advisors are doing."

Jack pressed a button. The tape clicked to a stop. "Do you recognize the voices?"

Agent Bailey chewed his lower lip. "It **sounds** like Vice President Martin. And the other guy, I know I've heard that voice before."

"There's more." Jack fast forwarded, then pressed play.

"Yeah, the money. You owe me thirty K."

There was crackling laughter under the static.

"Thirty thousand dollars payable on completion of the job, sir. I've completed, now I'm payable."

"Well, you have been paid. Quite well, in fact. I think I'd double-check with your wife."

Click.

Jack pressed the stop key. "Ms. Jeffries received this tape recording and the letter by FedEx yesterday morning." He smiled ruefully. "Luckily for us, Vice President Martin had just reamed her out a few minutes before. She told Bobby that she was tired of covering for the vice president."

"Covering what?" Agent Bailey asked.

Jack nodded at Axel, who jumped in his seat, then coughed. "Uh, well, you know Michael O'Hara? He's my man for dirt-digging. She's the one who tipped him off on the panty incident."

"Ms. Jeffries told Bobby that the vice president is still nursing a grudge against Senator Carver," Jack said. "In fact, in her words, it has become an obsession."

"He tried to use blackmail to get me to put him on my Cabinet, if I'm elected," the senator interjected.

"I still don't understand what this has to do with my agents."

"She claims the vice president was working with an inside member of our team." Jack shrugged, then sipped his coffee. "It makes sense. Each e-mailed threat we received was from a location close to us on the campaign trail."

"Only someone who knew of the senator's schedule would know that he was planning a big rally in Union Square today," Annika said. She bit her lip, then folded her hands on the table. "We believe that both the threats and the marijuana were carried out by one of the secret service agents."

Agent Bailey shook his head in disbelief. "These are highly trained agents—"

"Who are being bribed by the vice president," Jack said. "Ms. Jeffries gave Bobby a photocopy of a withdrawal slip. For thirty thousand dollars. That's a lot of spare change."

"Half of a government salary," Agent Bailey mumbled, staring at his clasped hands.

Annika leaned against the table. "The Fed-Ex and letter are written in a feminine scroll, while the taped phone message is of a man. We think there are two of them working together."

"But the only way to know for sure is to get this tape and letter to the FBI," Jack said. He pinched the bridge of his nose and shut his eyes. "Once they're analyzed, we'll have our man. Or our woman."

"But there's only one woman working on this detail," Agent Bailey said. He looked around the table. None of the faces registered surprise or shock. Annika held his stare grimly.

"We know."

He stared at her, frozen like an ice sculpture. Finally, he pushed his coffee cup away from him. "What do you want me to do?" he asked, resigned.

Jack and Annika looked at each other, then at the senator. Steven Carver placed a hand on the muscled arm of the agent. "I want you to be my bodyguard tomorrow. We'll keep all the agents on duty, but your job will be to watch for them to make their move.

"Then, we'll know for sure."

*   *   *

"Thank you, keep the confidence." Senator Carver shook the hands of supporters waiting outside the hotel. Jack found himself marveling yet again at the sincerity of this man. While shaking the hand of a young African-American woman, professionally dressed in a long brown skirt and pale yellow blouse, Senator Carver paused, head bent, listening to her story. As he had done so many times before, in so many locations.

Super Tuesday beckoned. Over fifteen states would hold primaries, but only two really mattered to their campaign—New York and California. The senator had spent twice as much time in flight between the two states than on the land.

But, if Axel's tracking data were correct, they would lose in New York. Governor deMarco had only a short drive to woo voters there, and had been doing so since November.

Californians, however, proved to be a difficult group to categorize. Jack remembered Axel shaking his head that morning while he looked at the numbers.

"Darn if I know what's goin' on in their heads. Could go either way."

Now, as he watched the senator, he wondered guiltily if he should have told Annika to leak the story of the stalker sooner. While the sympathy votes would feel like grease in his hand, at least Senator Carver would be safe. Jack swore silently at the senator's stubbornness.

"Thank you and remember to vote. Much appreciated. Thank you so much."

He held his left hand in a tight fist, something Jack noticed the senator did when his right hand hurt from the constant stream of enthusiastic greetings. Other than the faint bags under his brown eyes, which were nearly eliminated by one of Pam's secret potions, the senator looked at ease, comfortable with the mass of people reaching for him, touching him. It was as if Senator Carver had forgotten all about the death threats leading to this day.

Jack quickly glanced over to Agent Bailey. He surveyed the crowd casually, eyes hidden by the dark sunglasses all the special agents wore. Jack knew by experience that Bailey could be facing away from you, while all the time tracking you with those serious eyes. That skill would be especially helpful today, when he not only had to watch the crowd, but watch his own agents.

"The secret is to never let them know if you're looking at them," Bailey had told Jack once. They had been in a hotel gym room, spotting each other on the bench press. Who knew which city, which state. But traveling cemented friendships and loosened tongues.

"That's why we wear the sunglasses. The perp can't tell if we're watching or not." He'd added nearly double the weight Jack had just benched, then squirmed under the bar. "The other thing we look for is someone out of place. A woman who stays silent at a pro-choice rally. A guy who is spending more time watching the agents than the candidate. Sometimes, it's unexplainable. Just someone who looks a little off."

Thinking back to this tidbit of information, Jack found himself scanning the crowd. But all he saw were jubilant faces, arms reaching to shake hands or touch Senator Carver.

Then, he looked over at the secret service agents. Agents Bostitch and Barrington were posted behind the senator, both scanning the crowd with equal caution. Or were they looking for an opportunity? His nerves screamed at the strain.

"It's time." Gem nudged Jack toward the first car in the row of black Lincolns. Senator Carver, Richard Schwinn and Cleo Speros would be riding in the third car. A fourth car completed their motorcade.

With a last look at the senator, Jack walked quickly to the first car. Agent O'Malley opened the back door. Sliding in, briefcase placed on the floor, he took a deep breath to try and calm the jumping beans residing in his stomach.

"Hey, you." The sultry voice, honey smooth, ran over his raw nerves like a soothing waterfall. Annika sat, nearly hidden in the dark corner of the Lincoln's enormous backseat. He reached out to smooth a wayward ebony curl.

"You all right?" she asked, blue eyes darkening with concern. Sliding closer, she rested her hand on his thigh. His stomach jumped, relieved of its fear and replaced by rising heat. Could he ever get enough of her? Would a day go by where he wouldn't want her, need her so desperately?

Jack cupped her face in his hand, bringing her closer for a kiss. A casual peck instantly sparked, like flint. He wished he could bury himself within her, hiding from the fear that held his throat in a chokehold.

Reluctantly, he pulled away, leaning his forehead against hers. "You're worried about the senator," she said, her words a whisper against his skin.

Sitting back, he nodded. "Do you know how many of us it took to get him to wear a bulletproof vest today? Three."

"Two to hold him down and one to dress him?"

Jack glared at her. "It's not a joke, Annika."

"I know, I know. I'm just so…edgy. It's like right before a huge thunderstorm when you can smell the ozone in the air." She tapped her thumb against her skirt distractedly. "Or the greenish tinge of the light before the tornado sirens start blowing." Her eyes rounded, staring off into her own thoughts.

"What are you talking about?"

Blinking, she snapped out of it. "I don't know. Just rambling, I guess." She crossed her legs. "I can't help wondering if I'm missing something. Like there's an itch that I can't quite reach."

Jack slid over until their hips touched. "Turn around and I'll see if I can scratch it for you."

He caught her lips mid-laugh. She pressed against him, then pulled away. "Do you know how much I want you?" he breathed, running his hands lightly over her hair, her arms, her thighs.

"Yes," she whispered in return, a note of sadness edging her voice like lace.

Vanilla and almonds. He would never again smell those scents without imagining Annika. "I'm not pushing you."

"I know."

"I'm not even trying to pull you."

Annika sighed and folded her hands in her lap. Dressed in a dark navy suit, her ankles delicately crossed, she looked every inch the press secretary.

His voice softened, his hands dropping to hers and squeezing tightly. "I love you, Annika. More than I've needed or loved anyone." She sucked in her breath, but he pressed on. "You and I are like the moon and ocean. Your pull creates my waves. And I worship you."

A tear trickled down her cheek, but she steadfastly stared out the window at the distant Golden Gate Bridge. Jack moved closer. "Do you hear me? I worship you. I am completely, infinitely in love with you, and could not stop if I tried." Choking back a laugh, he said, "Believe me, I've tried. Please, Annika. Look at me."

To his surprise, she did. Her eyes sparkled like Caribbean waters and she smiled naturally. "Jack, you are such a creative speaker. We should use more of your work."

When he started to protest, she held up a hand. "I'm just kidding." As her hand dropped back into her lap, her voice fell in volume. "Look, I know we need to talk. But I just don't feel that this is the right time. I can't think about this right now when there's a chance a psychopath is out there with his gun trained on Senator Carver." She raised her eyebrows in a silent plea. "Can we talk over dinner?"

The Lincoln turned on to the crowded street, waved on by police officers in fluorescent orange vests. Throngs of people were hurriedly walking to the makeshift arena, some carrying homemade banners, most bearing the standard "Carver Can!"

Annika swiftly wiped her eyes and patted down her cheeks, rubbing her lips together to reset her lipstick. She turned to Jack, meeting his eyes directly. But it wasn't his Annika that looked at him. It was Annika Andersen, press secretary for Senator Steven Carver.

"I...love...you."

"Jack." Her breath hitched, tears threatening to well up again. The crack in her façade widened, her eyes filled with emotion. "Later, Jack," she whispered.

Smoothly stepping back into her role, she reached across, thumbing his lips. "Got some on you, Wiese."

With a speed akin to that of a jaguar, she was out of the Lincoln and striding toward the press box.

Chapter 22

What idiots. They didn't even check his badge, just looked at the tag that said, "Press." It was almost a waste that he had to knock out the snob from the **LA Times**. The badge was so flimsy he could have created a false identity with contact paper and a photo. And these retired security guards, strutting around in their fluorescent orange vests. What a waste of the taxpayers money. Even let him cut through the line waiting for the magnetometers. That's what you get from calling rent-a-cop.

Following the stink of carrion, he found the press box. He'd already staked out its location yesterday while watching the setup of the arena. Carver, in his typical self-worshipping style, had set up an area especially for the press corps close to the stage. All the better to be seen on C-USN that night.

He squeezed past yakking reporters and avoided stepping on the snakes of electrical hookups. Pushing forward, he set up a spot for himself along the back of the wooden box. His best view would be of the candidate's ass, which was why his corner was relatively solitary.

Pulling out a notebook, he pretended to write some notes off of the sheet that the spin-doctors had prescribed that morning. Stricter laws on gun control, ha! He couldn't help but chuckle out loud.

"Something funny?" A sleek blonde in a short skirt and pumps sidled up next to him, holding her microphone in a XXX grip. His breath caught, but he pushed it out. Why should he stand out? His beard was neatly trimmed, the gray threading through it like tinsel. The small, oval-shaped glasses that he wore magnified his eyes into huge mud puddles. He had even remembered to wear a tie.

Then he realized, she wasn't looking at him. Slimy reporter that she was, she couldn't help but try to peek at what was written in his notebook.

Slamming it shut, he scowled, then tried to stretch his lips into a semblance of a smile. "Just laughing about this press packet. They're trying to keep us informed, but not telling us a damn thing."

The blonde tittered, mouth wide, lips a slash of blood red. He watched her mouth, fascinated. Silver fillings glittered in her molars, like razor blades. He imagined her jawing on-camera, the razors cutting into her gums as she gnashed her teeth.

Her lips moved, and he forced himself to focus. "I'm sorry, what?"

Squinting her eyes, she gave him a strange look. He smiled easily, and her face relaxed. "I was asking what paper you're from. I know everyone from the national and regional press corp."

"John Hardy, from the **Los Angeles Times**. You know Jerry Lichtenstein?"

"Yes, we both belong to the same public service group. Where is he?"

Damn. He shrugged, feigning nonchalance. "Heard he caught the flu or some stomach bug."

Flipping through the day's pages, he felt the blonde's stare piercing his skin. Sweat began to bead under his collar, slowly slipping down the back of his shirt.

"John Hardy. I'm from WSFL, and your name isn't familiar to me."

Glancing up, he looked past the blonde. The rivulets of sweat chilled, becoming slicks of ice. "I'm pretty green, yet. This is my first big campaign." He tried to smile, but wavered. "Anyway, I don't want to screw it up and have it be my last. Excuse me, but isn't that campaign manager Jack Wiese?"

The blonde spun so fast she screwed her heel into the sod. "Yes. If you'll excuse me..." He breathed a sigh of relief at the reporter's quick departure, and wedged himself into the corner of the press box. The hardness of the .32 Magnum dug into his ribs, reassuring his power, releasing the butterflies that flittered in his stomach.

His messages had been ignored. He could sense the laughter, the ridicule they must have received. Bright red spots burned in his eyes. He blinked them away, wishing for crystal vision for the next hour.

It was almost time for justice to be served.

*   *   *

Annika always tried to have a quick word with a representative of each major news medium. She fed the day's spin with grace and humor, managing to make it sound like an exclusive for each team. But behind her smile, her glib responses, her own mind was spinning.

Jack loved her. Completely and infinitely, he'd said, fitting a piece into her heart that she had thought was forever missing. And try as she might, the excuses and reasons were so transparent they were breaking apart like dried rice paper.

Her body desired him. Her needs were fulfilled by him. But it was her soul, her heart that would never survive without him. The aching love she'd fantasized about as a twelve-year-old girl paled in comparison to this gut-wrenching passion and devotion. Flashing forward through the life she wanted to live, Jack was always there beside her, whether dressed in black-tie for a fund-raiser or in his worn khakis, swinging a squealing child into the air.

With a dizziness in her head that made her almost faint, she suddenly recognized the incredible lightness emitted by her body. All of her past, all of her history, it meant nothing. No pain. No fear.

Jack's love had filled all the crevices and chased away the darkness. And she allowed herself to be worthy of that love, that devotion.

"I deserve it," she whispered, oblivious to the reporters chatting around her.

"Talking to yourself is the first sign of a great president." She woke from her trance, staring wide-eyed into the face of Bobby Lansky.

"In fact, most politicians talk to themselves. No one else will listen as much." He laughed, a wonderful, carefree sound. Annika broke out in a wide grin, feeling unsteady and delirious. The crowd's murmur sounded like the approval of angels, while the hazy sunshine anointed everyone with its golden glow.

"Speaking of listening," she said, "Thanks for the heads-up on Vice President Martin. We're doing all we can on our end to find out who is helping him."

Bobby frowned. "You mean you haven't caught him yet?"

"We don't know who it is." She glanced around and lowered her voice. "Senator Carver is using himself as bait to draw them out."

"Jesus, and I thought this was a crap assignment."

"Look, this is off the record." She paused. "For now."

"Damn right, 'for now.' This is going to print above the election results headline tomorrow."

She laughed. "Boy, you love your work."

"Hey, when you find a passion for something, it doesn't let go. Kind of like relationships, I guess. First you're drawn, and then you're hooked."

Suddenly, the air felt too muggy, too close. She weaved slightly.

Bobby caught her arm, keeping her balanced. "Hey, Annika. Are you OK?" Concern wrinkled his forehead and darkened his eyes, but she just laughed out loud, then startled him with a fierce hug.

"I love him, Bobby! I do, I love him!"

Bobby stammered, pushing her to arm length while glancing around at the other members of the press, some of whom were watching with obvious curiosity. "Who? What are you talking about?"

"Jack!" She laughed again, drawing even more stares. "Where is he? I have to tell him."

"Jack? He's talking to the senator, I think. Wait, Annika—"

* * *

"Jack! Wait up! Do you have a minute?"

He paused, tearing his thoughts away from the recent tracking polls. Senator Carver was up by five points, mainly among women aged 21 to 45. He was mentally reviewing today's speech, wondering where he could add a statement on women's health and choices.

"Jack."

Slightly irritated, he glanced up, then gave her his full attention. "Shea! How the hell are you?" Engulfing her in an enormous bearhug, he stepped back to give her a once-over. Wavy blonde hair, smooth features, all California style in clothing with Minnesota manners to boot. "Looking fantastic as always."

Shea laughed, shaking her microphone at him. "Such a flirt, even though you've got Annika falling for you hook, line and sinker. Poor girl."

His heart twisted painfully, and he forced a smile. "Wish that were true. Anyway, what are you doing here? Isn't this more of a peon job, unsuitable for the leading anchor of the top television broadcast in San Francisco?"

Shea pulled a sour face, completely out of character for someone in her position. Jack couldn't help but laugh. "You think I'd miss this? It's better than a class reunion, with Bobby here, too." Face suddenly neutral, Jack recognized the shift from personal to professional. "Jack, the news leaks have been saying that Senator Carver has received several death threats in recent weeks."

"Hasn't every political official?" Jack tossed back, slipping his hands in his pockets.

"Can you confirm this?"

He paused, considering. "On or off the record, Shea?"

"Off. For now."

"Is that thing on?" he asked, gesturing to her microphone. She shook her head. "Then, yes, it's true. The letters started in January, during the Iowa Caucus. Our headquarters received them through the e-mail. The secret service agents and FBI traced it back to a local library. The scary thing is, the 'changeling' followed us throughout the campaign, leaving special care packages at every major stop."

Shea frowned. "Changeling?"

"That's what this guy calls himself. We can't figure out why."

"Hmm," she said, scraping dirt from her shoes with her thumb. She stood up and flicked the dirt off. Jack offered a handkerchief, which she accepted and wiped her hands. "Changeling. I learned about that in a Celtic and Irish History class in college."

Jack shook his head at the proffered dirty handkerchief. "So you know what it means?"

Shea pursed her cherry-red lips. "If I remember right, it comes from old Celtic tales of baby snatching. Like if a child had colic, the parents thought it was a changeling."

"I still don't get it."

She tucked the handkerchief into her front pocket. "Basically, the theme revolved around replacing a new life with an old. Like the wicked fairies would take over the child's spirit." Smiling, she shrugged. "I can see that didn't help any."

Jack smiled. "Not a bit. Other than this guy is crazier than I thought."

"There's added security today," Shea said. "The corps has noticed."

Jack met her eyes directly. "The letters have increased in their violence, their hatred. We're just taking all necessary precautions, like extra security, more magnetometers. The place has been swept for bombs three times."

Shea turned, facing the enormous crowd gathered in front of the stage. A line of police officers and secret service agents had created a barrier between the people and the stage, their arms crossed, dark glasses in place. The people, their voices once a hum of activity, were beginning to chant, "Carver! Carver! Carver!"

Tossing her blond hair over her shoulder, she glanced at Jack. "There's some guy, a John Hardy. Says he's from the *LA Times*, covering for Jerry Lichtenstein." She paused, twisting her mike between her hands, wrestling with her thoughts.

Jack touched her arm. "What is it, Shea?"

Shaking her head, she rolled her eyes at him. "It's probably nothing, but there was something…familiar about him. Maybe we had met before. I don't know, but it gave me a funny feeling." She covered his hand with her own. "I'm sure it's nothing, but I just wanted you to know. Now, I've got to go find my crew. Good luck."

"Thanks," Jack murmured, brow wrinkling in thought. From the corner of his eye, he saw the large mass of Agent Bailey, making a last-minute check of the stage's underbelly.

"Bailey!" he shouted above the crowd's din. The agent turned and started toward him.

"Have all the members of the press corps been searched?" Jack asked.

Bailey muttered into his mouthpiece and paused. Nodding his head, he answered, "Affirmative. Special Agent Barrington had three extra cops assisting him at the magnetometer. Is there a problem?"

Jack shook his head, wishing the stone in the pit of his stomach would dissolve. "Just a report of a new member of the press corp. Unfamiliar face."

"Then he would have been checked as carefully as the rest," Agent Bailey answered.

"How about everything else?"

All he got for a few moments was a cold, dark look. "Perfectly normal," the agent finally said, then turned around to resume his search.

"Damn it," Jack said under his breath. Waiting was painfully suspenseful, but now the clock was ticking down to the event. An event where his boss and friend may be gunned down. His stomach rolled over.

Gem scampered up, her high heels creating three-inch divots in the grass. "Take your place, honey! The state senators and representatives are already up in their seats!"

"Jack!" Annika jogged up, nearly breathless. "I need to—"

"Not now, darlin'! This show's about to start." Gem patted them on their rears with her leather bound notebook. "Now, scoot."

Swallowing a bitterness he couldn't put his finger on, Jack led the way up the back staircase, nodding to the secret service agent on duty. At the top of the platform, he put on his game face, smiling and clapping, nodding respectfully to the state senators and representatives, waving to the now-hysterical crowd. The faces blended, a perfect palette of human color represented. Nothing struck him as odd, but as he took his place at the edge of the stage, the heaviness in his belly pitched and rolled.

Annika took her spot beside him, clapping loudly, her smile wide, happy. It took him off-guard. She never displayed her private smile, the one he'd only seen a handful of times.

Curiosity settled his stomach faster than an antacid, and he relaxed as the crowd reached a crescendo in enthusiasm as their candidate for the President of the United States appeared mid-stage.

Chapter 23

"And so, I vow to protect the rights of American people. The right for our children to be safe in our schools. The right to get a decent education. The right to protect our financial future with social security. The right for every child, man and woman to have decent health care.

"And the right for more dollars to be spent on women's issues, women's disease treatments, women's health, while still giving women the right to choose!" Senator Carver shook his fist in determination. The crowd screamed their support. Jack watched as old women wept with renewed faith, college students waved double-sided "Carver Can!" signs, a circle of pro-lifers applauded reluctantly, their anti-abortion signs fallen to their feet.

Pride surged through his chest; the confidence of the crowd and its candidate overpowered him. An honest politician in the office of the presidency, he mused.

Senator Carver bent down to shake a few hands through the wall of secret service agents. Glancing at Agent Bailey, Jack caught his grimace of dismay.

Regaining his stance, the senator waved to the crowd, arms outstretched, working them into a frenzy of cheers. "Give me your confidence and your vote, and I will make it happen!"

Across the stage, Agent Bostitch spoke into her collar discreetly. Working crowd control on the far side, she was nearly eclipsed by the senator's frame. Her dark hair was slicked back into a severe bun; her black arched eyebrows like coal smudges across her pale forehead. Quickly, she swiped her cheeks free of sweat.

She seemed worried. All the agents were a little more anxious. Was it because of the magnitude of people, or because of their own agendas. This was not just the biggest day for the senator, but the ultimate challenge for the secret service agents in the history of the campaign. Through the haze of self-congratulations, he felt as if a knife had twisted in his gut.

Annika was cheering as loudly as the others, clapping her hands wildly. Her cheeks were flushed with unrestrained excitement, while her eyes sparkled dangerously. She looked…real.

He wanted to pull her close to him, thrust his fingers through her wild curls and kiss her long and deeply, tasting her intimately while loving her publicly. He wanted to capture her, right at this moment, when her true self was shining, unafraid, unguarded.

Like the thickening of fog, the mood shifted. Jack saw it first in her eyes, widening in incomprehension. Her stance stiffened, hands fisted, poised for fight or flight.

Jack felt as if he were walking out of a lake after dropping through thin ice. Time, frozen in millisecond cubes, played out like a strange dream sequence.

*   *   *

God, these reporters were obnoxious. Between their tittering and scribbling, they mocked the more outlandish people in the crowd. If he had the chance, he'd take out a couple of them, too.

That blonde bitch was back. She stood farther down the barricade, but had stepped away from the wooden rails, giving up prime press real estate. Out of the corner of his eye, he felt the heat of her gaze. She was no dummy. He could imagine her gears shifting, working frantically to place him.

He glanced over and caught her gaze. She held it stubbornly. He smiled, showing his yellow teeth through his beard. With obvious repulsion, she looked back at the senator.

He chuckled. Leaning forward, he felt the barrier give against his weight. He wondered if he would have a better shot if he pushed through, then decided he'd already staked out the best spot.

The senator shook hands with people whose faces glowed as if they'd seen the next coming of Christ. Or the reunion show of the Beatles. Or whoever the latest pop star was. There was a wide range of ages in the crowd.

But nobody looked out of place or threatening. He watched the secret service mumble in their shirts and hold arms stiffly, a second away from withdrawing a weapon. Too bad they were looking in the wrong direction.

Slowly, he parted his jacket. He glanced over at Shea Sheldon, but she was leaning forward, whispering in some guy's ear. With infinite patience, he reached into his coat, pulling out the Magnum. He pressed it against his thigh, the folds of his jacket flapping around, shielding it from view.

*   *   *

The sunglasses that crowded Agent Bostitch's face seemed to make her almost buglike, alien. Jack felt as if he was magnified into several images, like a fly's view of the world.

She seemed to be staring at Senator Carver. Without a pause, she reached down, her movements slowed in Jack's warped thinking.

She was going to kill the senator. Oh, God.

"Gun!" Agent Bailey's deep voice carried across the high pitch of the crowd. The senator appeared not to hear him, still waving enthusiastically to his supporters, embracing their applause.

She raised her arms, ramrod straight in perfect form. The gun fit in her hands like a natural extension of her body, its blackness gleaming in the hazy sunshine.

Jack's thoughts moved at light speed, while his body responded as if comatose. Had she fired yet? Why wasn't Bailey going after her? How could a bulletproof vest protect the senator's head?

The California state senators and representatives slid ungracefully from their seats to the stage. In his surreal state of thinking, Jack noticed the former football star turned politician was screaming like a B-movie star, while Cleo Speros kneeled with a calm face, poised to strike.

The spectators reacted. Rippling like a flag in the wind, the crowd shifted and reallocated.

He felt his rubbery legs moving before it really registered in his thoughts. **No!** his mind screamed. **No! No! No!**

*   *   *

The elation of the crowd buoyed Annika's own feelings. The campaign was invincible, the senator was invincible. And her love for Jack.

Glancing at him, cheering loudly, she glowed with excitement. She couldn't wait to tell him, but there was so much to say. Where would she begin? That she had fallen in love with the freckle-nosed brain in fifth grade science class? Or that when she saw him again, on New Year's Eve, her heart pounded with renewed desire? Or that she wanted to love him, be with him, forever?

He laughed at one of the senator's jokes, the dimple playing in the corner of his cheek. She hoped their children would inherit his dimple, then became startled at the thought. Children. **Yes**, she decided. **I want to have children with this man.**

Senator Carver was reaching the fevered pitch of his speech, the crowd a frenzy of approval. This was the point she and Jack had worked on together, filling their work with the passion they shared in the bedroom. The crowd recognized the tone of honesty and truth, and they roared their support.

Tickling fingers stroked the back of her neck, raising goosebumps on her arms, though the day was warm. The feeling was familiar. Danger had its own scent, like the syrupy thick weight of honeysuckle. Her delight dropped to her stomach like dead weight, filling her with familiar dread.

She knew. She knew before Agent Bailey even shouted. Agent Bostitch was drawing her gun with extreme sluggishness. Annika felt the puff of breeze tremble her hair, the scent of fried food and salty ocean filling her senses.

The senator waved, oblivious to the inevitable chaos.

*   *   *

In his mind he was halfway across the stage. Unfortunately, his legs hadn't followed orders.

Jack stared helplessly as the senator turned away from the spectators, his gaze traveling across the downed politicians. From the corner of his vision, he saw the blurred bulk of Agent Bailey, throwing himself at Senator Carver.

Annika. Jack's legs suddenly connected to his brain and began to run mid-stage. He resisted momentum and tried to turn back. Agent Bostitch stood still, gun raised, its black eye unblinkingly somber.

He slipped on the slick plastic floor, his loafered foot sliding as if on ice. Like a bird, he held his arms out, fighting the fall. His other foot hit a crack in the stage, stopping him from sliding more. He caught his balance and twisted to look for Annika.

*   *   *

Slowly, she turned, searching him out from the spectrum of faces.

Wedged in the corner of the press box, he stood not twenty feet away, surrounded by reporters who were just beginning to understand what was occurring but unaware of the hunter among them. The gun was small, but she was sure its bullets were no less powerful.

Hairline receding, he stood perfectly still, a man whose face was nearly unrecognizable behind the thick, graying beard. He wore glasses, but they only magnified his eyes. Those cold, unmerciful, familiar steel gray eyes.

"Oh, Chet," she whispered. He blinked once, as if surprised he was recognized, then lifted the gun higher.

In some primal nook of her brain, she knew she should be frightened. But in the milliseconds that followed, the past years were peeled back, the fear released, leaving behind the sour taste of pity. The thought must have registered on her face, because Chet's hand began to shake, the barrel of the gun blurring with the tremors.

Whoosh. She felt the impact before she heard the firecracker report of the gun. **Pop! Pop!** The air was pushed out of her lungs in an enormous gasp and she was falling, falling, American flags waving in her peripheral vision, the stunned faces both familiar and strange. With a powerful crack, her head hit the plywood floor of the makeshift stage, and she fought the darkness that sucked at her consciousness like a tidal surge.

*　　　　　*　　　　　*

"No!"

Jack's legs gained superhuman strength as his thoughts flew at supernova speed. The death threats, the strange reporter Shea saw, the bits he knew of Annika's past. It was Annika's life that was in danger, not the senator's.

Shifting direction in mid-stride, he swiveled, turning toward the now-empty rows of folding chairs, still warm from the seats of politicians. He didn't even glance up, didn't want to face the bastard who was set on destroying the woman he loved. Jack only wanted to get to her before he did.

Annika stood proudly, head held high, arms at her sides. The breeze swept up her dark hair, the tousled curls illuminating her vulnerability. Eyes like chips of Arctic ice stared, unblinking.

Running as if through gelatin, he jumped, the first crack of the gun resounding in his ears. His shoulder hit Annika's ribs, and he tried to reach out to soften her fall. The message center from mind to body was closed. His arm refused to move.

A second shot followed, its report echoing off the surrounding buildings. He could still hear the general panic and screams of the crowd, but it seemed to be fading like summer twilight.

*   *   *

Agent Bailey's deep voice swelled into his consciousness. "Perp is down, I repeat, perp is down. We need emergency services ASAP."

The warmth of Annika's body seeped through his shirt. Exhausted from his spurt of adrenaline, and afraid of what he would see, Jack slowly rolled off her, cupping her body with his own.

Ivory skin tinged gray at the corners of her mouth and temples. The blood that trickled down her forehead contrasted like strawberries in snow. But her long dark lashes fluttered like butterfly wings against her cheeks, and Jack felt the stirring of hope.

He turned and shouted, "Bailey! Get someone over here!"

Agent Bailey's secret service team was quickly ushering out the remaining politicians through a human shield of agents. He turned to Jack, his flushed face draining of color when he saw Annika's lifeless form.

"Medic," he said curtly, gesturing to a paramedic heading toward the press corps box. "Leave that one for last. We have someone else for you to look at."

The paramedic, a short, wiry man in white, knelt next to Annika, quickly checking for breath sounds and heartbeat. She moaned, eyes fluttering open, but unseeing. He rocked back on his heels, his brown eyes falling on Jack.

"She's fine. Regaining consciousness, strong heartbeat and breath sounds. You, on the other hand…"

"Me?" Jack looked at the paramedic incredulously, then glanced at Agent Bailey. They both were ringed with hazy light. Jack blinked to clear his vision and saw Bailey staring, teeth clenched, at his shirt.

The remaining adrenaline gave out, and Jack slid bonelessly to the floor, fighting for each breath. Pain seared through him as he dropped. Stubbornly, he lifted his right hand, touching his upper chest and shoulder, trying to search out the center of the pain and remove it. The hand he brought back was stained with crimson.

Limp with fatigue, he stopped fighting it, letting the haze drop down like a curtain of fog. Voices broke through like rays of light.

"He's been shot through the shoulder…. serious blood loss…. thready pulse…"

"….the senator has been moved."

"Oh my God, Annika! Jack!"

"….killed immediately. Thank God Agent Bostitch's such a good shot or else—"

He let the voices lap him into semiconsciousness, the pain slipping into oblivion. Need to fight, he thought. Is this what it's like to die?

"Jack."

The voice, so soft, so sweet and husky, like honey and dawn, made him want to open his eyes. Struggling, he blinked, the agony of his injury biting into him like a giant monster's teeth.

"Jack, can you hear me?"

He was riding in a car, lying down, the smell of pure alcohol and plastic soaking his senses. A dark angel sat to his right, a halo of light creating fiery auburn streaks through her hair.

Jack tried to speak, but his voice came out as a croak. "Annika—"

"Sshh, don't talk right now. For once, just listen to me." She winked, but her eyes were dark with worry.

"You...OK?" he whispered.

"I'm fine. Just a little bump." Her strong features sagged, and she bit her lip as if to hold back her emotions. Tears filled her eyes, threatening to spill over. "I've been wanting to tell you something, and it just can't wait any longer, Jack."

"Excuse me, ma'am," the paramedic intervened smoothly. "I'm just going to give him a little more morphine for the trip." A prick and a sting, and the heat of the medicine spread through Jack's veins.

The ambulance soared over a bump, the impact jarring Jack into immediate agony. He gritted his teeth against the cry of pain. "Now?" he asked, molars grinding together.

"Yes, now," Annika answered haughtily, drawing herself up straighter. "Damn it, you are the most infuriating man I've ever met. You drive me absolutely insane. You are the complete opposite of the man I dreamed of sharing my life with."

Her voice dropped into a near-whisper. "But you are the only man I can dream of sharing my life with. Jack, what I'm trying to say is, I love you."

Morphine dreams, he thought blearily. "What?"

"I love you, Jack Wiese. I love you..." Fight as he might, Jack passed out, feasting on her delicious words that he had been starving to hear for so long.

*   *   *

"Jack. Jack!" Annika jogged after the gurney, her high heels clicking on the hospital floor.

A team of doctors and nurses had surrounded him until only brief peeks of his dark hair and crimson stained shirt could be seen. Fighting her desire to push them aside, she slowed her pace.

"Take him into Trauma three…"

"We need an I.V. here!"

"Pressure is falling."

Like a swarm of bees surrounding their queen, they moved fluidly around each other, plastic tubing and bags soon draping Jack's still form. They pushed the gurney into a room and Annika stepped forward to follow.

"I'm sorry, ma'am. If you'll just stay in the waiting room and let the doctors do their work." The nurse's face was sympathetic, his voice low.

Her head felt as if the inside had been filled with water, making sounds seem farther away. The pressure built, pain at her temples. On rubber legs she followed the nurse and sank into a hard, plastic chair.

"Oh my God, Annika! Have you heard anything?"

Forcing herself to concentrate, she looked up into the worried face of the senator. His eyes searched hers desperately.

Suddenly, she burst into tears.

Chapter 24

"...a record victory of 63 percent of votes in the California primary. The victory must be especially sweet for Senator Carver, after the recent drama at a San Francisco rally held last week. WUSF has the exclusive on the stalker who plagued the senator's campaign with terror..."

"Shea got her exclusive," Axel Gallo murmured.

"Well, darlin', at least we can trust her to keep it factual-like," Gem said, whirling by, depositing a fresh pot of coffee, plate of sandwiches and pile of polling data in one sweep. "Besides, it's not every day she'll be spoutin' off on C-USN. Plus, Bobby beat her to the punch. He'll be getting' the Pulitzer for sure."

Snow brushed against the windows with icy fingers. The wind whistled around the hotel's windows. Outside, the temperature was dropping below zero faster than the snow was falling. But, like stoic Minnesotans, they ignored the blizzard warnings and planned the next day's agenda.

Axel grabbed the papers. "I've never seen tracking numbers like these. There's a fifty point spread between Senator Carver and Governor deMarco."

"He's got to announce his departure soon," Richard answered, eyes glued to the television.

"It would be the smart thing to do," Agent Bailey remarked, gulping down his second sandwich. "We could use the extra agents."

"Especially new ones that won't try to screw over the senator," Gem said bitterly.

Agent Bailey shook his head. "I still can't believe Agent Garcia fell in with that slime."

"Vice President Martin is pretty convincing. Only forty percent of Americans really thought he wore the panties," Axel offered.

"Yeah, the other sixty percent thought the crotchless ones suited him better," Gem said.

"If I become president, those words will never be used in my presence again," Senator Carver remarked casually, easing himself into a wide chair and reaching for an egg-salad sandwich. Lauren perched casually on the arm of the chair, leaning an arm against its thick back. "Besides, the campaign isn't over yet. We still have to keep campaigning against deMarco."

"Well, I'd have to disagree with you, Senator. I'd say it's over when the president says it's over." Her green eyes danced with glee, but she tried to keep a straight face while she stared at Shea Sheldon's face on the television screen. The entire room paused, breathless, the weight of their expectation a palpable force. A gust of wind rattled the window.

The senator broke the silence with a great, joyous laugh and scooped Lauren into his lap. "Are you holding out on me?" he asked, holding her tightly.

"Not from the sounds that come through my hotel room walls at night," Gem murmured to Richard, who, in embarrassed shock, choked on his coffee.

"Let me go and I'll tell you," Lauren laughed, squirming on the senator's lap. She stood up, smoothing her skirt and honey-blonde hair. "The president called this morning. He is planning on announcing later today his support for Senator Carver's nomination at the Democratic National Convention."

A bare second passed before the room erupted. Richard shook hands enthusiastically with Axel and Nick, patting each of them on the back. Gem whisked into the kitchenette and returned with a couple bottles of champagne and a handful of glass flutes. And the Senator swept Lauren up, kissing her passionately and deeply.

"I guess we don't have to worry about the lack of a woman representative at the Senator's side any longer now, do we?"

Everyone turned, elated cheers evolving into enthusiastic welcomes for Jack and Annika, standing in the hallway. Jack's left arm was in a sling, but his right arm wound protectively around Annika, his hand resting possessively on her right hip.

"What's going on?" Annika asked, brushing aside Gem's worries for her health.

"Well, for starters, we won Super Tuesday," Axel announced.

Annika snorted unladylike, all business. "We know that. We were in the hospital, not some cave in Switzerland."

"Lauren and Steven are making their relationship a bit less private," Gem said, handing them each a glass of champagne. Annika raised a brow at her assistant, who blushed fiercely.

The senator laughed, pulling Lauren to his side. "And…the president is supporting my nomination as the Democratic presidential candidate."

Annika gasped, holding her hands to her mouth. Months of work, with long hours and short tempers, and they had succeeded. As a team. Looking around the room, she saw people who had pulled together like a family. Who she could even consider caring about like family.

Her throat burned with suppressed emotion, pride and joy that stretched the seams of her professional façade. Blinking back tears, she folded her hands in front of her. "Good work, everyone. I am so very proud of each and every one of you. Your dedication and strength is admirable." She paused, drawing a breath and allowing the tears to flow easily, as if it had always been her nature. "It has been an honor and a privilege to work with such a fantastic staff."

Immediately, she was surrounded. Gem tackled her waist, while Lauren sobbed openly on her shoulder, "We did it! We did it!" Axel gave her a huge bear hug, and even Richard patted her awkwardly on the shoulder.

"All right, everyone dry their eyes," Steven said, waving his arms and swiping a hand across his own. "This is a victory party! Where's my champagne?"

As everyone scattered, looking for his or her glasses, Annika felt a strong hand fall on her shoulder. For the first time in several years, she didn't flinch. Smiling, she turned to see the bulky frame of Agent Bailey.

Eyes downcast, he shuffled his feet slightly, then straightened and met her gaze directly. "Ms. Andersen, I just wanted to say I'm sorry. It was my responsibility to make sure the grounds were safe, and I failed. I hope that you can forgive me."

Annika reached up and held his wide shoulders in her hands. Surprise flashed in his eyes. "It was not your fault. There is nothing to forgive. In fact, I don't think I can ever repay you for rushing to Jack's side so quickly. Without your help, he could have lost more blood, and…" She let the sentence drift off with a shudder. Losing Jack was too horrible a thought to let spoil the day. Instead, she slipped her hands around Bailey, hugging him tightly.

She glanced up and saw Agent Bostitch, awkwardly standing in the corner. "And you!" Annika beckoned. After glancing around, Agent Bostitch reluctantly approached, eyes staring straight ahead.

Annika grabbed her hands. "You saved my life. If you hadn't shot…him…"

"Oh, ma'am." Agent Bostitch blinked, embarrassed. "It's just my job." She smiled wickedly. "Now, will you let me do it?"

Annika laughed. "You can be my bodyguard any time!" She turned and pulled Agent Bailey into another embrace.

"Hey, now, you two. Trying to woo away one of my sweethearts again, big guy?" Jack grinned at Agent Bailey, making him break apart with a "Puh-shaw."

As the special agents walked down the marble hallway to invite the other agents to the party, Jack pulled Annika into a tight embrace. She nestled into his chest, her ear right over his heart, making a silent prayer that it still beat its rhythm so strongly.

He tilted her head up with one finger, his eyes nearly gray in the artificial light, thick black hair still mussed like a twelve-year-old boy. His impish grin only added to the appearance, and Annika laughed.

Spinning her around, Jack cleared his throat loudly. "Everyone, can I have your attention, please?" He waited patiently for the room to quiet. "Lauren, when is the president making his announcement?"

"At the afternoon press conference."

"Great, that gives us time to prepare our own statement. Axel, who's the leading Republican candidate?"

"Uhh, Governor William Rutledge has a three point margin over Senator Michael Richardson."

"Well, get a hold of your buddy O'Hara and find out some stats about both of them." Jack pointed to Richard. "We need some research on what each candidate's media output history has been, so we know how to retaliate." Richard nodded seriously, grabbing his yellow legal pad to jot down notes.

"And Gem—"

"Darlin', I'm so far ahead of y'all you can only see my vapor trail," she drawled, bringing out a fresh stack of papers outlining the campaign highlights through election day. As she swept by Jack, he planted a kiss on her cheek.

"Finally, Senator." Jack paused, reached for Annika's hand and gripped it tightly. "Steven. I need you to be my best man."

Annika's heart dropped to her stomach, head spinning. She stared at Jack with amazement as he turned and dropped to one knee.

"We're getting married," he told her, lighting her fire like a match.

Fisted hands on her hips, she glared down at him. "You call that a proposal? And don't you think you should have consulted me before asking the best man? And for another thing—"

Swiftly as a cat, he pounced on her, covering her mouth with hot kisses, probing deeply until her anger steamed out of her in pure desire.

"Annika, will you kiss a donkey for the rest of your life?" he murmured against her lips before drawing her in for another rough assault. Dizzy from the siege on her senses, she could only respond by pressing against him.

He pulled away. "Is that a yes?"

She opened her eyes, looking into his own, a mirror of hope and desire and commitment. "Yes," she whispered, then laughed and hugged him. "Yes!"

They were surrounded by cheers and congratulations, while Gem called out, "No more champagne, or y'all be lookin' like fools at the press conference."

"She's right," Jack said, sweeping the room with his eyes. "We've got a lot of work to do.

"And I have to kiss my beautiful bride-to-be," he whispered to Annika, slipping a diamond ring from his sling and easing it onto her finger. "Of course, we'll have to draw up a prenup stating that I will forever be in the right."

Annika laughed, watching the ring sparkle like the snow outside. "Don't forget the clause where I have final say on anything."

Pulled into a firm embrace, Jack whispered in her ear. "And we definitely need to find a way to keep work and pleasure separated."

Kissing him deeply, Annika again felt the wave of happiness roar over her. "What, and spoil all our fun?" she asked, and pulled him closer.

About the Author

Kristin Dodge is the author of several novels, including the upcoming "Swept Away" trilogy. She lives in Minnesota.

Printed in the United States
6269